THE COMFORT OF BLACK

Also by Carter Wilson

Revelation

The Boy in the Woods

Final Crossing

THE COMFORT OF BLACK

A Novel

CARTER WILSON

Oceanview Publishing
Longboat Key, Florida

ISBN: 978-1-60809-222-2

Published in the United States of America by Oceanview Publishing
Longboat Key, Florida

www.oceanviewpub.com

10 9 8 7 6 5 4 3 2

PRINTED IN THE UNITED STATES OF AMERICA

For Pam

ACKNOWLEDGEMENTS

The book is dedicated to my wonderful agent, Pam Ahearn. Your feedback, tireless effort, and most of all your belief in my writing are all forever appreciated. And thanks to Pat Gussin, Bob Gussin, Frank Troncale and all the other staff at Oceanview for reading this book and wanting to take it on.

I hugely appreciate all the feedback from the steadfast members of my critique group. Ed, Dirk, Sean and Linda, here's to you.

Ili and Sawyer, you can't read this one either. But thanks for being amazing children and inspiring me on a daily basis. I love you endlessly. Now, stop picking up my books and looking for the bad words.

Jessica, you are awesome in all sorts of ways. We are good together, and I simply couldn't do any of this without you. Henry, thanks for making me smile and being just a good kid.

Mom, I appreciate you reading the draft with a keen eye, as always. Sole, this one would freak you out as well, so I'll just give you the CliffsNotes version sometime. But you give me tequila, and that's a good thing.

Dad, I think about you every day, and there are always bits of you reflected in my writing.

Finally, thanks to all the readers who have been following me since my first novel. I hope this one lives up to your expectations. Knowing there are folks out there buying my books and enjoying the stories I create is pretty much writer-heaven. Let's keep this relationship going for a long time.

THE COMFORT OF BLACK

PROLOGUE

Hannah didn't have a plan beyond setting her father on fire.

She hid in her closet tonight as Billy rampaged, cloaked in the dark among shoes too small to wear, clothes reeking of cigarette smoke no matter how many times she washed them, and a memory box containing only dried, blackened roses from her first and only boyfriend, a romance that lasted not much longer than the flowers. Hannah had spent much time in this closet before, and time itself stretched into magical proportions in the cramped darkness. Seconds were minutes, minutes were hours. But it would finally be over. Billy was predictable. When his rage ended, it would leave him fatigued, like a cheetah after a kill. He would sleep, and when he did, it would be Hannah's turn to act.

Forever later, when the house finally fell silent around her, Hannah slowly counted to one hundred and opened the closet door. She left her room and crept through the house, the rough floorboards creaking beneath her bare feet. She found her mother in bed, an empty glass of gin on the night table, her nightly anesthetic. Hannah draped an arm around her and felt her mother shake with stifled sobs. Hannah told her it was time to do something. Time to stop living like this.

"Go brush your teeth and get to sleep," her mother said. She spoke into her pillow. "Things will be better in the morning."

Things were always promised to be better in the morning.

Hannah stroked her mother's hair.

"Yes, they will," Hannah said. It was the first time she ever believed it.

Her father's abuse stretched as far back as Hannah could remember. Now Hannah was fifteen, the assaults had become routine, and Hannah no longer called him Daddy. Justine still called him Daddy, but Hannah only called him Billy. To Hannah, she had no daddy.

Hannah left her mother and walked softly into the room she shared with Justine and found her twelve-year-old sister asleep, her hair pasted in sweat to the side of her face, her favorite stuffed rabbit clutched against her chest like a newborn child in its mother's arms. The rabbit was missing its left ear, the stuffing held in by a piece of duct tape pasted over the hole. Billy had torn the ear off one night as punishment for a chore left undone. Ripped it off the creature's head right in front of a crying Justine, then fed the ear down the garbage disposal. Hannah leaned down and kissed Justine on the forehead and whispered in her ear. "Tonight, Justine. It's gonna be over tonight." Justine didn't stir.

Hannah then walked through the living room and stared briefly at her father, who, even in sleep, seemed tensed in rage, ready to spring at any moment like the toy snake inside the fake can of nuts. He had finally passed out in his favorite chair, the shitty green one that smelled of mold and cigarettes. Billy's final Pall Mall of the night had burned to the filter as he slept, the ash scattered in gray motes around his dirty work boots. An empty whiskey glass rested on the arm of the chair, remnants of the drink visible on Billy's t-shirt, streaks of dull caramel against grayed white.

Hannah continued to the garage and found a can of gasoline. She picked it up and crept back into the house, leaving the door open behind her. She lifted Billy's lighter off the kitchen table and held it tight in her fist. Back in the living room now, the smell of turkey was heavy and stale from the kitchen. She unscrewed the top of the gas can, the acrid fumes attacking her nostrils. But it smelled *good*. It smelled like a last-chance gas station on a long, desert road, one final opportunity to refuel before heading west toward something new, vast, and different.

As she looked down on her father, Hannah's rage swelled. This was the rage Hannah inherited from Billy, and as she got older she found herself fighting against it, convincing herself she was not like him, but still the anger flooded her more often than she could remember. She usually found a way to dam it up. But not tonight. Tonight she was thankful for it. It would allow her to do what needed to be done.

As gently as she could, Hannah sloshed the contents of the bottle over Billy's lower legs and along the base of his chair. Billy was a hard sleeper. Hannah was pretty certain the noise would not wake him, but the smell was strong. The fumes might arouse him, so she needed to move fast. She trembled as the gas can lost weight in her hands. But Billy didn't move, and the only sound he offered was a steady, rhythmic snore, the song of the drunk. Hannah had poured a long trail of the gas leading toward the dining room table, next to where the uneaten turkey remained there, nobody having even bothered to put it in the refrigerator. She had poured the final drops inside the hole in the carcass.

She stared at Billy and squeezed the lighter in her right hand, her palm sweaty against the hard plastic. She heard his yells from earlier in the evening echo in her memory. *You ruined the fuckin' turkey, you stupid bitch.* Billy's open palm had connected with his wife's face, one more biting sting piled on top of hundreds—maybe thousands—before it. That was his preferred method of assault. Never a closed fist. Always open-palmed, as if somehow that made it a correction rather than a beating.

The fire would spread quickly, and Hannah would have to run and get her mother and sister. Would they try to help him? Or would they jump into the car and drive, drive as far and as fast as they could go, crying at the horror of what they left behind but relieved by the freedom the flames had given them?

Hannah fantasized the latter. In this fantasy, Hannah would

be a hero, the girl who saved her family from a monster. Her mother would stop drinking and her sister would finally live in a world where the drunken shouts of *cunt* and *whore* weren't night-time rituals. In this same fantasy the police would say it was self-defense, because the cops in the small Kansas town knew Billy was an evil man and the world would be better without him. Things would be the kind of normal Hannah had always dreamed.

A world without Billy.

But Hannah had never experienced a dream coming true, not in the fifteen years she had been on this earth.

She needed to act but found her body frozen. Standing, not moving, not even breathing, a void of motion that seemed to transcend time. The moment held a religious kind of quiet. In her mind, she saw the reverend in their little Baptist church reading from the Bible, and in this moment, this darkness, she could hear the man's voice speaking with conviction, his gaze sweeping through the tiny congregation.

Be still, and know I am God.

Hannah blinked, breaking the spell, not wanting God to be a part of this moment. God hadn't been there for her before, so He wasn't allowed to be here now. Her hand began to shake as she stared down at her father and flicked the lighter. Once. Twice. On the third attempt, the flint sparked the gas, and the flame rose above her thumb. A drop of sweat beaded on her forehead and ran down her face, tickling the tip of her nose. She heard herself gasp in the silence of the tiny, broken house.

Billy's eyes shot open. They were wide at first, then narrowed as his gaze drilled into her. He smiled in the dark of the room, his teeth radiating against his unshaven face. *Cheshire Cat.* He sniffed the air and then spied the gasoline can on the floor near her feet.

"Good for you, Hannie," he said. "Maybe you just did learn a thing or two from me."

An invisible python wrapped itself around Hannah's chest and squeezed.

Billy coughed and cleared his throat. His voice was a soft

growl. "You realize, even on fire, I'm gonna come over there and break every bone in that beautiful, soft face of yours. You know that, right? With my last ounce of life I will make you suffer, baby. But you do what you gotta do, Hannie. I always thought you were soft, but maybe I was wrong. This is *your moment.* So do it, little girl." He straightened in the chair. *"Do it."*

The words repeated in her head. A mantra.

Do it, Hannah. Do it. Do it.

Billy rose from his chair as Hannah kept her arm held out in front of her. Billy's face danced behind the flickering flame. His bright-blue wolf's eyes gleamed with excitement. The smell of blood, of a meal soon to be had.

She had stopped breathing. She could not move. The stillness of moments before was back and it consumed her. All she could do was look at him.

Billy came toward her.

PART I

HANNAH

CHAPTER ONE

Hannah and her husband hadn't had sex in six weeks. Six weeks and three days, the longest span of abstinence in their entire relationship. Hannah knew, because she kept a calendar. Since the first time they had made love she made a little mark with a pen in her Day-Timer, black hashes adding up over the year, whiskers of sexual memories.

The past two years had been filled with ever-increasing gaps. Dallin was thirty-three and Hannah thirty-four. There was no good reason for gaps at that age, she thought.

He was working late. Or he was tired. Or the most common reason of all: he was stressed. That one, in particular, made no sense to her. What better cure for stress than sex? But she didn't understand, he would say. *It's not like that. Do you know how much pressure I'm under? I can't just perform on command.*

Bullshit, she thought. Two years ago I couldn't walk across the bedroom in a pair of baggy sweatpants without you attacking me.

But he had been distant recently, the kind of distant older couples might call comfortable. There was no comfort in it to Hannah. To her, it was simply confusing and sad. How long could a person blame every other part of life for the simple fact that, perhaps, they were actually falling out of love?

The increase in gaps didn't completely overlap with their decision to start a family, but there was a relationship between the two. She had questioned if he even wanted a child, and though he insisted he did, there was no denying they were doing less and less of what it took to actually make one.

But tonight she could put a mark in her calendar.

Dallin thrust up into her. She lay on her stomach on the king-size bed, the comforter pushed aside in a mound, half-hanging off the bed, spilling on the floor like a snow drift. Hannah turned her face to the side, one side hot from the blood pulsing through her cheeks, the other cool from the Turkish linen. Her eyes were closed. Dallin's fingers clutched hers—almost painfully—as he pushed up into her from behind. His thrusting came erratically, almost desperately, until he slowed to a stop. Hannah started to open her eyes when he shifted his weight. She felt his tongue draw a line from the small of her back to the valley between her shoulder blades, and then she understood. He needed to *consume* her.

When things were good, times like tonight, she never felt so desired by a man as she did by Dallin. When he was like this, he would prolong his pleasure by stopping himself and exploring her body with his tongue, toes to earlobes, as if he couldn't get enough. Sometimes he bit her, other times his fingers would dig deep into her skin. Never too hard, but deep enough. Deep enough to let her know he craved her more than anything else could be craved.

This was the Dallin of two years ago. All Hannah wanted was that version of him, all the time. She wanted to clench her entire body, keep him close, not let him disappear back into interminably long days of *corporate importance*. She no longer wanted to compete for her husband against his own success.

Dallin put himself back into her and pushed deeper, creating a rhythm she knew to the exact beat. She felt drops of sweat from his face drip onto her back...one...two...as his pace quickened. He grunted as he moved quicker, his hips moving faster and pushing harder against her, almost violently, until she knew he was going to climax. She wanted to hear him say her name as he came inside her. She wanted it but she would never ask. She needed him to want to say it.

Dallin's body shuddered, tensed, and then eased. He came, but hadn't said a word. She felt him roll off her and collapse onto the sheets, and she remained trapped under a thousand-pound silence.

The idea of how good a drink would taste struck her. A Manhattan. Margarita. Even just a glass of pinot. It was so predictable, the urge for a vice at the slightest hint of unease. It was an urge of habit, and not just because alcohol was commonly a post-sex consumption. It was because alcohol itself was a habit, and her one drink a day had grown to three or more. But she hadn't had a drop in a week, knowing she could soon be pregnant. The seven days without alcohol had been maddeningly difficult, forcing her to label her habit a problem, but that was all over now. She had a reason to be sober.

Hannah finally opened her eyes and looked over at her husband. She reached out with her hand and brushed back his hair, which was just showing signs of early gray.

"I love you," she said.

"I love you, Hannah."

Hannah.

She remembered the first time she heard him say it. Her move from a life in Redemption, Kansas, to Seattle for college hadn't been insignificant. She'd grown up in the arms of white, small-town, God-fearing America, never having traveled to more than the neighboring states for the first eighteen years of her life, never having flown on a plane, never knowing the world she had only read about. But how she had read. Anything and everything. From Jane Austen to *OK Magazine*. Stephen King to Fitzgerald. Hannah dreamed of traveling the world, but the rare trip to a crowded mall in Kansas City overwhelmed her. What she couldn't experience in life she tried to compensate for in academics, and so Hannah had nearly perfect SAT scores and an emptiness in her soul because she didn't know how any of her knowledge mattered.

Billy never understood Hannah's attraction to books when she was a little girl. *You want a story? Here's a story. I work my ass off twelve hours a day so you, your sister, and your momma can sit around and read books and go shopping. The-fucking-end. How's that for a story?* It didn't matter if any of it was true or not, but that was Billy. What he said was the truth to him, and with a man like Billy, little else matters.

You're just a rube, Hannie. That's what all those folks in Seattle gonna say about you. Just a rube from Kansas, all she is. That's what Billy would have said about Hannah's decision to move, but Billy was no longer around, and Hannah never had to listen to him again. Billy had been out of her life since Hannah was fifteen, sent away to prison for beating her to near death. That night, Thanksgiving 1995, was the last time she had seen him. That was the night Hannah finally decided to do something about Billy. On that night Hannah touched the lighter to the gas, but Billy pounced before the flame reached him. On that night the fire did not start, and Billy beat her far beyond what he had ever done to her mother.

Billy was gone, but Hannah's fantasy of a perfect world never came. Three years later, Hannah's mother killed herself, binging on gin until blood filled her eyes. Her mother had always blamed Hannah for Billy's absence, blamed her for breaking up a violently dysfunctional family that was all she knew. And after Billy was sent away, there was nothing Hannah nor her younger sister could do to stop their mother's downward spiral of self-destruction. Hannah never understood the addiction to abuse her mother inhabited, but some things just defied logic. Like Hannah's own love of booze despite it having been her mother's choice of suicide weapon.

Soon after her mother's death, eighteen-year-old Hannah and fifteen-year-old Justine took the modest insurance payout and left Kansas for Seattle, trading in a small town for a big one. The following four years changed her in ways she never imagined, and she stayed there after graduating, using an English degree to keep her dream of being a writer alive while she made money working the front desk of a four-star hotel in downtown Seattle.

Hello, Hannah.

Dallin had said her name when he checked in that day, eight years ago. She had looked up from behind the counter and saw him. Crooked smile, moppy black hair, Black Lab energy barely restrained. She had been thrown off by his use of her name before remembering the small gold name tag pinned to her uniform. He had flown in from Boston, he told her. A meeting with potential investors for an idea he had, something he started working on his senior year at M.I.T. If they funded him he'd be moving out here, to Seattle. Sometimes a guest would tell their life story during check-in, but Dallin's was the first to which she had truly listened. He compelled her in that indefinable way that couldn't just be ascribed to purely physical attraction.

Tonight, Hannah lowered her hand to her husband's chest, brushing through the thin layer of hair with her fingertips, feeling his skin cooling, the softness associated with drying sweat. She thought about how he had changed in those eight years. He had grown heavier, more muscular, due to a love affair with exercise he'd begun four years ago. At his peak physical shape, his chest and arms had grown larger, his stomach muscles more defined. Six days a week. That was his exercise routine, or at least used to be. His rapid success in the world of Internet security had eaten at this aspect of him as well. The last year he'd had many more early mornings at the office rather than the gym. He'd lost some of that muscle and his frame was thinner and more angular than ever before. Not quite skinny, but close.

The initial seed funding had been just a stepping-stone to get him started out in Seattle. Hannah remembered when he had come back after his first trip. Stayed at her hotel again. He had walked up to the front desk and said he'd just gotten a check for two million dollars and he was going to take her out to dinner.

That had been a really good dinner.

She had used her day off to help him look for an apartment. He kissed her that day for the first time, kissed her in the empty walk-in closet of a loft apartment downtown, a stolen moment while the rental agent took a phone call in the hallway. She didn't know how to react, so she just dissolved into his lips, breathing him in, feeling him bite softly on her lower lip. She hadn't seen it coming, which was often the best kind of kiss there was.

After their first kiss ended, Dallin had simply looked her in the eyes and said, "I'm going to be wildly successful, and I want you to enjoy it all with me." It seemed an almost obnoxious statement, but to Hannah it wasn't. He was telling the truth. And she wanted him. She wanted it all. She had replied with one word.

Yes.

A week later they made love in that closet.

The distant memory made her smile tonight as Hannah stroked her husband's chest and looked down on his face. He looked back with half-open lids.

"I'm sorry," he said.

The words were so soft she wasn't certain what he'd said.

"What?" she whispered. Seconds passed.

He didn't answer.

"Sorry for what?"

Silence. His breathing slowed and his eyes were closed. Dallin was either asleep or didn't want to answer. Hannah didn't press it. He had been saying sorry a lot lately.

Sorry for being gone so much.

Sorry for long silences and touchless nights.

Sorry for letting you drink so much.

Sorry for not being the husband you need me to be.

Sorry for not giving you a baby yet.

Whatever he was sorry for tonight, Hannah decided she would accept it without explanation. She wanted to stay in a good mood. A hopeful mood. A Dallin-of-two-years-ago mood. It was strange, she thought, the power of transient happiness. The feeling of clinging to a brief moment of peace and assuming the rest of her life could possibly feel the same way. Such feelings gave people hope, Hannah thought. They also made the inevitable fall more horrifying.

Minutes later he was asleep, his breathing steady and deep. Hannah got up to use the bathroom. Zoo was there, paws on the toilet seat, leaning in for a drink. The dog pulled away at the sight of her and gave Hannah his famous *Blue Steel* thousand-yard stare, a look that had earned him the name after the character from the movie *Zoolander*. Neither a happy nor an aggressive look, Zoo's gaze was simply vacant, distant, and posed, as if the dog were frozen in place by a fashion photographer's directive. Hannah reached down and stroked Zoo's neck, which broke the stare into the closest thing to a smile the dog could give. Hannah had wanted a large dog, but it just wasn't practical in a condo, even a condo of this size. In short time she discovered a good mid-size dog was perfect, especially when the dog was a mutt—the animal shelter had guessed some kind of Airedale and Jack Russell mix. Zoo could be perfectly cast as a happy-go-lucky stray from the 1920s.

She returned to bed and Zoo followed. Hannah placed her head on Dallin's bare shoulder as Zoo leapt to the foot of the bed, circled three times, and collapsed in a tight ball near her feet. As Hannah listened to the steady rhythm of her husband's breaths, her mind took her to thoughts of a baby, wondering if tonight was the night she'd become pregnant. She counted the months in her head. *August.* It would be an August baby. She would go through the heat of the summer, though that was never much of a problem in Seattle anyway. She would start showing in, what, March? With her slight frame it might even be sooner, and she couldn't wait until it was obvious, where others, strangers even, would remark on it, asking her when she was due. Was it a boy or girl? Have you picked out names yet? As tedious as her friends told her all the questions were, Hannah knew she would never tire of them. *Ask away.*

Sudden thoughts pierced her brain like a bullet, shattering and dispersing all the good thoughts she clung to about having a baby:

What if your baby turns out like Billy, Hannah? What are you going to do then? You going to try to set your own baby on fire?

She tried to force the thoughts aside and focus on happy ones instead, of shopping for baby clothes and preparing a nursery. A baby shower. Holding her baby for the first time against her chest, feeling the tiny mouth take her nipple, needing her. As she lost herself in the convoy of thoughts that would take her until she fell asleep, she almost imagined it was Dallin's voice she was hearing. But it wasn't her imagination.

He had said something.

"What?" she asked him. She raised her head and looked at his outline in the silky moon- and city-light that filtered into the room through sheer, spilling drapes. She wondered if he had woken to explain his earlier apology.

He mumbled, twitched. His left arm lifted a few inches off the mattress and then fell. Then his right. He repeated a few words, which sounded like *yeah*, but she couldn't be certain.

He wasn't talking to her. He was having a dream. His twitching became more animated, and Hannah wondered if she should wake him.

Dallin had never spoken in his sleep before.

It certainly doesn't seem like a nightmare, she thought. He doesn't seem scared.

"You like that, don't you, baby?" The words, mumbled through a state of suppressed consciousness, surprised Hannah. It sounded like a sex dream. Was he reliving the past hour, or was she just being naive? She liked to think it was her face he was seeing. She liked to think he wanted her even in his sleep, and though she shouldn't grow jealous of his dreams, she worked hard to convince herself he was thinking of her and no one else. Hannah felt herself turned on by it. Maybe he was growing hard in his sleep.

She reached under the sheets to find out and discovered he wasn't. Maybe she would crawl under the sheets and go down on him, making him hard. Then she would mount him, and he would wake up to find his dream coming true. How amazing would that feel, she wondered, to dream about fucking your wife and to wake up and that actually be happening?

And he would come inside her again. Another chance.

As she slipped off her thong and pulled back the sheets to put her mouth on him, Dallin's limbs shook more violently. He was no longer twitching, his whole body seemed in a spasm. Hannah placed her hand on his chest, as if her touch could calm the shaking body. But Dallin came to life in his sleep, his arms suddenly flailing, his fists clenching, his head snapping from side to side.

Hannah lifted her hand and leaned away from him.

"Baby?" she said. "Dallin, are you okay? Are you awake?"

Dallin's voice was clear but quiet, as if he was whispering into a lover's ear.

"Yeah, you like that, bitch? You like my cock and my knife? That feel good, cunt? I want you to tell me what it's like to bleed out. *Tell me everything.*"

Hannah stared into the darkness, wanting to believe she only imagined what she'd just heard. *He didn't just say that. He couldn't have.*

"Dallin?" she said. "Dallin?" Her voice was fearful, a person asking a ghost to make his presence known. She said his name one last time, but did not touch him again.

Dallin was silent until, about a minute later, he began to softly snore.

Hannah pulled her knees up to her chest, wrapped her arms around them, and stared away from Dallin and out the window, over Puget Sound, as her husband's words tumbled over and over in her mind without stopping.

The moon climbed.

CHAPTER TWO

"So, tell me what's going on?"

Hannah looked at her therapist for a moment before shifting her gaze downward. Looking away was always the easiest option. Hannah sat in the same oversized leather chair she had been sitting in once a week for four years. It felt the same, *smelled* the same, as it always did and always would. There was usually comfort here in the office of Dr. Madeline Britel, but today Hannah didn't feel it. She shifted in her seat, trying to find support.

"I...I'm not sure what to say. Something happened yesterday."

Hannah had tossed fitfully in bed last night, finally allowing herself an Ambien and a glass of wine when she hadn't fallen asleep by one in the morning. She woke up after nine. Dallin had already left for work, and a small blue Post-it note was on top of his pillow. *I love you!* Hannah normally kept these notes. This one she threw away, but not out of anger. She just had a strong sense of not wanting to keep it.

Hannah was both eager and afraid to tell Dr. Britel about what Dallin had said in his sleep. Not telling her wasn't really an option. What was the point of coming here if she held back what had happened? But the fear existed she was making far too much of this. It was a dream, after all. Did she not have her own dreams of violence, rage, and fear, dreams fueled by the memories of her father, who, after all, was really the reason she came to therapy to begin with?

Dr. Britel would tell her it was nothing to worry about. Then it would all be better again.

"What happened?"

Hannah sucked in a breath and then told her. Just as she had rehearsed it in her mind. Word for word, though she softened her voice when she said *cunt*. It took maybe two minutes to relate the story. When she finished, Hannah laced her fingers together tightly and looked down at her wedding ring.

"I see," Dr. Britel said, her expression impressively unchanged. "What do you think that means?"

"I have no idea."

"Don't you? Doesn't it make you think something?"

Hannah anticipated the question. Many of the arrows in a therapist's quiver were such questions.

"I'm not sure. Maybe...maybe it makes me think there's something about him I don't know."

"Something like what?"

"I don't *know*. Why would he say that?"

"Do you have dreams that are incongruous with your character?"

"Of course I do. I mean...you know I do."

"Have you ever had a dream you were hurting someone?"

Hannah felt anger creeping over her. "You know the answer to that as well," Hannah said.

"Your dreams about Billy." The doctor leaned forward just a few extra degrees over her crossed legs. "But those dreams are just you playing out what happened in reality. And in reality, you never actually hurt him."

"I tried to kill him."

It felt good to say aloud. Dr. Britel was the only living person outside of Dallin, Hannah's sister, and Billy himself who knew the full details of what had really happened that night. Hannah didn't tell the police, nor had Billy.

"But do you ever dream you succeeded in killing him? Or even hurting him?"

This is getting off point, Hannah thought. She wanted the doctor to tell her something clearly was wrong with Dallin. She wanted to feel justified anger at her husband, because for Hannah getting angry was as satisfying as scratching a deep itch. Her anger was one of the reasons she came to Dr. Britel in the first place, and now Hannah was simmering at her own therapist. "I don't know. Maybe. I mean, I'm sure I do."

"Does that make you a murderer?"

"That's different. This isn't about Billy."

Dr. Britel shifted in her seat and cleared her throat, an indication she was going to make a statement rather than ask a question. Statements were rare.

"Your concern is understandable. You lived under the rage of your father for years, and the action you took...*almost* took...was a stand against a monster. So it makes sense something like what happened last night triggered your feelings of insecurity, fear. Dread, even. But I think what we need to explore is not what Dallin said. You're smart, Hannah. You know dreams can be meaningless, at least in context of a person's true nature. Our subconscious rules our nights, but that doesn't define us as a person. If he had a dream about, say, sleeping with his own mother, I'm sure you wouldn't fear that was actually happening."

"God, of course not."

"So I wonder if there's something about your relationship—your relationship with Dallin, and not your father—causing you to pay particular attention to what happened last night."

Hannah sat up a bit more. "Are you saying that, in a healthy marriage, a person shouldn't question or be concerned about their spouse having a rape-murder fantasy dream?"

Dr. Britel left the question unanswered.

"How's the drinking?" she asked, instead.

Hannah bristled, hated having to feel shame at the question. Sometimes she wished she drank more than she did so she could just call herself an alcoholic and get on with her life, rather than seesaw between good and bad nights, toeing the line between buzz-chasing and self-medicating.

"I stopped like I told you. For the pregnancy. But I had a glass of wine last night. Late. I needed it to sleep." She paused and scratched her arm. "Maybe two glasses."

"How's the anger?" the therapist asked.

"*Fine*," Hannah said.

"It's okay to be angry, Hannah. You and I have discussed this many times. But you have to channel it. Find a healthy target for it. You grew up around rage and anger. It's understandable."

"This isn't about my anger," Hannah said. "It's about my husband fantasizing about raping and killing someone. Why does everything have to be about my fucking anger issues?"

Dr. Britel stared at her for a moment to let the irony sink in before speaking.

"You've used the word 'mysterious' to describe Dallin in several of our sessions, since we first started. That's not a word commonly used by a spouse to describe the other. Most couples would say their marriages contain very little mystery. Spouses often think they know everything about each other, whether that's the actual case or not."

Hannah was beginning to regret bringing the topic up. She felt her weight shifting, her back now pressing harder against the chair, assuming a retreating, defensive position. "I always meant that in a good way," she said. "Mostly about his work. He's quiet about it. He's quiet in general. I've always been attracted to that quality in him."

"But mystery can create doubt."

"Are you asking me if I trust my husband?"

"Haven't you had questions about him before?"

Hannah paused, digested the question, and thought about the best way to respond.

"I'm getting the witness-stand feeling here."

"I'm not prosecuting you, Hannah. We can move on to another subject if you prefer."

That's right, Hannah. Shove all those doubts aside, just like you always do. Because this isn't the first time you've wondered about him, is it?

"That was different," Hannah finally said. "I questioned why he had a second phone that he hadn't told me about. It turned out to be another phone for work."

"If I recall," Dr. Britel said, "you found the phone in his jacket pocket. You asked him why he hadn't told you about it, and he got defensive about it."

Defensive. Is that what it was? She remembered Dallin dismissing her question casually. *It's a work phone. Emergency stuff. I rarely use it.* But when she pressed even a little harder, he had angered. *Jesus, Hannah, you can look at the phone if you want to. Do I have to give you an inventory of all my office equipment, too?*

"There are two different issues here," Dr. Britel said. "One is your concern about Dallin's fidelity."

"I'm *not* concerned about his fidelity."

"Forgive me. Let's just say there might exist some trust issues."

Hannah wanted to argue but didn't.

"The other issue is the violence. Have there ever been any other situations where he's done something that seemed...unusual? Aggressive in a physical way?"

"No. No, of course not." *Is that true, Hannah?* "I mean...I don't know. Sometimes he can get a little rough with sex, but I encourage it. It can be fun."

Dr. Britel wrote in her notepad, and it made Hannah feel like she was giving a confession to the police.

"Rough in what way?"

"Nothing, really. I mean, I think I've mentioned it before. Sometimes he bites, but not too hard. Or wants to try something a little more experimental." Hannah sucked in a deep breath and let go in one short, fast burst. "A couple of years ago he wanted to try choking me during sex. It's supposed to increase the intensity of the orgasm. I actually researched it. But...but I just wasn't comfortable with it, so he let it go. It was no big deal. He asked a couple more times, but not in a while."

"I see." More note scribbling. "Did he ever ask you to choke *him*?"

"No."

"And this dream last night. The talking in his sleep. Did you ask him about it?"

"No. I haven't seen him today. He'd left for work by the time I woke up."

"Are you planning to?"

I don't know.

"Yes," Hannah said.

"Okay, then I suggest we move on from this subject for now. Let's wait until next week to explore this much further. I would like to see how you two discuss this first."

Hannah nodded, relieved to be able to move on. Though she felt a twinge of panic. *Now I have to ask him about it.* She truly wanted and intended to, but the idea of actually asking him filled her stomach with ice. If she asked him, he might tell her an answer she didn't want to hear.

The remainder of her session was filled with the usual back and forth that seemed routine but was the essence of why Hannah had started her weekly therapy. After Billy went to prison, Hannah had left her tiny Kansas town and had matured immensely, but perhaps too fast to be healthy. Dallin's company had grown at lightspeed pace, and by the time he'd proposed to Hannah almost six years ago, his net worth approached a million dollars. Today, that number was nearly forty times that, at least on paper. Growing up, Hannah's understanding of money came from Billy's profane outbursts about how they *didn't fuckin' have any*. Forty million was an incomprehensible number to Hannah, and the richer they became, the more detached she became from all of it. Now they had *people* to tend to the finances. Accountants. Advisors. And she had her sister nearby, who hadn't been nearly as prosperous. Their relationship strained as Hannah's wealth rocketed.

She could hear Billy in her head in these moments, saying she should have turned out more like her sister, Justine. Single mother of two kids from two different fathers. Decent job but hardly what one would call successful. Outward bitterness towards life.

But Hannah was not Justine.

"We're nearly out of time," Dr. Britel said, "and I want to resume next week with our discussion earlier today. But let me ask you one last question before you leave." Dr. Britel stared at her, those cold, clinical eyes framed by wrinkles of years asking a thousand patients a million questions about their most desperate thoughts and feelings. "Do you feel safe at home?"

"Safe?"

Dr. Britel nodded.

Hannah hadn't thought about that. For all the horrible things that her imagination let her paint in her mind, she had never questioned her own safety. Until now.

"Yes," she said. "I feel safe. Dallin would never hurt me." As if to convince herself, she then added, "Ever. Why?"

A small, polite smile from the doctor. "It's just something I need to ask."

Throughout the rest of Hannah's day, the question kept coming back to her.

Am I safe?

Of course she felt safe. Even though everyone had a side darker than they often let show, she *knew* Dallin. They knew *each other*.

Then she heard Billy in her head.

Ain't true, Hannie. Everyone has secrets. Tra-la-la, is what I say. Tra-la-fuckin'-la.

Hannah looked down at her left forearm. She just realized she'd been unconsciously scratching at it all day, and now it was red with fingernail tracks.

Of course I feel safe.

CHAPTER THREE

Hannah stood on the balcony of their downtown Seattle condo, watching Puget Sound fade slowly into darkness. The half-hour before the sun disappeared always seemed the loneliest to her. There was something about how the waning sunlight turned the Sound gray that made everything feel cold and empty to her. Hannah preferred even blackness to gray. Blackness could at least be defined. She could hide in black. Wrap it around her. Disappear.

She took a sip of her wine. Really, a gulp. She was on her second glass, which, most likely, would be a full bottle by the end of the night, followed by a small headache but larger sense of regret in the morning. But tonight she wasn't thinking about conceiving a child. She was wondering about secrets.

The sliding glass door slid open. Dallin was home.

"There you are," he said.

She didn't turn around. A few moments later she felt his hands slip around her waist and grasp around her belly. She kept her gaze straight, watching the gray mercifully turn to black.

"What's wrong?"

"Nothing."

He leaned his face around to hers, and she saw his blue eyes shine brighter than they should have in the faded light coming from in the condo. His intentionally disheveled brown hair faded into a smoky five o'clock shadow that accentuated his jawline. She smelled him, breathed him in. He didn't smell like the Dallin from two days ago. She didn't know why, but he just didn't smell the same. In fact, he seemed completely devoid of any scent at all.

"When you say *nothing*, it's always *something*," he said, a thin smile on his mouth. "You've been distant for a couple of days. What's going on?"

It was true, she had been avoiding him since the night he spoke in his sleep. She knew she needed to say something about it, but yesterday she just avoided it altogether. She had kept conversation minimal and gone to bed early while he worked in the study. Tonight, though, was different. Tonight she had to say something, or this would continue to gnaw at her until it ate her from the inside out.

"Two nights ago you spoke in your sleep," she said.

His head pulled back, just an inch. Caution. "Did I?"

"You did."

She waited for him to ask her what he said. He didn't.

"You...you were talking to a woman," she said. "I...think you were...Dallin, I don't even know how to say this. I think you were raping and killing her."

Dallin pushed away from her, and Hannah felt a flash of anger at him doing so. "Jesus," he said.

She turned and searched his eyes, looking for panic. Looking for explanation. Even looking for bemusement. But there was nothing in them at all, and she didn't know what to do with that.

"I must have been having a bad dream," he said.

"You've never talked in your sleep before."

"So?"

"So you called the woman a cunt."

The word shocked him silent for a moment. "Are you asking me to apologize for what I said in my sleep?"

"I'm just trying to understand. You don't remember anything?"

The normal, analytical Dallin would have asked her exactly what it was he said. The Dallin on the balcony with empty eyes did not.

"No."

Dallin took a step back from the edge of the balcony and let his arms hang at his sides. It seemed to Hannah a studied posture. *Non-threatening.*

"Dallin, just...I don't know. I realize you were sleeping, and you can't control what you dream. But doesn't this seem weird to you? I mean, do you...do you have fantasies that are..."

"Violent?"

She hated that the word came so quickly from his mouth.

"Yes," she said.

"What would you do if I did?"

It was as if someone reached out and slapped her open-palmed across the face. She had asked the question so she could judge the quality of his denial, but she had at least expected a denial. Not a question directed back at her. Hannah took a step backwards.

"Please tell me it's not true," she said. "Don't tell me the idea of...of hurting someone turns you on."

"I'm not saying that at all. I'm simply asking what you would do if I said it was true." He shifted his weight to one leg, his posture more casual than his words. "Look, Hannah, you're asking me to defend something I did when I was unconscious. So if you're going to stand here and ask me to justify words I couldn't control, then I'm asking you to deal with my answers. So I'm asking you, if I had violent fantasies that I never acted upon, what would you do? Would you explore them with me?"

"God, *no.*"

"Then what?" His voice rose just a few decibels. "Would you leave me?"

She shook her head. "*No,* Dallin. I just want to understand. Why are you asking me this?"

There was a moment in his eyes, a brief flash of desperation, of pleading. The moment in the interrogation room where the suspect wanted to confess, considered it for a moment, lured by the promise of *It's okay. Tell us what happened and it'll make things better for you.*

Then the moment was gone.

"Well, I don't have an answer except to tell you I'm the man you've always known. Who is *not* a rapist and murderer. I mean, are you even kidding me about this? You know I have bad dreams from time to time."

"Sometimes I feel you only show me what you want me to see."

"What does that mean?"

"Like you never telling me about your second phone."

"The two-phone argument again? I told you it was for work." Dallin balled his fists and then released them. "Do you tell me about every part of your life?"

She hesitated. "I tell you about every part of my life here," she continued, quietly adding the "here" as her loophole. "You know why? Because I love you and want to share with you. You know what I do all day, because I *tell* you. But you come home and tell me work was good, or some meeting was great, or maybe a small piece of something that's bothering you. Other than that, I don't get anything from you. That's if I'm lucky enough to see you before I go to bed."

"Hannah, I just don't think you would—"

"What, *understand*?" *Hannie, you dumb rube.* "I'm too stupid to understand your work?"

"Calm down. I was going to say find it interesting."

Was there anything more enraging than to be told to calm down? Hannah felt her neck muscles tighten. "I just don't want to feel like this."

"Feel like what?"

"That you have secrets from me."

"I'm confused. I have a bad dream and you think I'm full of secrets all of a sudden? Well, shit, Hannah, maybe I should start sleeping in another room. Better yet, I'll just stay awake from now on. Would that help?"

"You basically admitted you have violent fantasies."

"I didn't say that at all."

"Then tell me you don't."

He leaned in, almost predatory.

"I *don't.*"

"It's more than just what you said. The past two years. You've been distant. I hardly see you. We go weeks without sex—"

Dallin pushed his fingers up through his hair and let out a sigh of exasperation, the sigh of someone who had the same argument a thousand times before and had to have it yet once again.

"I know I work a lot. But by the time I get home, you've already lost yourself in a bottle of wine. You've replaced me with that glass. How do you think that makes me feel?"

She moved to set the wine glass down but held it defiantly, as if proving her drinking wasn't the problem.

"Maybe I drink because I'm bored and lonely. You spend longer hours away from me as each month passes. Jesus, it's such a cliché. The richer we get the emptier I feel."

"Hannah, do you want me to leave Echo? Leave what I've built?"

Echo. His company. Everything was about Echo.

"Actually, sometimes I do," she said. "We have more money than we'll ever be able to spend."

"If I left, the value of our stock goes with it. And how could you even want me to leave? You know how passionate I am about it."

"I want you to be passionate about more than just Echo. About us. About our life together," Hannah said.

"I *am.* The other night was great. And we're...we're trying, you know?" He reached out and stroked her hair, and she suddenly felt like a trophy being admired on a shelf. Then his thumb lowered and traced the faded scar above her right eye, the scar Billy put there when she was fifteen. Hannah pulled his hand down.

"What about when you wanted to choke me during sex?" she said. "Why would you want that?"

"That was years ago."

"But still, you wanted it. You wanted to choke me."

"That's supposed to be pleasurable for you, not for me."

"I can't see how that would be pleasurable."

"And you've used handcuffs on me before," he countered. "Does that mean you secretly want to restrain men, fuck them, and then slit their throats?"

The coarseness of his words attacked her. He wasn't just trying to make a point. He was trying to make her mad. It was working. She couldn't let herself be baited, because she would lose her temper completely and he would win. He would win because he could then say she was irrational and he could no longer reason with her.

"Those were...stupid fuzzy handcuffs. I thought it would be fun. Different. I wasn't trying to *hurt* you." She felt the warmth of tears spilling over her face and she hated it. "It was more than a dream," she continued. "You were talking. You were enjoying yourself. You were causing pain and it made you happy. I *heard* it make you happy. Do you have any idea how awful a feeling that is? What if it were me saying things like that in my sleep? Wouldn't that make you wonder things about me?"

He took a step forward and jabbed his finger toward her face. "It wouldn't make me question the nature of who you were as a person. I would see it for what it was. Your subconscious taking over. This whole thing is ridiculous."

These last words were spoken with a voice that seemed not her husband's and with a facial expression more of an amateurish actor than someone who believed in what he was saying. Dallin was suddenly distant, as if reading the lines off cue cards placed behind Hannah.

"Don't call me ridiculous," she said. "And don't just dismiss me."

"Hannah, I'm *not*."

"Dallin, what the hell is happening here? None of this makes sense. What's going on with us?" She looked in his eyes, searching for a flicker of change. "What's going on with *you*?"

He closed his eyes, took a deep breath, and then slowly exhaled. When he opened his eyes again he appeared more focused, more committed to the moment. Calm face, but body tensed to the point of explosion.

"You tell me, Hannah. You brought this whole fucking thing up."

There was a tipping point here. Hannah knew her husband would either escalate things or remove himself from the situation. Nine times out of ten Dallin chose to back down, apologize, or extract himself from an argument. He either knew he was wrong or, she conceded, sometimes it wasn't worth the effort to him. He'd told her as much before. Then there was the one time out of ten he pushed on, harder, with conviction, not letting go until he felt his point was very *clearly* made. That's when he shouted. Three months ago he had even punched a wall.

She had never seen that side of him before, the sudden violence. It had been the low point of a hard year, a time of seeing him less and less as his company grew astronomically. Their happiness strained as their fortune blossomed, and the stress was tearing at him. She could see it in his eyes, hear it in his voice. Late nights, early mornings, meals alone. He hadn't been the same Dallin. But the past month he had changed, as if he recommitted himself to their happiness. Things had been better. *Good.* Until the moment he had talked in his sleep.

Hannah looked in his face and wondered if this was going to be a one-in-ten moment.

"I'm going to get a drink," he said. Dallin turned and walked into the condo, sliding the glass door behind him.

She watched him walk up to the bar and pull out the scotch. She was relieved. She didn't want to talk more about the dream now, anyway. Hannah had to process what little he had already said. She would have to replay the evening over and over in her mind, combing through his words and his gestures, finding those bits that assured her and the pieces that made her want to ask him more questions.

Hannah turned and looked back at the water in the distance. Things were darker now, but there was still a dusting of gray. She no longer wanted to be out on the balcony. As much as she preferred the darkness, she suddenly sensed how long a fall it would be if she went over the edge.

CHAPTER FOUR

DAY 4

Hannah woke to a tongue on her face and the smell of dog breath pushing up her nostrils. Zoo stood over her, his body shaking in canine excitement, acting as if Hannah had finally awakened from a month-long coma. She reached out, simultaneously giving herself a long stretch and scratching his rump, which stirred him into a small frenzy. Finally, she pushed him away and sat up. Dust danced in sunbeams streaming through the bedroom window. She looked over and discovered Dallin's side of the bed empty. She glanced at the clock on the wall. Five after nine.

That was the second time in three days she'd remained in bed longer than usual. The bedsheet could have been lead-lined considering how heavy her body felt. She forced her bare feet to the floor, stood, and headed to the kitchen where the coffee maker seemed to shine like a beacon of hope. Zoo pursued, his nails click-clicking on the hardwood floors.

She saw the Post-it pressed against the coffee machine.

I really love you.

Do you? she wondered. Such an easy note to write, but it takes a lot more than a few handstrokes to actually mean it.

The theme song from *Six Feet Under* emanated from her cell phone. Hannah looked at the screen. Justine.

"Hey there," Hannah said.

"Morning. How's the view from the top of the castle today?"

Hannah bristled. She loved her sister but could do without

the constant references to Hannah's wealth. Hannah and her sister had had vastly different lives since moving from Kansas together. Justine finished high school but never went to college. When she turned eighteen, she had moved in with her boyfriend, the first in a series of many of the following decade. Justine's last relationship resulted in a brief marriage that ended with her ex leaving both her and their son, Aikman, behind. As Justine struggled, Hannah thrived. A little over a year and a half ago Justine was pregnant again, this time by an almost-boyfriend who had disappeared two weeks after Justine told him the news. She had kept the baby, and Connor was now nearly a year old.

Hannah knew her bond with Justine was based more on shared childhood hardship than true love and friendship. They had both cowered under the shadow of Billy when they were growing up, though Justine had never felt the hand of her father. Hannah only had once, but that had created a chasm between their childhoods. Billy never directed his rage at Justine, which had always made Hannah jealous. How strange to hate your father but also long for his approval.

"Same as it usually is, Justine. Cloudy."

"Just wanted to call and check in on you. Haven't heard from you in a few days."

Hannah sighed. "Yeah, I know. Just...I don't know. Stuff going on."

"Stuff?"

"Yeah. Stuff."

"Want to be more specific?"

"Not right now. Later, okay?" She would tell her sister about Dallin. Of course she would, because she always did. But at the moment Hannah didn't want to talk about what Dallin had said in his sleep.

"Did something happen with Dallin?"

Hannah paused. "What makes you say that?"

"Because you're rarely quiet, and when you are, it's either something with Dallin or it's around Mom's birthday. And that's not for another four months."

"Yes, Justine. I'm fine."

"Coffee later? After work and I pick up the kiddos?"

"Sure, that'd be great."

"Oh, and also, I wanted to know if I could borrow a laptop for a few days. Mine just died and my company can't get me a new one for a few days. I'm sure you guys have a spare that you don't use."

Don't you rich folks have spares of everything just in case?

It was true, though. She and Dallin each had their own laptops, iPads, iPods, and a spare laptop and desktop. That wasn't because they were rich. It made them like most Americans. Sometimes Hannah thought her sister chose to live on a shoestring budget just to appear to be struggling more than she actually was. Her job as an event planner paid well enough. And hadn't they just given her ten thousand dollars a few months ago? Moreover, Justine hadn't paid back any of the home loan they had given her. Not that Hannah would ever ask—she would never do that—but still...shouldn't Justine at least make the effort?

"Sure," Hannah said. "I'll bring it this afternoon. It's not real new or anything."

"Oh, I'm sure it's better than what I had. Thanks, sis. That's a huge help."

In addition to asking for money, Justine always, but subtly, reminded Hannah how hard it was being a single mom, and how lucky Hannah was to be able to have the freedom not to worry about paying bills. Hannah had retaliated at times, once even telling Justine no one had forced her to have two kids with two different men who clearly had no intention of sticking around. They didn't speak for a week after that fight. Justine had been the first to apologize, but it wasn't long after that Justine also needed help buying a car.

Relax, Hannah told herself. *You're fortunate to have so much after being raised with so little. Appreciate what you have and share it with your sister. You're family, after all.*

Zoo followed Hannah into the office. For a condo, the office was large, nearly three hundred square feet. Floor-to-ceiling bookshelves comprised two of the walls, half filled with technical volumes on computer science, the other half with the kind of escapist literature Hannah used since the time she learned to read. *Pride and Prejudice. Last of the Mohicans. Of Mice and Men.* These were complemented by a whole row of comic books, a lifetime of Sunday newspapers and memories of locking herself in her room and disappearing into the abstract lives of Garfield, Calvin and Hobbes, and Cathy. Cathy was especially unfunny, but Cathy had been there with her simple problems to distract a young Hannah when screams of anger filled their small Kansas home. *Ack!* was much more pleasant to read than *fuck you, whore* was to hear Billy yell at her mother.

There were two desks in the office, one for Dallin and one for her. Dallin's desk was littered with Post-it notes—each containing half-thoughts or reminders understood only by its author—iPad and cell phone accessories, and documents with titles like *Adaptive Behavior-Based Malware Protection.* Hannah's desk was empty save for her laptop and a neatly organized pile of things *To Get To*, which never grew too high.

The spare laptop was in a drawer in Dallin's desk, or was at least the last time she had seen it. She reached down and pulled at the drawer, and then was surprised when it resisted. She tried again with no effect. The drawer was locked. She tried the other drawers. Also locked.

Hannah straightened and stared at the desk as if it was a math problem to solve. Dallin had never locked the desk before. His sensitive work information wasn't stored on his hard drive, much less printed out and filed inside a desk drawer. Most of what was inside the drawers was clutter, the office-supply flotsam and jetsam accumulated over the years.

He *had* mentioned something about the cleaning woman, Hannah remembered. Said something a couple of weeks ago. *I don't trust her.* Maybe he had started locking the desk to keep her out. But what was he keeping her from?

Hannah normally would have waited for Dallin to come

home and have him retrieve the laptop. But now she wanted to know what was in there.

The desks were only about a year old, purchased together. Each came with its own set of two keys, and after they were delivered Hannah took one of his keys and put it with hers, and one of hers with his, so if either lost their set a spare would still exist. It was a smart idea proceeded by neither of them ever actually bothering to lock their desks. Until now.

She opened the top drawer of her desk and found the two brass keys on the thin wire loop, tucked back behind a box of paper clips. She tried the first key on his desk and it slid into the keyhole but did not turn. She tried the second key. It turned easily.

Hannah opened the top desk drawer, the wide, shallow one that could not possibly hold a laptop. As soon as it opened she closed it again, her eyes having only scanned a drawer of office-supply clutter.

She reached down and opened the larger, bottom drawer, the one she had tried earlier. This time the drawer slid easily on its rollers. The spare laptop was there on top of a pile of blank printer paper, just where she remembered it. She lifted it out, along with its power cord, then locked Dallin's desk and put the keys back where she kept them. She would tell Dallin she had opened his desk in order to retrieve the computer. She'd say it matter-of-factly, and might ask why he locked the desk but wouldn't be accusatory about it. That's how married couples were supposed to be. Matter-of-fact. Benefit of the doubt.

Hannah wrapped the cord around the laptop and then noticed something sticking out of the side of it. She recognized what it was, though she had never seen this one before. It was a flash drive, a small storage device no longer than an inch or so.

She pulled it out of the USB slot and turned it over in her hand. Small. Silver. *HP* etched into the side. *16GB.*

I wonder what's on there, she thought. It wouldn't be hard to solve the mystery. Just plug it into her computer and see what was on it. Dallin had probably grabbed the spare for a presentation he needed to give and put his presentation on the portable drive. There were probably a host of PowerPoint files on it.

She hesitated a moment, as if she had no right to look. But then she assured herself *she* wouldn't mind if he looked at her files. She plugged the flash drive into her computer, took a deep breath, and then sat at her desk. Hannah launched her file browser and navigated to the new device, which the computer told her was named *HP ProStor*.

She clicked on the device name and opened it up. There were only two files. She double-clicked on the first one, the one with a .wmv extension. She was pretty sure that was some kind of video file.

When the video opened, she immediately saw it was footage of Dallin speaking at a conference. He would save these to watch and critique himself. He was a wonderful speaker, but was never happy when he watched these, looking for imperfections, ways to improve. She thought he obsessed over the matter. Truth was, he was compelling to look at and listen to, but he wouldn't ever let himself be happy with his performance.

He used to practice in front of her, in those early days when he wasn't as polished as he was now. She missed those moments, her sitting on the couch, an audience of one, Dallin looking to her for any bit of advice she could give him. Now he just watched video of himself alone.

The other file was much larger than the first, nearly four hundred megabytes, and was an *.avi* file. She double-clicked on it.

At first she didn't think it was going to open, but after a few seconds it did. Another video.

This time, it wasn't Dallin.

CHAPTER FIVE

The woman in the video was young, probably a decade younger than Hannah. Twenty-two, perhaps. She had brown, kinked hair that fell loosely around perfectly smooth, alabaster cheeks, reminding Hannah vaguely of a woman from the Renaissance. The woman was sitting at her computer staring into a webcam, and the image capture stopped just above the top of her breasts. She seemed to be in a bedroom. A framed Coldplay concert poster adorned the wall behind her.

Her voice was fresh and young, hopeful. Playful. "You want to talk or type, sweetie?"

A long pause.

"Talk." A man's voice. Dallin.

Hannah's stomach twisted.

The woman—just a girl, really—nodded and smiled. "Okay, then. Your name is Samuel?"

Another pause.

"Samuel, yes."

Hannah looked at the top rim of the laptop screen to the small circle where the built-in web camera existed. The girl viewed Hannah's husband through this tiny lens.

"Okay, Samuel. I'm Rebecca. Thanks for finding me."

Silence.

"Are you shy, Samuel?"

"A little."

"Well, if you're shy now, could be a problem when we meet up." A crooked, not-so-innocent smile.

Hannah felt sick. She wanted to pretend to have no idea of what any of this was, but she knew. She just *knew*.

"I'm okay," Dallin said. "It's just a little new for me."

"Are you married?"

No hesitation. "No."

Hannah squeezed the mouse in her hand. A thin film of sweat coated her palm.

"Okay, Samuel. Well, no need to be nervous. Let me tell you how all this works." Rebecca brushed a long strand of hair back behind her ear, which remained for a moment before falling in front of her face again. "First, some ground rules. This is a pre-screen I require of all my clients. Someone who is willing to let me see them on camera is as concerned about being safe and smart as I am. You'd be surprised how many men refuse to do this pre-screen. It also lets us get to know each other a bit, so when we do meet in person we're able to let ourselves fully relax and enjoy... our time together."

"I understand," he said. "Makes perfect sense."

"Also, you can record this video stream if you want—just click on the button on the bottom of the screen. But you cannot distribute it in any way or form. I am also recording this, which is for my own protection, but I value confidentiality as much as I do safety, so as long as we're respectful of each other we won't have any issues. Finally, I won't discuss anything overtly explicit during this conversation nor over the phone, and know that, should we meet, you will be paying for my time and not in exchange for anything of a sexual nature."

Then Rebecca gave a little wink, and that slight flutter of her eyelid may have well been a knife plunging into Hannah's bowels.

Dallin's brief chuckle rumbled through the laptop speaker.

"I get it," he said.

"You fucking asshole," Hannah whispered to the screen. "You motherfucking asshole."

"Good," Rebecca said, smiling at Hannah. "Now that's out of the way, let me tell you a little about myself." Then Rebecca launched into a couple of minutes of what things she liked and didn't like, from a loose description of her educational background to the kind of dogs she rescued. It was scripted but convincing, the portrait of a young, strong, independent woman who was willing to share but not share too much. Rebecca sounded mature beyond what her age must be, and she smiled enough to seem genuinely interested in the person at the other end of the video stream.

She wrapped up her speech with, "and I really like to make people happy. It's why I do what I do. I consider myself a kind of therapist. I help people. I want to be able to give you what you want, Samuel."

Hannah could hear Dallin's breathing. Loud and fast, like some kind of goddamned fucking *animal*.

"So, Samuel. Tell me a little about yourself. What kind of work do you do?"

"I'm...in technology. Computers."

She smiled. "You must be very smart. I could never figure them out. Maybe you can look at my laptop and tell me why it keeps crashing."

He's not a fucking computer repairman, you whore. He runs one of the largest Internet security firms in North America. Hannah didn't know why she felt like defending her husband, but this girl was making him sound like he was some kind of plumber.

Dallin's laugh sounded nervous and uncertain, two adjectives Hannah would never typically associate with her husband. But in front of Rebecca, he was just a shy little boy. Hannah's stomach continued to collapse in on itself into a tiny, fiery pit.

"I have to say, Samuel, you are damn sexy. Why do you want to see me?"

"You came recommended."

Recommended? By whom?

"I know," Rebecca said. "I will thank our mutual friend for that later. But I mean, what is it that you want to do with me? Is it something you can't do otherwise? And please don't be too explicit in your answer."

"It's...unconventional."

"Unconventional is my specialty, Samuel. I'm sure you've heard that from your friend. I'm very open minded. That's another reason I require a thorough pre-screen. It's also why my rates are what they are. Tell me, Samuel." Rebecca leaned slightly forward toward the camera and her face filled the screen. She pursed her lips and widened her eyes just enough to make it clear she was up for anything. "Do you like to be in control?"

The next words Dallin said were louder than all the others. And they didn't come from the laptop speaker. They came from directly behind Hannah.

"What are you doing?"

CHAPTER SIX

Hannah screamed. Or thought she did. She didn't even know. She turned and saw Dallin standing in the doorway to the room, looking at her with confusion.

What was he doing home?

Zoo jumped up. Eyes wide. Whiskers bristling.

The video kept playing, though Hannah only heard it. Her gaze was locked on her husband's face. The Dallin on the computer—*Samuel*—spoke with the quiet conviction of a child in Santa's lap.

"The kind of control I desire is...somewhat extreme. It's something I've never asked of any partner. Money isn't an issue."

The Dallin in the room was far less controlled. His expression immediately changed from confusion to anger as he raced toward Hannah and snatched the laptop off the desk. As he yanked it, the power cord and mouse went along with it, whipping up into Hannah's face. Dallin yanked out the cords and hit the power button, killing the conversation between Samuel and Rebecca.

"Dallin, what the hell was that? *Who is she?*"

"Where did you find this?"

"Are you kidding me? Who the hell is she?"

"No one."

"Don't you dare do that, Dallin, *who is Rebecca?*" She hated hearing the whore's name come off her lips.

His face softened into one she recognized, and Hannah was suddenly chilled by the thought that this was actually his pretend face. The one he used when he needed to get what he wanted.

Maybe the question wasn't who Rebecca was, but rather *who was Samuel?*

"You went through my stuff?"

Dallin didn't wait for an answer. He walked out of the room, taking the laptop and flash drive with him. Anger welled through Hannah as she followed him into the master bedroom.

"Don't walk away from me," she said. "And don't turn this around on me. I needed the spare laptop for Justine. I have a key to your desk. Now I know why you kept it locked. Now I know why you really have a second cell phone. How long have you been doing this?"

"Hannah, calm down."

They stood at the foot of their bed. She kept her gaze locked with his, refusing to look down or away.

"Don't tell me to calm down. Don't you *dare* tell me to calm down. Did you *fuck* her?" The word *fuck* sent a pain through her core. Saying it out loud made the possibility so much more real.

"I don't want to discuss this when you're hysterical."

The word *hysterical* attacked her, making her skin itch with a thousand ravaging fire ants. Hannah was her father's daughter in this moment, and how she wanted to control the temper she had so often successfully reined in. But there were moments when it was just too much, when Billy's DNA controlled her, and Hannah didn't just want to argue. She wanted to pick up something heavy and destroy. She longed to hear the sound of something fragile shattering into a thousand pieces.

"*Who...is...she?*"

Dallin turned, slipped his hands into his pockets, and gazed out the window at Puget Sound.

Hannah crossed her arms, stared at the floor, and willed herself not to cry. She looked over to Zoo, who, while not whining, was wide-eyed and alert, his muscles tensed in rapt attention.

"Why would you do this to me?"

"It's nothing," he whispered to the window.

"How long, Dallin? How long have you been cheating on me?" Now she approached him and spoke to the back of his head. "How many other web girls have there been? And what the hell kind of fantasies are you into that you can't tell me about them? When did I become not enough for you?"

He let out a long breath, the sound of a parent trying to be patient with a child. "You're too upset to discuss this right now. Let's talk about it later."

For the second time in two days Dallin suddenly seemed as if he was reading lines off cue cards, an actor in some stage production about love and betrayal. His voice, sounding not at all like it should, made everything dreamlike. Well, *nightmarish* would be more precise.

She wanted to touch him, ground herself, something she was so used to doing, but Hannah kept her hands at her side. She so desperately wanted him to tell her it was all a joke, made up, some kind of sick prank, but in her soul she couldn't conceive of how that could even be a remote possibility.

"You're not seeing this for what it is," he said.

Hannah dropped her hand, the hope for any assurances or comfort dissolved. "Seeing it for what it is? Dallin, you won't even answer my questions. We're talking about this now. I don't even know if there *will* be a 'later.'"

Finally, Dallin turned to her. His face had the smooth plastic expression of a mannequin. "What does that mean?"

She threw her arms out. "Do you seriously think I'm just going to allow you to do this to me? What if I was talking dirty with some guy on the Internet? You'd lose your fucking *mind*."

"We'll talk later." Dallin started to walk around her.

"Don't leave this room. You don't get to make that decision. *You don't get to leave.*"

"Hannah, we'll talk later."

"No, we will talk *now*."

He took another step. She grabbed his arm, and in that moment, it was Billy's arm. Hannah was fifteen again. In her mind, her hand held a lighter with a flame that glowed in a dark room. *You don't get to do this anymore. You don't get to hurt any of us ever again. It ends tonight.*

Like Billy, Dallin looked down and yanked his arm free. Unlike Billy, Dallin then kept walking and disappeared into the other room.

Now Hannah screamed.

"I'm the one who gets to leave you!"

Silence for a moment. Then Dallin reappeared. He stood there in the doorway, hands in his pockets, perfectly still. It wasn't that he was merely quiet, observing. He was completely motionless. The way he looked at Hannah was something she had never experienced from her husband. In that look, in that absence of life in his body, he wielded all power in the room, as if, telepathically, he commanded the sound and the air to leave the room. And Dallin just stared. He just fucking *stared* at her. Then very quietly he said, "What did you say?"

Her voice was coarse and dry. "I'm the one who gets to leave you."

Dallin stormed into the room. That's the word that came to her mind in the seconds before he grabbed her. He's *storming*. The twisted face of rage, the anger at the inconsideration of someone defying him, the need to punish the insolent, the disobedient.

She heard his sharp, fast breaths—*jackal*—as she saw him raise his hand.

Then it was around her throat, and he used that hand to shove her against a wall. The pain in her throat as he squeezed dwarfed the concussive slam of her head against the sheetrock. A framed picture from their honeymoon fell and shattered on the floor, shards of glass scattering around her feet.

Zoo roared to life, barking furiously, the yapping piercing Hannah's brain. *Bite him!* her mind screamed, as her voice was unable. *Fucking bite him!* But Zoo only barked.

"Leave me?" Dallin said. His voice was calm, controlled, as his fingers squeezed her throat. "That's what you're going to do?

You think you can *leave* me, Hannah? Just like that? With every-thing I've done for you? Saved you from a shitty white-trash exis-tence. Made you wealthy. Given you everything you wanted, just so you can sit here and drink all day. And you get to leave me? No, I don't think so."

His fingers squeezed into her neck. Hannah reached up and grabbed his forearm with both hands and dug her nails in as hard as she could.

Dallin's eyes widened barely more than a hair. "You have no idea what's good for you," he whispered.

He wasn't squeezing hard enough to block her air passage. Yet. She sucked in a shallow breath and asked the only question that existed in her mind at that moment.

"*Who are you?*"

Dallin studied her. There was no joy in his eyes, yet neither was there menace. There was just a complete sadness, a resigna-tion, the look of someone lost deep in the woods who finally re-alized they weren't ever going to make it out. He leaned in and Hannah felt his breath on her ear as he spoke. The words came on such a light whisper she wasn't even convinced she heard what he said.

"I'm so sorry."

Then, without saying anything else, he released his grip. She fell forward, almost to the ground before catching herself, regain-ing her balance just as she saw Dallin turn and walk into the liv-ing room. Hannah stared out vacantly in that direction, unable to move, gasping. Zoo came up and whimpered softly as he licked the top of her right foot, the small, wet tongue rolling over the ridges of her bones.

You don't touch me, she thought, thinking not of her dog but her husband. The last man who had hurt her physically was Billy, and the emotion, the adrenaline, the heat from the rage, which created millions of pinpricks across her skin, it all came back in this moment. In this moment Hannah was nearly blinded from anger, and despite all the love and history she had with Dallin, she wanted to smash in the teeth of whoever that man was in the other room.

She steadied herself, breathing more slowly. Hannah reached down and patted the top of Zoo's head, and he licked her fingers greedily.

Hannah held her breath and listened, her body tensed, ready to spring.

Silence for a minute. Then the sound of the TV turning on in the other room. Dallin was watching the news.

CHAPTER SEVEN

Hannah raced into the master closet and pulled down a leather overnight bag. Zoo followed her every step, staying so close Hannah twice tripped over him. He barked and nipped at her feet, trying to get her attention. Hannah shushed him.

She turned her attention to the task at hand, frantically grabbing at clothes on the racks and stuffing them into the bag. Now into the bathroom. She snatched items off the counter indiscriminately, cramming them in the bag wherever they would fit. She risked a glance at herself in the mirror. Her face was puffy and red from crying, her eyes bloodshot. Her long blond hair, which was so fine it could rarely ever fall anywhere but straight down, was disheveled, as if she had just rolled out of bed. She leaned in and saw the marks around the base of her neck, where Dallin's hand had been just minutes earlier. They were a sunset red, the kind that would eventually turn into a gunmetal gray as bruises flowered.

She turned away, wanting to see no more.

Leave, Hannah. Leave now.

Her purse was by the front door, and in it was everything else she needed: wallet, keys, phone. She had to go through the living room.

She slung the overnight bag over her shoulder and went back into the bedroom. She still heard the TV in the other room. Financial news. Dallin loved to watch the goddamn financial news. Loved to follow the markets. See what was happening in the various tech industry silos. Echo Systems—Dallin's company, of which he was the Chairman and CEO—was a security tech company, and he feasted on information. She pictured him out there, on the couch, shoes off, feet propped on the table, watching the news. As if nothing had happened.

Hannah steeled herself to make her way to the front door. What if he wasn't on the couch? What if he was standing by the door with a knife? She only heard the TV, the sound of some talking head droning on about post-market closing corporate announcements of the day.

She couldn't even call 9-1-1 if she wanted to. Hannah and Dallin only had cell phones. No landline. Hannah's cell phone was in her purse.

Hannah looked at the shattered photo on the floor. The picture was from Bora Bora, when they had sailed around the Tahitian islands on their honeymoon five years ago. She had taken the picture herself: the shot was from the front of their beach villa, which had been so close to the water the morning-tide waves had licked their feet just a few steps out the door. The Pacific Ocean stretched out endlessly in the photo, the water smooth and the blue color of a robin's egg. They had made love right before the photo was taken, and every time she looked at the picture on the wall she could feel him inside her, which always made her feel wanted.

Hannah bent down and reached out to Zoo. "We're leaving, Zoo. Stay close." Then Hannah picked up the longest of the broken shards of glass. The side of it was sharper than she expected, and it nipped her skin, cutting her hand. A small droplet of blood grew until it ran down her palm. She made her way back into the bathroom and grabbed a white washcloth hanging near the sink. She covered all but the top few inches of the shard in the cloth and then secured her grip around it. She held the piece of glass upside down. Dagger-like.

Hannah returned to the bedroom and again looked at the doorway into the living room. Zoo, as commanded, remained close. Again, only the sound of the TV. She could do this one of two ways. She could go slowly, peering around the door, assessing his position, and try to sneak out quietly. Or she could just go.

Not even look at him. Just walk quickly to the entryway, grab her purse, and get out of there.

She took a deep breath, counted to three, and walked into the living room. Hannah's gaze locked on the front door. Dallin wasn't blocking it. And her purse was there, right where she had left it. She headed directly for it, not turning her head to look where Dallin was. If she saw him, she might lose her nerve. She might get scared, and maybe he would sense her fear and would pounce.

Ten steps. She counted them as she walked as fast as she could without running.

Nothing.

On her tenth step she grabbed her purse and yanked open the front door. Zoo bolted into the hallway.

Hannah chanced a glance back into the room. Dallin was exactly as her mind pictured, on the couch, back turned toward her. He seemed oblivious that she had entered the room, or was on her way out. It was as if, for him, Hannah had simply ceased to exist.

Zoo's toenails clicked on the wood floors of the condo corridor as they walked away from her home and toward the elevator. She pushed the button to go down and waited a lifetime for the elevator cab to arrive at her floor. The whole time, she expected Dallin to come storming from the condo towards her, face twisted in rage, ready to attack.

Leave me? I don't think so.

But he never did. The empty corridor remained empty. As the elevator finally arrived and its doors opened, Hannah looked down at the glass shard in her hand. Her grip on it was slightly loosened, and the small cut on her hand had oozed more blood onto the white washcloth, the stain spreading and growing like an oil slick on a lake.

Hannah stepped inside.

CHAPTER EIGHT

She stared out the restaurant window, through the gray of a fall day in Seattle, to the electronic readout board on the bank across the street. Fifty-two degrees outside. Just after eleven in the morning.

The waiter set a glass of ice water in front of her and Hannah shivered, wanting nothing to do with anything else cold. She noticed the wedding band on the waiter's finger and wondered what kind of husband he was, then decided she didn't care.

Justine, sitting across the booth from her, ordered them both coffee while Hannah stared at the top of the table. When the waiter left, Justine leaned in.

"Hannah, what's going on?"

Hannah had told her nothing on the phone, not because she was worried about privacy, but because she didn't think she could do it without crying. She cried now.

Justine came to Hannah's side of the booth and held her. Hannah didn't want to cry any more, not because she was stoic, but because it exhausted her. Justine squeezed her sister.

"It's okay, Hannah. Whatever it is, I'm sure it'll be okay."

No it won't, Hannah thought.

Hannah wiped her face and then eyed the waiter coming toward them with their coffee. She felt embarrassment for her tears and then anger at her embarrassment. She looked down as he set the coffee on the table and walked away without saying anything.

Hannah lifted her head and looked into her sister's eyes. "I don't know. It's just...Jesus, you left work and everything."

"Screw work. *What's going on?*"

Deep breath. Then tell it straight. Just as it happened.

Justine's eyes widened as Hannah's words came forth, and her mouth opened to interject, but Hannah stopped her.

"Let me just talk. Please."

Justine nodded.

When she finished, Hannah stopped crying.

"What a fucking *monster*," Justine said.

Hannah let her gaze fall to the table.

"I can't believe this," Justine added.

"I know," Hannah said. "It made me think...you know. Of the night with Billy. I don't think I've been this mad since back then."

"You need to go to the police. He *assaulted* you."

"I...I know that. But then I was thinking how that never did any good for Mom."

Three times the police had come out to their small Kansas home when Hannah and Justine were just girls. Three visits, all from phone calls placed by Hannah. Three raps at the door, three light interrogations of the man of the house, asking if everything was okay. Always talked to Billy, never to Hannah's mother, who remained in sight but never spoke unless spoken to. And each of those three times the police walked away without doing a goddamned thing.

And why should they have, Hannie? There weren't no bruises on her face. No blood to be seen. Just one big happy family. Well, maybe not happy all the time. I was the only rooster in that henhouse, and that means I had to keep order, didn't I? You was way too eager to call 9-1-1. But it didn't do you any good, did it?

"That was in Kansas," Justine said. "Not here. And that was a lifetime ago."

"Justine, I don't know what to do."

"He *hurt* you, Hannah. If he's capable of that, who knows what he might do next."

Hannah knew.

"You have to leave."

The words made Hannah dizzy with disbelief. "I've...we've been married five years. Together for longer. This isn't him. I *know* him."

"Apparently you don't. He's *cheating* on you, Hannah. And he hurt you. He *strangled* you. Are you fucking kidding me?"

The family in the booth behind them spoke excitedly of a trip to Disney World they were planning for Christmas. The boy wanted to go on the Haunted House ride. The little girl: Teacups.

Hannah flagged down the waiter and ordered a Jack and Coke, and Justine thankfully said nothing about it not even being noon yet. Coffee just wasn't enough right now. "I feel like I'm not even sure this really happened."

"I can see the marks on your neck, Hannah. It happened."

Hannah looked outside and toward Zoo, who was leashed to a small tree in front of the restaurant. He caught her eye and gave her his vacant stare, but was soon distracted by a passerby stooping to pet him. Hannah hadn't taken his leash when she left the condo, so her first stop was a boutique pet store two blocks from her building. Strange how her whole world disintegrated in minutes and the first thing she thought of when leaving was needing a leash for her dog.

"Can I stay with you, just until I figure things out? I know I could afford a hotel, but I don't know what to do with Zoo. And I don't think I want to be alone. I know Aikman is allergic, but maybe we can—"

"Of course you can stay with us. Don't worry about Zoo. We'll think of something. Hell, he's small enough we can keep him in a bag or something. Aikman won't be able to pet him that way."

Hannah laughed, not because the thought of her dog suffocating in a bag was particularly funny, but because laughing was cheaper relief than crying.

Justine gave her another squeeze and then returned to the other side of the booth. "Hannah, this is not a marriage-counselor kind of situation. This is a get-the-fuck-out kind of situation. It'll be messy because of all the goddamn money you two have, but you need to get out."

"This is crazy. We have a *good* marriage. We're planning a family."

"Hannah, how many times over the past two years have you told me about fights you've been having? About the second cell phone, the late nights, his lack of communication? It seems like every month there was something new."

Hannah squeezed her temple with her right hand. "Things were good for the last few weeks. It felt like it was at the beginning. Before—"

"Before the money?"

Hannah felt her back muscles tighten.

"I was going to say before he had to start traveling so much. Right after we got married, it was perfect. It was feeling like that again. He's been leaving me notes, we finally had sex after six weeks, and we—"

"You're trying to rationalize an irrational situation, Hannah. Mom did that for years. If she was here, she would tell you the same thing. Get out before it gets worse. Hannah, he could be Daddy."

"Don't call him that."

"Okay. He could be *Billy*, and you're just finding out now. Or he could be worse. I know this is hard to hear, but that hooker shit, and the dream? What if he's a psychopath and you're just learning that now? Hell, Hannah, he could *kill* you."

Kill. Such a short, simple word. Like *cut* or *run*.

"Mom should have done a better job disappearing with us. Changed our names, even," Justine said. "We should have driven all the way to California."

Hannah thought of the night her mother had told the girls to come for a car ride. Billy wasn't home from his construction job yet. Hannah's mother smiled despite the horror from the previous night, a night of open palms and screams. The station wagon had two suitcases loaded in the back—the large yellow

Samsonite ones, their hard plastic exteriors cracked and peeling. Hannah asked what they were for, and her mother had smiled and said they were taking a little trip. Justine asked if Billy was coming, and Mom said he wasn't. That it was a special girls-only trip.

Hannah had been ten.

They hadn't gone far, just a few towns away. Billy found them four days later and used his charm to lure her mother back home. Said he couldn't live without her. Said he would change. Even promised it right there in the dingy motel room, its smell a mixture of cigarettes, trucker cologne, and empty years. Billy was looking at Hannah when he said it, though his words were directed at her mother. *You know I can change. Be a better man. Be the man you need me to be. Ya know I got it in me, babe.*

He did change. He got worse. For some reason he never touched Justine or Hannah, as if that would be crossing some kind of moral boundary. How many times Hannah wished for her skin to tingle with the hot flashes of pain rather than her mother's. But Billy saved his best verbal abuse for Hannah, cutting her into pieces with every sentence directed at her. It took another five years before they finally rid themselves of Billy, and the bitter irony was by that point their mother was so reliant on the abuse, it turned out she couldn't live without it. Today, her mother was dead. Hannah had no idea where Billy even was. Maybe still in prison. Maybe dead. Billy was just the name of a ghost that whispered in her ear from time to time.

"Dallin's never done anything like this before," Hannah said. "And Dallin isn't like Billy."

"Holy shit, Hannah. Are you seriously listening to yourself?"

But Hannah didn't hear her sister. She was gazing through her, existing deep within her own mind. She was replaying the scenes over in her mind. Rebecca winking. Dallin leering. Fighter's stance. The sudden hand to the throat, the slam against the wall. Zoo barking. Glass breaking.

You have no idea what's good for you.

A thought jolted her from the imagery.

Why had he come back home that morning? Dallin was usually out the door by eight, and he certainly wasn't home when she had woken. But then, there he was, sneaking up on her just moments after starting to watch the video of him and the web slut.

Justine said something. Hannah only heard sound. She lifted the cocktail glass to her lips.

"What?" she asked.

Justine peered over Hannah's shoulder.

"I said there's a guy over there. Sitting alone. He keeps watching us."

Hannah felt herself turning but pulled back. "What does he look like?"

Justine kept staring, assessing. After a few moments, she quietly said, "A problem."

CHAPTER NINE

Hannah turned. The man was three tables away, seated alone at a four-top, a glass of water on the table and nothing else. He was not a small man. His black sport coat was squared sharply at the shoulders, giving him the look of a linebacker. Shaved head, thin, dark goatee, and searching eyes that probably were most comfortable behind sunglasses.

The man sipped his water and offered a single nod at Hannah.

"Who is he?" Justine asked.

Hannah turned back to her sister. "I have no idea." She was suddenly worried about Zoo, and she looked back outside to find him. He was still there, and now he was facing away from her, staring off toward the street. "But I don't think I want to be here anymore."

"Agreed." They didn't bother asking for the check. Hannah reached into her purse and dropped two twenties on the table. As they got up to leave, the man stood.

"What is going on?" Justine asked.

"I'm going to find out." Hannah began walking toward him. She was in the mood for confrontation, even though she had no idea who this man was or what, if any, threat he represented. Justine followed.

They were dwarfed by him. A waiter carrying a tray slipped deftly around the small circle the three of them formed in the middle of the restaurant.

"Can we help you?" Hannah asked. Her tone didn't suggest helpfulness in the least.

The man looked down on Hannah with a barely restrained

smile, a parent amused by a child's defiance. "Most women wouldn't have come up to me," he said. His voice was deep and purposeful. "So you saved me from having to follow you outside."

"What do you want?"

"I want to talk to you."

"Why?"

"Because it's my job. My name is Peter. I work for Echo."

"Dallin..." Hannah said.

"That's right."

"I've never seen you," Hannah said.

"It's a pleasure to meet you." Peter stuck out his fielder's-glove-sized hand. Hannah took it without thinking. His fingers consumed her entire hand as he gave it a light pump. "I certainly didn't mean to interrupt you."

"You just said you were going to follow us outside," Justine said.

Peter ignored her. "Is there a place we can go to talk?"

"About what?"

"A favor."

Justine said, "We can talk here."

Peter studied her for a moment. Finally he nodded, then pulled a chair from the table where he had been sitting. He motioned for Hannah to sit. She looked to her sister, who sat first. Hannah followed suit. Peter slid back into the chair he'd been in, defying its delicate wood frame to withstand him. He looked directly across the table to Hannah.

"I'm in charge of Risk Management for your husband's company. Simply put, I make sure everyone is happy in their jobs, and if there's a problem, it's my job to handle it quickly, efficiently, and to an agreeable end."

Justine said, "You're a thug for Echo."

His black gaze shifted to her. "I'm not a person you want to make simple assumptions about, Ms. Parks."

Hannah looked at her sister. Peter's use of Justine's last name was effective in further unnerving Hannah, though Justine herself didn't seem fazed in the least.

"You still haven't told us what you want," Justine said.

"I mitigate risk for Echo. This, of course, is the primary objective. Company first. *Your husband's company*, Mrs. Leighton."

"I don't go by Leighton," Hannah said. "I kept my maiden name. Parks."

"My apologies." Peter held a hand up. "Bad intelligence on my part. Ms. *Parks.*"

That's purposeful, Hannah thought. He's telling me Dallin owns me. This is about Dallin.

"I want to know everyone with whom you discussed your recent altercation with Mr. Leighton," he said. "I assume your sister is one of them, which is why I feel comfortable bringing this up in front of her. Have you called anyone?"

Hannah only said, "What altercation?"

"I believe you know to what I'm referring. Do I need to specify it?"

"Yes," Justine said. "Tell us what he did. I want to hear you *specify* it."

Peter didn't seem the least bit bothered to comply. "Very well, two hours ago, give or take, Mr. Leighton slammed Ms. Parks against a wall, squeezed her throat, and made threatening remarks before releasing her and walking away." He looked at Hannah's neck and, for the first time, a small crack of emotion—*was it pity?*—appeared on his face. "The marks on your throat are consistent with that story."

"So you admit it?" Justine interjected. "He admits it? That he tried to kill her?"

The pity disappeared as Peter set his face blank once more, as if willing himself back into his dispassionate corporate role. "I can't opine if he tried to kill her," he said. "My professional opinion is if that was his intent she would be very much dead by now. Nonetheless, he told me the events as described, so he certainly acknowledges assaulting and threatening Ms. Parks."

"So I assume you're going to the police, then?" Justine asked.

Peter seemed both genuinely surprised by her question and

oblivious to the sarcasm Hannah detected. "No, Ms. Parks. That would be contrary to the primary objective of my position. I would never go to the police with this, and if confronted by them, I would deny everything I've said here. I'm quite good at denying." Peter pulled a small piece of lint off his jacket sleeve and let it drift to the floor. "My job is to find a reasonable solution."

Justine said, "How the hell are you supposed to find a solution that makes her happy? Her husband is a *monster*."

"I admit I'm not always able to solve a problem to everyone's satisfaction. Nonetheless, there is a problem that needs solving. So I'll ask you again: aside from your sister, who else knows about your altercation?"

"First, it's none of your business," Hannah said. "Second, your *boss* nearly strangled me. Doesn't that concern you?"

"It does, indeed. Which is why I mobilized so quickly."

"So he called you right after this happened? I left him watching the news, then his first thought was to call his Risk Management manager?"

"Apparently, yes."

Hannah felt like screaming at the insanity of it all. "How did you even find us here?" she asked. "I didn't tell anyone where I was going."

"Again, that's part of my job."

Hannah felt a tapping on her arm.

"Hannah, let's go."

Peter kept on. "You went to your therapist the day before yesterday. Dr. Britel. Clearly, the incident hadn't happened yet, but perhaps you were having some other concerns about Mr. Leighton of late. What did you tell her?"

"I'm not telling *you*. Now leave us alone."

"Any other friends? Family? I believe your only living parent is your father, is that correct?"

More poking. "Hannah, let's *go*."

Peter said, "Two nights ago, you had intercourse with Mr. Leighton. You are in discussions with him—*trying*—to conceive a child. I realize this is very recent, but do you have any reason to believe you are, or could be, pregnant?"

Heat flashed through Hannah as she leaned across the table. "He told you about our *sex life*?" She said it loud enough that a diner at the table to her left turned and looked. *Good, let them hear me. Let them see the petite blond getting harassed by the hulk.* "Fuck you, *Peter*."

Now Justine grabbed her arm. "Hannah, *let's go*." Justine stood and pushed her chair back. Hannah stood, but slowly. The anger within her made her want to stay and fight.

"He can't send you to make sure everything just disappears. He has to pay for what he did. And he will."

Peter gave another look of confusion. "I'm not here to buy you off, Ms. Parks."

"And I'm not asking to be bought." Anger coursed through her. "I'm telling you he can't just pretend he didn't hurt me. He can't just make it all go away."

"I'm simply collecting facts about the situation. Wise decisions are rarely arrived at hastily. Without complete information, it's often necessary to err on the side of caution when formulating a conclusion. In war, an appropriate analogy would be opting for a carpet bombing rather than a surgical strike."

"Is that what this is, Peter?" Hannah felt her arm being yanked by her sister. "Is this war?"

For some reason that comment seemed to make an impact. A small crack in the mighty exterior of Peter's face. A twitch on one side, just below his left eye. If this were a boxing match, Hannah would have just scored a point.

Hannah finally succumbed to her sister's pleas and followed her out of the restaurant, to the sidewalk, and into a cool, gray October day. Zoo shuffled with apparent glee as Hannah unwrapped his leash from the tree. They walked toward Justine's car at a pace faster than normal, and the dog, sensing something wasn't quite right, gave out a long, low whine as his small legs struggled to keep up.

CHAPTER TEN

She's having the Billy Dream.

Hannah feels it coming on and deep in her mind, beyond the sleep, she tries to tell herself to wake up. Sometimes this works, but not tonight. Tonight that small part of her brain with the power to wake her or steer her mind toward more pleasant images instead ignores her. Perhaps even laughs a little.

It's Thanksgiving night, 1995. Hannah is fifteen. Outside the small house, a cold wind bites and scrapes at the clapboard siding, taking with it flecks of decades-old peeling paint.

Billy is drunk again, and not the sloppy kind of drunk. That's not how Billy was when he drank. Billy got quiet, though there was nothing about his body language suggesting relaxation.

Every sip he takes out of his longneck seems to take more of his words away, until he just sits back in his favorite ripped-fabric chair and looks around at his little world, surveying, waiting for something to require his judgment. It won't take long. Billy is a strong, lean man, ropy veins always bulging from his constantly tensed arms. His deep olive skin seems perpetually tanned, and his dark complexion makes his eyes glow from his face. They are a washed, transparent blue, the color of ghosts in the snow. Despite the pervasive scowl on his face, he is a handsome man—model-like, even—which makes the reality of him all the more ugly. A beautiful monster.

People used to say the same thing about Ted Bundy.

Hannah has her mother's blond hair and pale skin. She doesn't have any of her father's physical traits, but she knows she has more than a touch of Billy's blood inside her.

That fuckin' bird done yet?

In the dream, he takes another swig from the bottle and lets his arm dangle off the chair, spilling a trickle of beer on the cigarette-burned rug. *Dinner's ready*, Hannah hears off in the distance. It is her mother's voice. Hannah floats to the kitchen where the Thanksgiving meal is beautifully presented, the dream version an exaggeration of the reality from that actual night. The turkey, glowing in a golden hue, is surrounded by a multitude of side dishes of various colors and textures, together creating a perfect Rockwellian image of a holiday feast. Of warmth and abundance. Thankfulness.

Billy pulls his chair out and sits down before anyone else. Then he dips into his torn shirt pocket for a Pall Mall and lights it, coughing out the first puff.

Where's the goddamn carvin' knife?

Hannah's mother walks—no, *scurries*—across the kitchen and hands him a long silver blade and a sharpening stick. Hannah thinks she sees hesitation in her mother's face as she passes the knife over, as if handing a loaded gun to a child. Billy takes the knife in one hand and with slow, practiced movements he scrapes the blade against the sharpening stick, alternating sides.

Sssskkk. Sssskkk.

Hannah sits at the table next to her father. Justine is not there. In the dream, Justine is never there.

Billy looks up from the blade, his long, soft hair dangling down to his nose. He glares at her, the cigarette perched on his lower lip, a small fleck of ash drifting like a leaf falling from a dying tree, floating and falling onto the deep-brown skin of the turkey.

Your momma overcooked this thing, I just know it.

Back to the blade.

Sssskkk. Sssskkk.

Billy stops, tests the blade with a calloused thumb, then rests the edge of the knife against the crisped flesh of the bird. He sets down the sharpener and picks up a fork, then slowly pushes the tines into the flesh. His right hand draws the blade back along the skin, and Hannah watches the heat rise from the open wound like steam from an urban sewer grate. He peels back the meat and peers inside. After a few seconds of silence, Billy draws his gaze up to his wife, and Hannah sees the pupils in his eyes constrict into little black dots.

You ruined our Thanksgiving, you worthless bitch.

* * *

Hannah woke to a familiar ringtone. It took her a moment to orient herself, to realize she wasn't in the past but having a dream. Sweat glazed her face and chest, and as she pushed herself up in bed, the sheets fell off her, her skin instantly cooling in the bedroom's midnight air. She'd been having the Billy Dream but didn't make it to the really bad part. Thank God for small favors.

Hannah reached over to the bedside table and seized the phone. The glow cast a shallow spotlight on Zoo, who slept next to her on the bed.

She was in her sister's house, in the guest bedroom. For a half a second she didn't remember why, but it all flooded back to her the instant she saw the name on the screen.

Dallin.

She didn't answer, and a few seconds later the ringing stopped. The name on the screen disappeared, replaced with the time. Just after two in the morning. Hannah stared at the phone and waited to see if the voice mail icon appeared. It took her a moment before she realized she was holding her breath. As she exhaled, she was aware of how rapidly her heart was beating.

No voice mail. Either he was leaving her an exceptionally long message, or none at all. Hannah released a more controlled breath, grounded herself in her thoughts, and loosened her grip on the phone. Minutes passed, and as her mind raced with the possibilities of what he wanted to say to her, sleep began to creep up over her once again. She fought it weakly, powerless against her fatigue but not wanting to return to the dream.

Hannah reached a hand out to Zoo and rested it on his side, wanting to feel his bristly fur, his warmth, as she drifted back into the void. Finally, the long fingers of sleep reached out and pulled her underneath the surface.

The phone rang again.

Hannah bolted awake, and this time Zoo stirred with her, raising his head in alert.

She grabbed the phone and, without allowing herself to mull over the decision, answered.

"What?" she said.

"Are you coming home?" His voice was dry and distant.

"What?" She pushed herself upright in bed, jostling Zoo from his position.

"I'm asking you a question. Are you coming home?"

"Dallin, what's happening? I don't understand what's wrong with you."

"We need to talk."

"Talk to me *now*, Dallin. Tell me who that was earlier, because that wasn't you. I can't believe you did that to me."

"Hannah—"

"And you sent a man after me today."

An audible exhale. "Peter."

"Yes, *Peter*. I'm surprised you told him what happened. And everything else you told him. Our sex life?"

"This might be hard for you to understand, Hannah, but anything that threatens the reputation of the company, no matter how personal, has to be addressed by our Risk Management department. I had a responsibility to inform them of our...incident."

"Dallin, I don't think you understand. We're...we're different now. You've been cheating on me. I'm fucking crushed, Dallin. Doesn't that mean anything to you?"

In the silence on the other end of the line, she thought she heard a small gasp. Then he said something in a voice soft and different, yet similar to the *I'm so sorry* voice he had used before he released the grip on her throat. One sentence, a hush of jumbled words. Hannah's mind seized on the voice in the dark and the still of the bedroom, and if she was asked to repeat what he'd said she would have recited what she thought she heard, which was:

They're making me do this.

"What?" she asked.

Dallin was silent.

"What did you say?"

A few seconds of nothing, then in a louder and clearer voice than before, Dallin said, "Don't make me go through this."

Was that what he had truly said? Neither possibility made any sense to her. "What does that even mean? I'm not making you go through anything. You're doing this to *me*. Dallin...just please make me understand. Tell me what's happening."

Now his voice was louder. Firm. Resolved. "We need to meet. If we meet, I can explain things to you."

Her mind screamed *no*, but it wasn't what came out.

"Not at the condo," she said. "In fact, I want to move into the condo, and I want you out. At least until we figure this out. I shouldn't have to run away."

"Fine. Yes. You can move back whenever you want, and I can go to a hotel. But first we need to talk. There are some things I need to tell you."

That sounded like a conversation she didn't want to have.

"Fine," she said. "Where? Someplace public."

"You act like I'm going to murder you."

"I don't know *what* you're going to do. I didn't expect you to slam me against a wall. To put your hands around my neck hard enough to give me bruises. I didn't expect you to have some...I don't even know...sick rape fantasies. I expected a caring, loving, faithful husband. Until yesterday, I thought I had that. So, yeah, when I say I want to meet in a public place, I would expect you to understand."

"Fine," he said. Then the call disconnected.

Hannah stared at the phone, wondering if the call had dropped. But she knew it hadn't. The bastard had hung up on her. A minute later a text appeared on her screen.

Four Seasons. Lobby. 3pm.

She didn't reply and instead turned off her phone and waited for a sleep that never came.

CHAPTER ELEVEN

At fifteen before three in the afternoon, Hannah set her half-consumed mocha on the table next to her. She'd been in the coffee shop for half an hour already and couldn't drink any more—she was jittery enough. The place hummed with post-school activity. Mothers, trailed by their kids, loaded up on caffeine to steel themselves for a couple more hours until they could switch to alcohol. The barista shouted her filled orders with the energy of a train conductor.

Every time the door opened Hannah looked up, hoping to see Justine walking in. But person after person it was someone else.

That morning she had told Justine her plan to meet Dallin, expecting her sister to tell Hannah she was crazy. *Don't be stupid,* Hannah had expected to be told. *He's just going to try to talk you into coming back to him. That's what happened to Mom.* But that's not how her sister had reacted. Instead, Justine had sat in silence for a few moments, mulling over Hannah's decision, and had finally said she would go with her. Hannah had weakly protested before Justine insisted. Justine had even given Hannah a can of mace. *Just in case,* Justine had said. Hannah didn't think the mace was necessary but took it anyway, and was comforted by the fact she wouldn't be confronting Dallin alone. As much as Hannah wanted to deal with the problems herself, she wasn't so blindly strong she couldn't admit when she needed help.

But Justine hadn't arrived yet, and it was nearly time.

The Four Seasons was just around the corner. It would only take a minute to get there, and she didn't want to show up early. She looked at her watch again, and then scanned the e-mail on her phone. No one had decided to send her anything in the thirty seconds or so since she last checked.

She glanced over for perhaps the third time at the man sitting in the adjacent oversized chair, reading the *New York Times*. He had lifted his gaze from the pages to her more than once, smiling on the last instance. It was near the moment she was certain he would say something to her, some kind of innocent ice-breaker, something to establish conversation. She should have kept looking away, which is what she usually did in moments like these. But she found herself glancing over, perhaps because of his good looks, but maybe it was because of where she found herself in that exact moment. The confluence of all things that had happened. Maybe she needed a little boost of confidence.

She remembered she wasn't wearing her wedding ring, having left it at Justine's house on purpose. But rare was the man who was deterred by a diamond on her finger.

Her cell phone vibrated and Hannah looked down. Justine sent a text.

Connor threw up at daycare. I have to pick him up early. Can't make it. I'm SO sorry. Can you postpone with him?

"Fuck," Hannah muttered softly. She let the idea of meeting with Dallin alone swim around her head for a few moments. *Should I postpone?* she wondered. *Should I just talk to him on the phone?*

No, she decided. *I'm here. I'm ready to see him. I need to see him. Face to face. I'm going to get the answers I need now. Hell, I was planning to do it alone anyway until Justine insisted on coming. I'll be fine.*

Hannah glanced at the time on her phone once more before putting it back into her purse, leaving her sister's text unanswered. She felt like throwing up.

"If we were sitting in an airport, I'd say you were nervous about flying."

It was the man next to her.

Hannah snapped her head to him. "I'm sorry?"

"You seem nervous. Sorry, hope that's not too...obnoxious. I was just wondering what there is to be nervous about in a coffee shop."

Hannah held her face as tight as a mannequin's. "If you're trying to flirt, I can tell you you've picked the absolute worst time to do it."

His body shifted back in his seat. "Wow," he said. "I'm really sorry. I wasn't trying to flirt. You just...I don't know. You just seemed upset. I'll leave you alone."

His gaze went back to his paper and Hannah stared straight ahead. A minute passed, maybe two. Hannah couldn't handle the crawling of the time anymore. She needed a distraction.

"Look, I'm sorry," she said. "I'm not usually that rude to strangers."

The man looked up and held out a hand.

"I'm Black," he said. "Black Morrow. Now we're not strangers."

She hesitated and then gave his hand a brief pump. "Black like coffee?" she asked.

"Black like Betty."

"I don't get it."

"It's a song."

"Oh." She hated not knowing references. "I'm Hannah," she said.

"Pleased to meet you, Hannah."

"Is Black a nickname?"

"Short for Blackstone."

"I see. Well. Blackstone Morrow. It's...nice. Different."

"Thank you, Hannah. And I'm sorry you're having a bad day."

Hannah looked at the time on her phone.

"I'm about ten minutes away from seeing which direction my life will go next," she said.

Black sat up in his chair. He wore a black sport coat over a pressed white Oxford shirt, which was tucked into a faded pair of Levis. His slightly disheveled hair was espresso black, and his pale green eyes shone out from behind a smooth complexion and a couple of days' worth of sculpted stubble.

"Well, that's about the most intriguing thing I've heard in a long time," he said.

"Do you start chatting up women in coffee shops all the time?"

"I rarely make it into public, so no. And don't worry, I won't ask the obvious follow-up question. Something big is happening in your life, and that makes it officially none of my business."

The tone of his last sentence made Hannah feel the tears start to well within her, tears she had spent all day damming up just so she would be strong when she faced Dallin. She shook her head and locked her gaze on Black, almost as if rehearsing for confronting the other stranger in her life.

"Yes, something big and bad. And I'm about to find out how bad it really is."

Black leaned forward. "I'm sorry to hear that. I don't even know you, and you just broke my heart a little."

One tear escaped and she quickly wiped it away, then smiled and looked down. "Great," she said. "Way to make it all about you."

He sat in silence for a moment and then started to laugh, a deep-throated soulful laugh, one that seemed beyond his age, which Hannah guessed wasn't far off from her own. Hannah was immediately taken in by it, as if the delight he was experiencing draped a comforting blanket, however briefly, over all the ugliness.

He let the following silence settle for a moment before speaking again.

"Well, Hannah, I'll let you to your business. May I ask one other question?"

She looked at her phone yet again. She had seven minutes left. *Why the hell am I concerned about being punctual?*

"Why not?"

"Whatever you are doing in a few minutes from now—do you feel safe?"

"Safe?"

He nodded. "Safe. Physically safe."

"What makes you ask me that?"

Her mind flashed to her visit with Dr. Britel. *Do you feel safe at home?*

He nodded down to her purse. "You've got mace in there—I can see it. Not that that's unusual. You also have a visible line on your ring finger where I'm guessing a wedding band sat until recently. And you have a certain twitch on your face that suggests a spike in adrenaline, as if your heart is preparing itself for some kind of event. Now, absent the mace, you might be meeting someone for an affair. Maybe at the Four Seasons next door. You know, come to Room 1401 at three o'clock, that kind of thing. In that case, you might be experiencing a nervous excitement. But you told me something bad is happening to you."

Hannah's impulse was to tell this man, in the polite kind of way she could always manage, to fuck off. Who the hell was he to assume she was having an affair, or otherwise? And was she really so readable? His arrogance in drawing together clues should have annoyed her more than it did. But this man wasn't really being arrogant. She didn't even think he was flirting with her. Black was actually concerned about her.

"I don't need protecting, if that's what you're asking," she said.

"No, that wasn't what I was asking. I asked you if you felt safe. And I wasn't offering protection. Do you feel the need to be protected?"

She felt herself leaning forward. "Who are you?"

"I told you. My name is Black."

"And why do you care if I feel safe?"

"Is there a reason I shouldn't care?"

"Yes. Because you don't know me."

Black smiled, a teacher's restrained smile of frustration with an ignorant but well-meaning student.

"There are a lot of different things I could say to that. Suffice to say, my not knowing you isn't a reason not to care."

"I have to go," she said.

He nodded. "Of course." He stuck out his hand, and Hannah took it for a second time. This time her grip was more firm, and she felt his heat course through her. She looked at his face as he held her hand and she wondered what kind of work this Black did. A lawyer, perhaps? Maybe, but he looked more honest than that.

She dropped her hand first. "And what do you do, Black Morrow?"

He sighed. "The answer to that question would cause you to be late." He looked down at his watch. "Which, if it's due to begin at three, is in one minute. Hannah, it was a pleasure meeting you."

"You too, Black." She let her gaze rest on his for a moment longer than she normally would have. It was just enough time, a second or two at most, for something to be communicated between them. Hannah wasn't sure what exactly it was, but it was more than *it was a pleasure meeting you.*

She liked to think he was still looking at her as she walked out the door of the coffee shop. Once outside, the momentary warmth she'd imagined seconds before was gone. Once outside, there was only reality.

Justine wasn't coming.

Hannah looked up at the digital clock on the bank directly across the street.

It was one past three.

Dallin didn't like it when she was late.

CHAPTER TWELVE

Hannah walked into the lobby of the Four Seasons, sensing, as she always did here, that she entered a luxurious cave. The décor inside was sleek and modern, stone-like, a mix of various shades of tan and gray, as if the builders had constructed the hotel within a huge piece of slate. Modern enough to be cool, but not cold. Everything geometric, particularly rectangular, long shapes along the walls and floor all pieced together, the perfectly achieved Tetris board.

Hannah knew the hotel well. Sometimes, after going to dinner on a Friday or Saturday night, she and Dallin would come and spend the night here on a whim, and their neighbor Cynthia had always been kind enough to take Zoo for the night.

No change of clothes. No toiletries. Just check into a suite, devour one another, then fall asleep naked in each other's arms. And really, wasn't luxury-hotel sex the best kind of all? The different type of furniture, nooks of the room to explore, the king bed with more pillows than seemed necessary until you realized the myriad ways you could contort a body against or around them. Every stay in a hotel, even just for a few hours, was a mini-vacation for them.

They hadn't been to the Four Seasons in a long time. Hannah used to love this hotel. Today, the cool, modern stone felt cold and lifeless, like she was entering a mausoleum. As she stepped inside the lobby, she cursed Dallin for ruining this place for her. Every night they had spent here now was another night Hannah had to reevaluate in her mind, dozens of nights where she no longer knew who it was she'd been naked with.

A sleek, elongated fireplace spat gas-fueled flames at one end of the lobby. It seemed neither cozy nor warm, but instead sterile, utilitarian, simply a device with which to burn things. Dallin was seated on the marble hearth extending from the fireplace, rising when he saw Hannah walking toward him. He wore a suit, something he rarely did at work, not even when there was an investor meeting or a media interview. Dallin only wore suits for special occasions, times of fun: weddings, special dinners, holidays out with his parents. When he wore a tie, it meant there was something to celebrate.

Seeing him in a tie now chilled her, just like the frozen fire he stood before. His face was expressionless.

Hannah clutched her purse and stole a look down into its partially open pocket, eying the can of mace.

He took only one step forward. It was up to her to walk the rest of the way to him. The lobby was quiet, one guest at the front desk, the clerk tapping away on an unseen keyboard. The sound of water falling came from behind her, a rock wall of cascading water she did not see but remembered, the melody of it making her think of a country stream surviving a cold snap, flowing freely, unfrozen, along narrow banks of snow and smoothed rock. Her heels clicked on the marble floor, then fell silent at the transition to the area rug in front of her husband.

She stopped a few feet short of him. Beyond arm distance.

"I'm here," she said.

"Thanks for coming. How are you?"

"I'm a fucking wreck, Dallin. How are *you*?"

He grimaced and then held an arm out to the side. "Let's go somewhere a little more private."

"Where?"

"Follow me."

"I asked where."

"There's a small meeting room off the lobby. I reserved it."

"You need a meeting room to explain to me why you cheated and then assaulted me?"

He took a deep breath and looked down at the floor. "Please, Hannah? Can we just go sit and talk?"

"Fine," she said. "But the door stays open."

She studied the outline of her husband as they passed through the lobby. The slope of his shoulders. The gait of his walk. All the things about him she knew so well. So intimately. And it had all been a sham. The extent of his masquerade left her feeling not just vulnerable, but incredibly stupid. *How could I not have known?*

Past the lobby, down a carpet-lined corridor. Double doors on each side, beside which meeting room placards displayed the name of the various rooms. *Maple Room. Birch Room. Sycamore Room.*

They stopped at *Ash Room*. Beneath the room name was another card-stock sign with one word on it.

Reserved.

Dallin opened the door and propped it against the outside wall, where it clicked against a magnet and remained open. He gestured her inside.

She walked around him and stood at the entrance to the room. It was just large enough to house a sleek conference table in the center of the room with ten black leather chairs placed around it. They were going to decide their future in a fucking boardroom.

Hannah entered and pulled out the chair closest to the door. She sat down but kept her purse in her lap. In the middle of the table, a silver pitcher wept condensation from the ice water within it. Hannah noticed an empty glass at each chair. She didn't touch hers. The last thing she wanted right now was ice water coursing through her body.

Dallin sat next to her and poured water for both of them, then took a sip of his. Even though the door was open, there was only the faintest murmur of activity from outside the room. Inside, it was quiet as a tomb. She sensed him preparing to talk, so she spoke first. She didn't want him to control the conversation.

"Yesterday morning you attacked me," she said. "You slammed me against the wall and put your hand on my throat. Do you have any idea what those seconds did to completely change everything about us?"

"Yes," he said. "I do."

"Do you, Dallin? Because I can't imagine you're feeling what I am. The confusion. The betrayal."

He looked as if he wanted to say something, but he remained silent.

"I'm here alone," she said. "I didn't have to come. Or I could have come with a lawyer. Or the police. But I didn't." Though I wish Justine had showed up, she thought. "This is your chance, Dallin. If you have something to say to me, in private, now's the time."

Dallin took a deep breath and studied her. He looked at her the way he used to, a look of wanting. Of hopefulness. The look that said *I'm so happy you chose me.* But he said nothing. Not a word. He just sat there and stared, and Hannah could do nothing but stare back and fight against a blind, stupid hope that he could explain it all away with the one excuse she hadn't thought of, the one that somehow made sense and put everything back to normal. The only one she could think of was that everything was a long nightmare. Or perhaps she was dead and in some kind of purgatory. Maybe she had died after they had sex, and this was all part of a slow journey to heaven. Hannah didn't like the thought of being dead, but somehow it was more a relief than falling helplessly through a bottomless pit.

"Are you going to say anything?"

Dallin reached into his coat pocket and pulled out a business card and a pen. He scribbled on the back of it and showed it to her.

I'm doing this for you.

Then he put both items back in his pocket.

"What does that even mean?" she asked. "Why won't you talk to me?"

He shook his head and then looked to his left, at the doorway.

Hannah turned around to see what he was looking at.

Peter stood in the doorway, his hulking body seeming to fill it entirely.

"What is he doing here?"

Dallin reached out and put his right hand on top of hers.

"I'm sorry, Hannah."

She yanked her hand back as she heard the door close. That single click was the sound of something permanent. She looked down at the purse in her lap. The can of mace was still visible.

Stall.

"Who are you, Dallin? Who are you really?"

Dallin just shook his head. "I'm sorry. That's all I can say."

She heard his words, and she thought of his note.

I'm doing this for you.

She had to get out of this room. She didn't know what they planned to do to her, but she was pretty sure Dallin shoving her against the wall would pale in comparison. Peter was there for a reason, and it wasn't mediation.

Dallin looked up at Peter. "She has mace in her purse," he said.

"Got it."

"Everything else secure?" Dallin asked him.

"Cameras won't be a problem," Peter said. "We're good."

Peter stood behind Hannah, in front of the door, and Dallin sat to her side. She sensed Peter stepping forward so he stood directly behind her chair, so she wouldn't be able to push backward if she tried.

His massive arm snaked around in front of her. Hannah tensed and pushed back into her chair, steeling herself. Peter plucked the purse out of her lap and dropped it to the floor.

She turned to Dallin. "I'll scream."

Peter's voice in her ear. "Not for very long, you won't."

Still looking at Dallin, she said, "I'm leaving now."

Dallin held her gaze for only a moment. "No, Hannah."

A spike of electricity shot through her, adrenaline telling her to attack or flee. With the spike came anger, the rage of Billy.

Most of her life she learned to curb this impulse, to deny herself the satisfaction of the uncontrolled rage Billy got high from every night. But now, here, trapped in this tiny room, there was no reason for control. There was only rage, and Hannah wanted to kill.

I'm going to rip your fucking eyes out and get the hell out of this room.

Hannah lunged.

Her scream lasted as long as it took for her fingernails to arc toward Dallin's face. The last thing she saw was the surprise in his eyes, as if he believed she wasn't really capable of anything so aggressive. Little, pretty Hannah, the wife who had supported her brilliant husband, through good times and bad, through the last two years as he had been distant and cold to her, through all the empty liquor bottles in her wake, she had always been there for him. Even after he shoved her against a wall and had nearly strangled her, she hadn't fought back. All she asked was *why*. But now there were no more questions. There was only feral anger.

Before her nails reached his face, Hannah felt herself lift from the chair, a seemingly supernatural force sweeping her up. Then, for a few seconds, she was being smothered, and a deep chemical smell invaded her entire being.

Before there was only blackness, she had a fractured thought that it smelled like nail polish remover.

PART II

BLACK

CHAPTER THIRTEEN

Bacon.

The aroma swam in her head, awakening her senses. Then she heard it, the spitting of the grease on the pan, the sizzling as the strips flipped to a raw side. If this was a dream, it was a good one. Or maybe she was dead and this was heaven. Heaven would definitely have bacon.

Hannah opened her eyes. The room was dark, but enough light spilled in through the edges of a door and a window shade that she could make out shapes. Her head throbbed, a small victory. *Okay, probably not dead,* she thought. *Dead people don't get headaches.*

Where am I?

She felt around her. She was in a bed, and a quick check with her hands confirmed she still had clothes on. She did a mental scan of her body and moved her limbs. No physical problems, except a bad headache.

Wait. There was something else. Pain in her left arm. Localized. Hannah looked down and saw what looked like a fading bee sting in the crook of her elbow. She rubbed at it and found it sore, like a day-old bruise.

The last thing she remembered was being lifted from the chair, right before she slashed at Dallin with her nails. Then the smell of nail polish remover and then the darkness. And then...bacon. That was it.

Hannah sat up in the bed looked around. Her eyes had adjusted and she could now see more clearly in the partial darkness. The room was small, maybe ten by fifteen, and sparsely furnished. An armoire. Mirror on the wall. One window, one door.

Hannah swung her legs around and placed her bare feet on the cool hardwood floor. She spotted her shoes placed neatly next to the bed and slipped into them.

The smell of bacon grew and made her intensely hungry.

Where's my purse?

She looked around, not seeing it.

She had no concept of what time it was. She had met Dallin at three in the afternoon and had been attacked not long after that. Was it even still the same day?

Hannah walked to the window and pulled the shade to the side. Her view from the ground level was of an endless expanse of trees. She wasn't staring into someone's backyard. She was somewhere in the woods. The pine trees painted a swath of forest green across the landscape, and the smattering of deciduous trees had shed most of their leaves, the ground beneath them coated in spongy layers of red and yellow.

There was no screen behind the window. She scanned the woods again and saw no sign of anyone. Hannah unlatched the window and lifted. It opened with ease. Cool outdoor air flowed into her lungs.

If she was being held against her will, her captors weren't very good at it. She could just open the window and run. But where? How far was she from the next house? Or road? Or even city?

Hannah turned and looked at the door. There was no lock on it. Back to the window, she lifted the shade fully. She searched for the sun above the spiny fingers of the pine trees and found it low in the sky off to her right. She had no idea if that was east or west.

The sound of movement outside the bedroom door. The sound of plates rattling against each other. Clanking metal, a skillet scraping against an cast-iron burner.

Hannah lifted the window a few more inches.

"Good morning."

Hannah spun.

She hadn't even heard the door opening. A man stood holding two coffee mugs. He offered a nervous smile, the kind used when reaching fingers out to a strange dog.

It's okay, girl. It's okay.

Black. The man who had asked her if she felt safe, and she didn't have an answer.

But she did now. Whatever any of this was, Hannah did not feel safe.

She turned and scrambled out the open window. As soon as her shoes touched the soft dirt, Hannah ran as fast as she could.

CHAPTER FOURTEEN

"Wait!"

She heard the shout and Hannah only chanced a brief glance back as she sprinted. The cabin she escaped was small, old, with a rock-wall foundation and aging wood siding. A simple cabin in the woods, the kind a family visited a few days every summer. Or the kind someone spent their last days in, afraid of society. Or a place to hide from those searching for you. Or maybe a place to hide a body.

She saw Black leaning out the window, his hands perched on the sill. He shouted again for her to wait, but Hannah didn't obey him. She was done obeying.

Her fists pumped in rhythm with her legs. *Just run, Hannah. Run hard and fast, constant speed and one stride at a time. Just like long-distance running back in high school, back in Kansas, when the sun burned on the track and the rhythmic slapping of feet on the spongy surface almost became hypnotic. Back then, you could run forever. Now you have to do it again. Just run and don't look back.*

But she wasn't in high school anymore, and she certainly wasn't on a smooth, flat track and wearing running shoes. She was running in pumps over layers of moist leaves and pine needles covering rocks and branches. Twice she slipped and nearly fell but was able to catch herself, but with each falter she lost momentum.

She could hear him. He was coming fast.

"Hannah, stop!"

The woods were dense with trees, but not enough for her to zigzag and lose herself among them. She knew she would not out-run him. She spotted a narrow creek bed up ahead of her, a snake of land that once held water but now only nestled river rocks, smoothed by years of passing currents. She made it to the creek before stopping. Hannah bent and picked up two of the rocks, each about the size of a baseball, before turning to make a stand.

Black slowed.

Hannah sucked in the moist air of the woods, cooling her burning lungs. Her headache was gone, or at least pushed aside by the adrenaline and rage. *How dare you*, she thought. *How dare you bring me here against my will.* Hannah held the rock in her right hand up at shoulder height, perched to throw. It was a desperate move, she knew, because she couldn't throw for shit. But if he came close, maybe she could smash it into his skull.

Black came within twenty feet and stopped. Hannah waved the rock above her head, ready to let it fly. She was panting. He hardly seemed out of breath.

"I was hoping for a thank you," he said.

"What did you do to me?"

He held his hands up. "I saved you."

She launched the rock at him. It had the distance but went far right. Black didn't even move as it sailed past him. Hannah shifted the other rock to her throwing hand.

"Look," he said. "You can keep running if you want. We're in the middle of nowhere. You can run and run until you are so lost your only option is to die of exposure. Then you'd give those men exactly what they wanted. Or you can give me two minutes to tell you what happened."

She threw the other rock. Wide left. Frustration seared her.

"Let me guess," he said. "You never played softball growing up."

She bent and snatched two more rocks.

"What did you do to me?"

"I followed you to the hotel," he said. "Do you remember me? From the coffee shop?"

"Yeah," she said. Hannah pushed the hair out of her face with her free hand. "Black like Betty. Did you abduct me, you pervert?"

"Look, Hannah. What I do...for a living. It involves being able to read situations with very little information. I could tell you were scared about whatever meeting you were going to."

"I wasn't scared." She heaved another rock and felt good about this one. Perfect aim. Black casually sidestepped to avoid having it hit him in the head.

"Will you stop that?" he said.

"Why did you follow me?"

"I was worried about you."

"I didn't need your help."

This time Black outright laughed at her and her anger—Billy's anger—crested over her.

"*Don't laugh at me!*"

His laughing stopped and his face lost all expression. "You needed all the help in the world," he said. "I watched you talk with that man in the lobby, and I could tell right away he was bad news. Slick. Confident. Definitely not friendly. Then I watched you cross the lobby with him, and I followed until I saw you disappear in the meeting room. A moment later, another man approached the room, and I knew he was ex-military. It's in the walk." Black took a couple of steps forward and Hannah threatened another throw. He backed up, holding up his hands in a *take-it-easy* gesture. "He had a big steel case with him, the kind roadies use for music equipment. He wheeled it outside the room. It was big enough to hold a body. He left it in the hallway and then I saw him open the door. Now, you can stand there with a rock in your hand and tell me you don't need help, but you sure as hell did back in that hotel."

Hannah kept the rock held high and her arm was starting to tire.

"He drugged me," she said. "Smelled like nail polish."

"Sounds like ether. I thought I heard a muffled scream but I wasn't sure. A moment later the door opened and the big guy pulled the case inside the room. When he did that, Slick left the room and walked to the service elevator, then disappeared. I waited.

A couple of minutes after that, the big guy came out of the room, wheeling the case behind him."

"Why didn't you call the police?"

"They wouldn't have responded fast enough. You would have been long gone before the cops got to the hotel."

"So, how did—"

"I checked the room and you weren't in there. Three people went in, two came out. Easy math. I knew you were in that case. I followed him to the garage. He loaded the case into the back of a van. If I had tried to jump him, he would have torn me to pieces. Fortunately for you, I have a good habit of never leaving the house unarmed." He patted his waist as if looking for something. "Well, almost never." Then he took a step forward and a twig snapped beneath his boot. "I forced him out of the van and then took it. Drove straight here."

"You brought me here instead of taking me to the police?"

"I don't trust the police."

"You kidnapped me."

"I saved you. And that guy, the one who took you? He's not an amateur. Wherever he was taking you, I'm thinking you weren't coming back. If I had taken you to the police, it was probably just a matter of time before he tried to take you again. Don't ever assume the police will be able to help you."

"But *you* can, right?"

"You're alive, aren't you?"

Hannah finally lowered the rock. Whether his story was true or not, she was certain a rock wasn't going to be a game-changer. "The slick one. The one I was talking to in the lobby. He's my husband."

"I know."

"How do you know?"

"Your purse. Found your ID. Wasn't hard for me to find out everything about you."

"You went through my purse?"

"You're seriously surprised by this?"

She wasn't surprised at all. Hannah heard the leaves rustle to her left and she spotted a squirrel foraging. "He...the other guy...Peter. He works for my husband. *Risk management.* He said something about the cameras being secure."

Black nodded. "He probably made sure the security cameras in the hotel that would have picked up his exit were non-operational. Like I said, not an amateur." He took another step forward. "They were kidnapping you."

"I don't know what they were doing."

"People are taken away against their will usually for one of two reasons," Black said. "One is to hold for hostage or ransom, but that doesn't make as much sense when it's the husband kidnapping the wife."

Hannah guessed the second reason before he said it.

"The second reason is to kill the person at another location. One less traceable. Or to sexually assault them."

Hannah was suddenly exhausted, the adrenaline spike draining from her, leaving her wobbly legged. She didn't know if she could trust Black, but she didn't see much of a choice at the moment. She let the rock fall from her hand, which landed by her side and rolled down into the dry creek bed. Then she sat on a much larger rock, its surface cold and hard. She brought her knees up to her chest and wrapped her arms around them. The contact with her own body made her aware of how cold she was.

"We're having some...issues," she said.

"Most people just get lawyers."

Hannah laughed and it threatened to turn into tears, but she didn't have any energy left to cry. She just wanted to sleep for a long, long time.

"I'm learning Dallin is far from being a 'most people' kind of guy."

Black walked up to her and Hannah didn't look up. As he stood next to her, she could smell his scent. Faint aroma of spice.

"Let's go back inside," he said.

She looked up.

"Can we call the police now?"

He reached out his hand.

She was torn between distrust and an overwhelming feeling of helplessness. Finally, she closed her eyes and sucked in a breath.

It's going to be okay. It's going to be okay.

She took his hand. The warmth of his skin radiated throughout her.

"Let's just get inside. And then we'll talk about your options. Do you like bacon?"

CHAPTER FIFTEEN

She desperately had to pee. Once inside, Black pointed her to the one and only bathroom. She found it immaculate but sparse, a roll of toilet paper and a year-old issue of *Popular Science* the only contents inside. No soap, no hand towel. She opened the cabinet underneath the sink. Empty.

She washed her hands in the kitchen sink as Black cooked at the stove. His back was turned to her as he added more bacon to the pan. Based on the smell in the room, the last batch burned when he was chasing after her in the woods. She quickly scanned the cabin. A simple, functional living space, but that was it. There was no hint of a home. Nothing personal, not one thing revealing anything about the person who lived there. No art on the walls. No mail on the counter. No family photos. Not even a TV or, from what she could see, a computer of any type.

No clock. The digital clocks on both the stove and microwave flashed an eternal 12:00.

"What time is it?" she asked.

Black checked the watch on his wrist.

"Just after seven," he said.

Hannah glanced at the light streaming through the curtain on the kitchen window. Seven p.m. was dark this time of year. And the light had only grown brighter since she had tried to escape.

"Seven in the morning?"

He flipped some bacon, which spat and hissed at him. "That's right."

She rubbed her head. "I was out all night? All yesterday

afternoon?" Which explained why her need to pee had felt like a knife in her bladder.

"Yes."

"But...how?" Could ether have knocked her out for so long?

Black wiped his hands on a paper towel, turned, and walked up to her, which took all of six strides. She shifted her weight to her back foot but she stood her ground. He reached out to her.

"Give me your right hand."

"Why?"

"Just give me your hand. Dammit, Hannah, if you're going to trust me you have to...to trust me."

After a moment she put her hand in his. He pulled her arm straight and pointed at the small bruise in the crook of her elbow. He touched it lightly and she could feel the tenderness of the skin.

"My guess is after they knocked you out with the ether, they injected you with something to keep you unconscious. Probably some kind of anesthetic, like propofol, chased with a longer-lasting barbiturate. They didn't want you waking up anytime soon, which means they were probably planning on transporting you somewhere distant."

"Distant like where?"

"I don't know," Black said. "But somewhere far, I'm guessing. They would have used that." He pointed to the cargo van he'd taken from Peter.

"Can't they track me?"

He shook his head. "No GPS in that thing. And they would have ditched your phone soon enough. There would be no trace of you. I still have your phone, but I drained it. We don't want them finding you again."

Hannah pulled back her arm and ran her finger over the spot where she'd been injected. Dallin had drugged her. He fucking *drugged* her. He didn't just assault her in a momentary loss of control. He plotted to have his own wife kidnapped.

Hannah tried to understand. She found out he was cheating

on her and that he had some dark sexual fetishes. Then he had attacked her. Was he so afraid she was going to have him arrested for assault that Dallin decided it was simply easier to make her disappear? It was possible, but she just couldn't reconcile that idea with the man she thought she knew.

"I need to get out of here," she said.

Black nodded, handed her a plate of bacon, and said, "Sit. *Please*. Just for a few minutes. Eat something. Then you can do whatever you want. I'll drive you back to Seattle, take you anywhere you need to go."

She hesitated, then pulled out a heavy wooden chair from the table and sat. The chair, the floor, the bare tabletop: everything seemed cold. A shiver rippled through her shoulder blades as she picked up a piece of bacon.

"Breakfast of champions?" she asked.

"I didn't stop for groceries," he said. "And all I had up here was bacon and coffee. Sorry."

"What is this place?"

He handed her a mug of coffee and sat next to her, pushing his own chair a few inches back from the table.

"This place," he said, seeming to struggle to find the right words. "This place is a bit of an Underground Railroad station."

"Meaning?"

"Well, you know of the Underground Railroad?"

"Of course. That was almost two hundred years ago."

"The metaphor still works for this place. For what I do."

She finally crunched a piece of bacon and had to restrain herself from shoveling all of it into her mouth at once.

"So, you help black people escape their Seattle slave owners?"

He put his head down and chuckled. "Not exactly."

"So what, then? What exactly is it you do?"

"I help people start new lives," he said. "People in trouble. People who have gotten themselves into a situation with no other choices. Some of these people are criminals. Others are people who have been abused. Mothers with children. Men who have been framed, or don't trust witness protection. People who, if they were back in society under their own identities, would likely be killed or jailed. I help them disappear, and this place..." He looked around and took in the tight surroundings. "Well, this place is where many of my clients start their journey."

"So you help people to disappear?" she asked.

"I do."

"And how do you do that?"

"Through a series of intricate steps, none of which can be skipped. There's a formula for erasing one's existence, and if you leave out just one part it won't work."

"How much do you charge for such a thing?"

He shrugged. "Some clients pay me almost every penny they have to disappear. Others I do pro bono, depending on their circumstances. Overall, it balances out so I don't worry about paying bills. I live fairly humbly, after all."

"Why did you bring me here?" she asked.

"It was close and safe."

"I want to go home."

He nodded. "I know you do."

"You said you have my phone. Where is it?"

"In your purse, in the kitchen."

Hannah stood and moved to the kitchen. Her small black purse was hanging around the back of a chair. She picked it up and looked through it. Everything seemed to be there. She picked up her phone and pressed the side button, but nothing happened. She held it down a few seconds but it remained lifeless.

Black called over. "I told you I drained it. I didn't want you to be tracked. I only use prepaid cells without any GPS functionality."

Hannah felt like she was drifting further into space, with no tether left to stop her.

Black walked toward her in the kitchen and opened a cabinet above the sink. He pulled out a laptop and took it back to the table. Hannah followed. He booted it up and logged on with an impossibly long password.

"You can make a call on this if you want. The person you want to reach won't recognize the number so they might not answer, but it's anonymized and the only way to communicate out here. Or you can send an e-mail if you want. The IP address is untraceable."

"Or you can just take me back to civilization," she said. Hannah didn't know if she really meant that. Truth was, as much as she didn't want to trust this man, she was much more worried about being in a place where Dallin and his *risk-management employee* could find her. But she no longer believed in the concept of heroes, and she wasn't ready to freely accept Black as one.

Black reached out to touch her arm but seemed to decide against it. "Don't worry, Hannah. I'm not keeping you here. I saw you in trouble and just wanted to help."

Hannah's stomach let out another growl. "So you just happened to meet me in a Starbucks, where you sensed something bad was going to happen to me?"

"I didn't sense it," he interjected. "You told me yourself."

"And then you followed me for no other reason than your concern for a stranger," Hannah continued. "You overpowered a huge guy in a parking garage—"

"I didn't overpower him. I had a gun. Makes things easier."

"—and then you whisked me here, stealing a van in the process. All out of the goodness of your heart."

"Is there a question there somewhere?"

"No question. It seems staged, like you were waiting for me in that coffee shop. Like I'm some pawn in some bizarre game of yours." She squinted at him. "What do you *really* want with me?"

An emotion swept over Black's face, brief but distinct, that Hannah couldn't quite place. If she had to guess, it was frustration, but it didn't seem as simple as that.

"Like I said, a thank you would be nice," he said. "Believe what you want, but I saved your life."

"My life wasn't yours to save," she said. She didn't even know what she meant by that, but it felt so true. Maybe he saved her, maybe he didn't. All Hannah knew was she was in some remote cabin in the woods and couldn't leave without the help of a man she'd briefly met yesterday in a coffee shop.

Black gently shook his head. "Of course. You're right. I'm sorry. You have no reason to trust me or anything right now. Your world is in upheaval. I'm just trying to help. Please..." He gestured to the laptop. "Make as many phone calls as you want."

She sat and Black logged into software that looked like something out of the movie *War Games*. It ran on a DOS prompt, and after a few more series of 1980s-style menus and password prompts, he asked her for the number she wanted to call.

The first person who came to mind was her sister, and Hannah recited the phone number to him. After typing the number into the keypad, he passed her the headphones, which had a pull-down microphone. She eyed him and he took the hint, leaving the kitchen and giving her as much privacy as the small cabin afforded.

She didn't even know what she would say to Justine. *I've been kidnapped twice. Dallin had me drugged and shoved into a trunk. Now I'm somewhere in the woods with a man who helps people disappear.*

Four rings and no answer. Voice mail. Hannah felt another burst of panic.

Did they get to Justine, too?

After all, Justine had been there when Peter confronted them. Did that make Justine some kind of liability in whatever this was that was happening?

"Justine, it's me. I just want to tell you I'm fine. But things aren't good. Dallin...he...look, just stay away from him, okay? I hope you and the boys are okay. I'll call again soon when I can. Be safe and...just take care of Zoo, okay?"

She didn't know how to hang up using the software, so she

motioned Black for help. He walked back over, read her face, then typed \END CALL at the prompt and pressed return.

"She wasn't there," she said. "God, I hope she's okay."

Black said nothing to reassure her that Justine was fine.

"I don't know what to do," she said. "I can't go home. I don't want to stay here." She turned to Black. "Why don't you trust the police?"

"Because I used to be a cop," he said.

"That doesn't tell me anything."

His jaw muscles twitched. "Look, Hannah, all I know is you're a target, and the people after you are professionals. Filing a police report or even having your husband arrested won't protect you. If the people after you know what they're doing, and it seems they do, they've already planned for a failed abduction attempt. Despite the fact you were in a public place, I'm quite certain there won't be any evidence left behind. It will be your word against theirs, and, while the justice system figures it all out, you'll remain a target."

"I can't believe this is my husband we're talking about here. He...I *love* him. Or at least I loved the man I thought was him."

Black put a hand on her arm, and she let it remain.

"Hannah, in my work I deal with clients who are at the end of their ropes. Emotionally. Physically. It's my job to assess the situation analytically. Objectively. If I couldn't do that, most of my clients would be dead rather than living life happily and anonymously. I'm telling you, from a professional viewpoint, that you going home right now is not a good idea."

"So what am I supposed to do?" She moved her arm away from him. Suddenly she wanted nothing more than to hit something. She thought how good it would feel to hurl her mug of coffee at the wall and watch it shatter, watch the coffee spray like blood against the empty, undecorated, anonymous sheetrock, the wall of a safe house where people began the journey of leaving the only world they knew. "Am I supposed to disappear, too? You want me as a client, is that what you're saying? You went through my purse. You researched me. You know I have money. That's why you don't want me to go to the police, isn't it?" She heard her voice get louder and it felt *good*. It would feel better to scream, but she wasn't quite there. But she was close. "You don't trust the police? *Bullshit*. You want me in your control, because then you can fill me with fear so I can pay you for protection. Is that it? Hell, if it's money you want, I'll pay you just to *drive me the fuck away from here*."

But where would she go?

He nodded patiently. "I understand how you feel. I'm not suggesting you disappear. But I think you should stay here for a day or two until we can figure out why your husband tried to have you taken. It's unlikely, but maybe we will get lucky and be able to find some evidence of what they did to you. I can help with that. But I can't help you if—"

"Why are you helping me at all?" Now the yelling came. "I didn't ask for your help. I don't want it now. I didn't ask you to take me here and make me goddamn bacon and pretend you're my savior. I don't know who you are. Don't you understand that? You think you're my hero, and all I see is a man who chased me when I tried to escape this cabin." She felt the sweat on her forehead, but her skin felt cold. Clammy. Her stomach churned and she tasted a flood of saliva in her mouth.

Don't puke, she told herself. *Don't be weak.*

Hannah closed her eyes and stilled her body. A few moments later her stomach steadied.

When she opened her eyes she saw Black walking back to the kitchen. He picked up a set of keys off the counter and came back to her.

"Fine," he said. "I'll take you wherever you want. But they'll come for you again."

Black opened the front door and gestured for her to walk out. It almost seemed a bluff, but she believed he would take her back home. She had a momentary resistance, a brief pull that she did, in fact, want this man to protect her. She wasn't at all certain she should go home. But the door was open, and Hannah looked at the growing daylight and knew she would pass through that door, with a stride of defiance, whether it was the logical decision or not.

She looked straight as she walked outside, avoiding his glare. The daylight was strong and the smell of trees filled her senses. The white van, the one Black stole, sat in the dirt clearing in front of the cabin. In the distance, a group of birds chattered excitedly.

Hannah paused and sucked in a deep breath of air, holding it, steadying herself. Then she closed her eyes, soaked in the sun on her face, and slowly exhaled, letting the movement of the air from her lungs ground her. Stabilize her.

The moment she opened her eyes, something exploded next to her head.

CHAPTER SIXTEEN

At first, Hannah didn't know it was a bullet. All she knew was a chunk of wood frame exploded next to her head, sending splintered shrapnel into her face. As she instinctively reached to feel her cheeks, Black shouted, "Down!"

A second later he slammed into her from behind, pushing her to the ground, his weight grinding her against the dirt walkway. She then heard three muffled pops, each one followed by a concussive thump and spray of dirt on the ground near them. Black's weight shifted as he repositioned, and his elbow dug painfully into her lower back.

"Gunshots," he said. "Keep down."

A deafening bang exploded in her ear, and she realized Black was shooting back. Another distant pop and a chunk of ground erupted next to Hannah's face. She finally touched her cheek and felt the warmth of blood ooze beneath her fingertips.

Black squeezed off two more ear-shattering rounds and then leaned down and looked at her face. His eyes narrowed as he gently touched around her left cheek and the side of her neck. "It's not a deep cut," he said. "We can't go back inside. We'd be trapped." His words were steady and calm, reassuring, no hint the two of them were potentially seconds from death.

The firing from the woods ceased. For the moment.

"What the hell is happening?" she asked.

"I'm guessing your husband wasn't happy with how yesterday turned out, and somehow they found us." He paused. Hannah heard what he did from the woods: silence. "We have to get to the van out there," he continued. "It's our best chance." His voice was closer now, in her ear, his warm breath sweeping through her. "I saw the shooter—he's fifty meters away, maybe more. He's going to come in closer. I want you to get up and run to the van. I'll cover you. Open the side panel door and get down on the floor. There're no seats in the back so you'll be able to lie flat."

She nodded, but Black seemed to sense her fear. "Hannah, listen, I've been in some bad situations before. I know this is scary, but our best chance is to do what I'm telling you, okay? I know you have a whole trust-issue thing, but now's not the time to be defiant."

"I'm not scared," she said. The weird thing was, she meant it. She felt oddly in control, perhaps for the first time since Dallin had uttered those words in his sleep. Hannah had no choice but to take action, and even if that action for the moment was running for her life, at least she was doing *something*.

Black pressed his thumb against her cheek, wiping off some blood.

"Good," he said. "Ready?"

"Yes."

"Go, Hannah. *Now*."

She jumped up, hesitating only a moment before running. In that instant, she wondered if, like in a dream, she would run but go nowhere. If she would scream without making a sound, be shot but feel no pain. If she would wake before she died.

In that same instant, another shot lasered from the trees, another soft pop of a noise that seemed incapable of representing instant, powerful death. So much quieter than Black's gun, she thought. She heard a bullet whiz by her head, but that was all just part of the dream, wasn't it? And in this dream she saw movement behind a tree, saw the man who was trying to kill her. But she didn't really see him, she merely detected a shape briefly shift into view and then disappear.

The percussion of Black's gun firing back into the woods made her run even faster. She closed in on the van in seconds, and if the shooter fired more shots in that time, she had no idea. Black aimed and shot twice in rapid bursts. This time Hannah didn't flinch.

She grasped the faded chrome handle on the van's side panel door and yanked hard before sliding the door open. Somewhere in the recesses of her mind Hannah realized this was where she'd been briefly a passenger trapped in a large storage container, just a day ago.

She scrambled inside. As she turned to close the door, she saw Black running toward her, gun pointed up, left arm swinging, legs pumping. He didn't look panicked. He didn't even look worried. He moved with purpose, speed, and the seeming certainty that all would be fine, as long as they kept moving, and moving fast.

Black opened the driver's door and threw himself into the van. He turned the engine over, shifted into gear, and slammed down the accelerator. The van lunged and Hannah fell back in the empty cargo area, sliding against the bare metal floor.

"Hold on!"

But there was nothing to hold on to.

Black yanked the steering wheel to the left and turned away from the direction of the bullets. Hannah slammed against the right wall of the van and felt a sharp pain in her shoulder. She yelled out as she tried to brace herself, which was pointless.

"Sorry!" Black shouted. He steadied the direction of the van and accelerated. The road was unpaved, choppy, but relatively straight. Hannah lay flat on the floor of the cargo area, her arms spread wide, her body thumping with the bumps in the dirt road. She closed her eyes and just wanted him to keep driving, faster and farther away. She didn't even care where they went as long as it was somewhere else.

She expected to hear the sound of bullets *thunking* through the metal of the van's back door, releasing beams of bright dusty sunlight through fresh holes, but those shots never came. Seconds passed, then a minute.

She craned her neck and looked up at Black, who simply stared straight ahead, both hands on the wheel, silent as he sped them over bumpy earth into an increasingly uncertain future.

CHAPTER SEVENTEEN

The road changed from bumpy to smooth. The van slowed, and then stopped.

Hannah looked up. "What's going on?"

Black said nothing. He opened his door and stepped outside, leaving the van idling. Hannah heard scraping around the vehicle, one section at a time. A couple of minutes later he got back in.

"Just what I figured," he said. "I was sloppy not to have assumed it before."

Hannah rose to her knees, steadying herself with the palms of her hands along the metal floor. She could feel beads of sweat glaze her forehead.

"What are you talking about?"

"There's no built-in GPS device in the van, so I figured we were safe. But there *was* a planted GPS unit under the front carriage. That's how they found us at the cabin, which is now totally compromised. It's my fault. I should have checked." She caught his gaze in the rearview mirror. "Better yet, I shouldn't have taken this van at all."

"You had to," she said. "I was in it."

He nodded, but it didn't seem like agreement. "I think I found the only one, but I can't be certain. I tossed it in the woods, but we need to ditch this thing soon."

"Where are we going?"

"Seattle. Need to get my car." He looked at her again in the mirror. "Okay by you?"

"You still think it's a bad idea going to the police after someone just tried to kill us?"

"I know it sounds crazy, but it won't do any good," he said. "We can't ID the shooter, and the second you file a police report you make yourself visible, which means they can get to you again. But if you want me to drop you off at a police station, I can do that. I'm not holding you."

Hannah reached up and pressed her fingers against her cheek, feeling the sting of the cuts from the wood splinters. She moved her hand in front of her eyes and saw the red of the blood mixed with the grime on her hand. She didn't respond to Black. Instead, Hannah climbed forward to the passenger seat and stared out the window and into the side view mirror. Her face was smeared with blood and dirt, her hair a mess of tangled thatch, and she thought distantly of the savage boys from *Lord of the Flies*.

Hannah saw Billy's eyes in that mirror, and they seemed to glow even brighter than usual against the dark haze of her muddied complexion.

Kill the pig. Cut her throat. Spill her blood.

They didn't speak as Black drove them from forest to civilization, as trees gave way to billboards, and finally to buildings. The cabin in the woods was located roughly a half-hour east, maybe southeast, of Seattle, somewhere in the density of Tiger Mountain State Park. Or at least close to there, she figured. Hannah tried to calculate the route back from where they'd come and knew she could never do it exactly, nor even knew why she would need to bother with it, but the idea of being able to find Black's cabin from her own memory gave her some sense of control.

When they reached downtown Black pulled the van into a surface parking lot and used the sleeve of his shirt to wipe down the steering wheel and door handles. Hannah stood outside and looked around, knowing the area intimately but never having felt so much like she was in some other country. It was still morning and she heard the city murmur with activity as people went on with their daily lives, repeating their usual routines, ordering their same cups of coffee from the same Starbucks as they had the day before.

It was just yesterday afternoon Hannah had met with Dallin. She turned her head and noticed the edge of the Four Seasons sticking out from behind an apartment building. *Right there*, she thought. *It had all started right there.*

No, she corrected herself.

She turned her head the other direction and saw her own apartment tower a few blocks away, rising above the buildings in front of it. *That's where it all started.*

Black spoke. "Get back in the van and wait for a minute."

"Where are you going?"

"Just hang on," he said.

She watched him jog to a nearby 7-11 and disappear inside. Hannah returned to the van. She saw flashes of Black through the store window, and the last time she saw him he was on his cell phone. A few minutes later he came back and opened the passenger door. He handed her a bottle of water and a roll of paper towels.

"Clean the blood off your face," he said. "You shouldn't be walking around like that—it'll attract too much attention."

She opened the bottle and took a long draw of cold water, which tasted better than any martini she'd ever had. Then she poured some on a wad of paper towels and wiped the blood until the towels were streaked in red. She looked in the rearview mirror at the cut on her face. Black was right, it wasn't bad. About an inch long on her right cheek, not too deep. She had certainly had worse.

"Who were you calling?" she asked.

"It was business," he said. "Nothing about you."

"Why would it be about me?"

"Like I said, it wasn't. This little side excursion has delayed some of my other business dealings, so I had to let one of my clients know I need to postpone an appointment." He surveyed her face. "Better," he said, and then handed her a hair tie. "They didn't have brushes."

Hannah put her hair back in a ponytail.

"Police station is just a few blocks away if you still want to go there," Black said. "I'm guessing your ID is in your purse, though."

Hannah instinctively reached for her purse, finding nothing. "Shit. My purse is still at the cabin."

"I know. Well, it's gone now. No doubt they swept it up after we left. Probably combed through every piece of that place. They won't find much, but they'll take apart my laptop trying to figure it out. They won't find anything they can use, but they're probably expecting you to contact the police."

"So if it's such a bad idea to go to the police, what are my options?"

Black lifted his chin up just an inch, like an antelope suddenly sniffing out a lion hiding in the tall grass. "Let's walk," he said. "We can discuss your options when we aren't standing out in the open." Black started across the parking lot and she followed, and for a brief moment she had the sense of trailing Dallin through the lobby of the Four Seasons. Hannah had had about enough of men leading her to unknown places.

"Wait," she said.

"What?"

"When I got back in the van, I had to use the door handle. My prints will be on there. Shouldn't we wipe the handle like you did before?"

He stopped. Turned. Considered.

"It's okay," he replied. "We just need to keep going."

"Why the rush?"

"Not rushing," he answered. "Just not backtracking. Backtracking is usually a bad idea." He turned and kept walking away.

They walked the downtown streets, the buildings looming over them. Hannah felt a thousand eyes from the soaring windows all directed at her, watching her, a multitude of human security cameras, all relaying information to those who wished to harm her about where she was. *On the corner of 4th and Seneca, heading west...* She knew it wasn't true. No one was following her movements. No one cared about the blond woman with the small cut on her face.

Then she saw the cop.

Street cop, on foot. In uniform. Long sleeves, midnight blue. Brimmed cap. He had been staring at Hannah when she noticed him. He was on the other side of the street, walking parallel with them. Looking at them the whole time. Black turned right and led them into a side alley, away from the cop.

"Don't look back," Black said.

She ignored him and looked directly at the cop. The cop was staring intently at her. Then he began crossing the street.

"Keep following me," Black said.

"No," she said. "Goddammit, just stop. I'm going to talk to him."

"*Hannah.*"

She turned and walked slowly toward the cop as he approached them at a faster clip.

"Fine," Black said. "Stop walking and let him come to us. And let me do the talking."

Moments later the cop approached them. They were fifty feet into the alley, flanked by dumpsters and back entrances to coffee shops and retail stores. A few pedestrians walked along 4th Street, but no one else other than the cop came into the alley. They stood and watched him approach. He maintained a distance of ten feet.

"Morning," he said. The man's face was scarred by a smattering of ancient acne pits. His eyebrows were jet black and perfectly shaped, looking like they were drawn on with Sharpies. His voice was calm but his body rigid. "I need to ask for your IDs, please."

"Is there a problem?" Black said.

The cop took one step forward. "I just need to see your IDs."

"We have a right to know why," he said.

"Are you refusing to produce your identification, sir?"

"I'm asking to know why."

Hannah interjected. "I don't have my purse."

The cop flicked his gaze to her and studied her face. "Where'd you get that cut on your face from, ma'am?"

"Accident," she replied.

Black approached the cop, who put his hand up. "Please remain where you are, sir." Back to Hannah. "Are you in trouble, ma'am? Do you require assistance?"

There were so many answers to that question, and Hannah just wanted to say the first one that came to her mind. *Hell, yes, I need assistance. I need you to arrest my husband for assault and attempted kidnapping, maybe even attempted murder. I need you to conduct a thorough investigation that will tell me how everything in my world became so fucked up in so short a time. So, yeah, you could say I require assistance.*

In her peripheral vision, Hannah saw Black leaning toward the cop.

"I can't read your badge number."

"Sir, I will give you a card with my information on it in a moment. In the meantime, I need you to stay back and remain silent while I speak with Ms. Parks."

The sound of her name coming off this man's lips sent a rush of ice water through her belly. "How do you know my name?" she asked.

"You both need to come with me," the cop said.

"Why?"

"We're not going anywhere," Black said, this time taking a pronounced step forward.

The cop moved his right hand to the butt of his holstered gun. "Stay right there."

"Are we under arrest?" Black asked.

"Ms. Parks is wanted for questioning in conjunction with an embezzlement charge."

"*What?*"

"Ma'am, everything will be explained at the station. Now I need you both to come with—"

It happened in an instant. Hannah didn't even see Black move. All she saw was his body slamming into the cop, knocking him onto the ground. The cop reached for his gun but had no chance. Black removed it, held it by the barrel, and slammed the butt into the man's forehead. The cop shouted and reached for Black's arm, grasping for the weapon.

Hannah stared at the men struggling on the ground, and her instinct was to do *something*. She could kick. She could scream for help. She could stomp on the face of her enemy. But who the hell was her enemy? The cop? Black? Or maybe she should just run. Run and keep running. Stopping only when either her legs or her heart gave out, when she was at the point where nothing mattered anymore.

A gun spilled onto the ground, the metal and plastic clacking on the concrete. It was Black's gun, and it must have fallen out in the struggle. The cop, still struggling despite the blow to his head, seized the weapon. At this point, everything Hannah saw happened frame by frame, like a child thumbing the pages of a flip-book, making the animated figure dance.

The cop moved his arm from the ground. The gun in his hand slowly turned toward the man on top of him.

Black darted his eyes and saw the threat. Hannah saw a flash of something move over his face. Resolve. Decision. Instinct.

In one smooth movement, Black spun the cop's gun in his hand so it was no longer the barrel in his hand but the butt of the gun. Then, as easily as if stapling up a string of Christmas lights, Black pushed the tip of the gun hard against the cop's chest and fired.

The explosion was deafening.

This isn't real. This isn't real. This isn't—

Black sprang from the ground and grabbed her by the hand. "Come on!" he yelled. He yanked her arm so hard it pulled the darkness away, but not the disorientation. She saw people come into the alleyway. A woman screamed. Another woman yelled for someone to call 9-1-1. A young man just stood and stared, his Seattle Mariners cap crooked on his head, his t-shirt displaying the image of a jack-o'-lantern with blood coming from its eyes. He lifted a white phone in the unmistakable gesture of *I'm capturing this on video*.

Hannah ran.

CHAPTER EIGHTEEN

Black's car sat in a surface lot three blocks from where a cop was shot. They reached the sedan without anyone following them, and as they sped through downtown, Hannah stared out the window. Buildings lasted just moments in her field of vision before vanishing. Pedestrians were little more than plastic toy figurines set upon a city canvas play set. Beams of sunlight burst through holes in the clouds, spotlighting large swaths of street and structure.

She spoke first. "You shot him. No matter what happens now, we're criminals. You shot a *cop*."

Black kept his focus on the road. "Hannah, listen to me carefully, okay? Yes, I shot him, but I knew what I was doing. I didn't hurt him, at least not badly. He had a vest on, and I shot into it. He's probably got a couple of broken ribs, but that's it."

Relief passed through her, and she tried to suppress it, hesitant to believe him. She wanted to ask him if he was sure, but she knew Black's answer would be *of course I'm sure*.

"But you still shot a cop," she said. "That's a problem."

"That wasn't a cop."

"How do you know?"

"His shield was phony. Also, any street cop would have a radio on him, and he didn't."

"So who was he?"

"Had to be working for your husband," Black said. "I have no idea how they knew where to find us. Maybe a second tracker on the van I didn't find, though I looked pretty carefully."

Was it possible Dallin had some kind of army scouting for Hannah? It was hard enough to believe Dallin had turned into the monster he now seemed to be, but the logistics of his efforts to find her seemed like something out of a Cold War spy novel.

"That man said I was accused of embezzlement," Hannah said. "If he was planning to kidnap me, why would he even say something like that? I mean, what does that even mean?"

Black made another left and Hannah spotted the sign for the interstate a block away.

"There's a script," Black said. "Contingency plans. When they failed to abduct you yesterday, they went to Plan B. Pose as cops. Tell you you're under arrest, get you to come with them. They probably thought that would be enough to get me to let go of you, but they were wrong. But now we have more problems. I did shoot someone, and there were witnesses. A video will surface of the shooting, and both our faces will be on it. And that embezzlement thing? My guess is your husband's company managed a way to make that a real accusation against you, and if you go to the police you'll have to deal with that."

"You have an answer for everything," Hannah said.

"It makes sense, and it's what I would do if I were him. I'd make sure if Plan A failed, you'd have no safe harbor. Start building a story so if you came out against me, you would immediately have credibility issues."

The car started to close in on Hannah, shrinking smaller around her, suffocating her. She rolled down her window, but the rushing air whipping her face didn't help.

"I can't do this," she said. "I don't want to be here. I don't want to be in this car. I just need to stop and think for a few minutes."

Her chest tightened, and despite the chill in the air, her face flushed with a flu-like heat. Saliva suddenly started filling her mouth.

"Hannah, I don't see how stopping the—"

"Please, just let me out."

"Hannah, I'm not your enemy. You have to understand—"

"*Stop the fucking car!*"

Black said nothing for a moment and then swerved the car over to the curb, earning a blast of the horn from the person he'd just cut off. Black turned down a side street flanked by industrial buildings and warehouses, stopping in front a shop with a weathered metal sign reading *Amco Import Repairs*.

Hannah flung the door open, stood on wobbly legs, then bent over and dry-heaved onto the asphalt of the parking lot. She retched twice before catching her breath. Acid burned her throat, but she managed not to vomit. She stood to find Black staring at her. If he was sympathetic, she didn't read it on his face.

"I know your world is rocked," he said. "But this isn't the time to reflect on that. This is the time to keep moving."

She wiped her dry mouth with the back of her hand.

"I don't trust you," she said. Then she added, "I don't trust anyone right now."

"Hannah, I can't wait here while you figure it out. I need to keep moving."

Hannah looked around. She didn't welcome the idea of being stranded here.

"I don't have a wallet," she said. "Or phone."

"Yeah, I know. Which is why I wasn't just planning to abandon you. But that's what you want, so here you go. I'll even give you some cash."

Hannah looked around at the unfamiliar buildings, and as she did, memories of the past twenty-four hours flashed through her mind. She saw them as if they were sloppily stitched together in some grainy, out-of-focus movie, the scenes short and the storyline incomprehensible yet jolting.

She saw Dallin, his face so different than the man she knew. A mannequin.

I'm doing this for you.

Then the smell of bacon. The sunlight streaming through the trees in some swath of woods unknown to her. The voice of Black.

I help people disappear. That's what I do.

The bullets splintering the wood, the smell of morning air mixed with her own sweat. The coppery smell of blood smeared on her face. Concussive thumps against the bare metal floor of the van as Black drove them away.

She looked up at Black and wanted desperately for him to be one of the good guys.

"I don't know what to do," she said. "Can you understand that?"

Black held up his hands to her. "Of course I do, Hannah. But you have a choice to make, and it needs to happen now. You can walk right now. Walk away. I'm sure you can find someone who will let you use their phone. Then you can go to the police and take your chances. You can tell them everything you know about me. About what happened to you with your husband. I have no idea what will happen to you, but I have a lot of experience dealing with people who have shitty lives. My guess is you'll wind up dead. If not in the next few days, then certainly within a year." His voice grew in volume as he pointed to the distant buildings of downtown Seattle. "That fake cop back there? You'll probably be seeing him again."

A siren wailed in the distance. A few seconds later a second siren joined, both punctuated by the deep bass of a fire engine's horn.

"I can't stay," Black said, thumbing in the direction of the sound. "I shot a man back there and that's no small problem for me. I need to keep driving, and you can either come with me or stay here. I want to help you, but I'm done insisting."

Black didn't wait for an answer before he began walking back around the car. Hannah stood there with his words—his anger—in her head, and she couldn't help but flash back to Billy, the yelling, the insults. The disdain for her existence, a disdain Hannah never understood.

"I'm not helpless," she said just as Black opened the car door.

"What?"

"I said I'm not helpless."

She heard her father's voice in her head. So many years of

being called a rube, a good-for-nothing, and, the worst of all, a follower. *Little Hannie, just doin' what the cool kids tell her to do. You gonna end up pregnant by sixteen and that's prob'ly for the best.*

Black folded his arms onto the roof of the car. "You have to do what you think is best, Hannah. All I'm saying is I'm leaving right now, and if you're coming with me you need to move."

Black climbed into the car.

Hannah reached for the door handle. She was wary of following, but was swept in a current she couldn't seem to swim against.

CHAPTER NINETEEN

She scanned the car as Black drove. Spotless. No stray receipts on the floor, no water bottle in the cup holder, not a single pet hair on the upholstery. The car was as unadorned as the cabin had been. It served a function, but that was it.

"Can this car be tracked?" she asked.

"No."

"I thought the van couldn't either."

He shot her a look but said nothing.

"I want to use your phone," Hannah said.

"Who do you want to call?"

Anyone, she thought. *Everyone.* Call the police, tell them everything that happened. Call Dallin and give him a hearty *fuck you, I'm still alive.* Call—

"My sister."

"Who you called back at the cabin?"

"Yes. I have no idea if she got my last message. I mean, if they do anything to her family..."

"Is that your only sibling?"

"Yes."

"Where does she live?"

"Nearby."

He let out a deep sigh. "I wouldn't be surprised if they have her line monitored. Or someone watching her house. Better not make contact. At least not yet. Let's get a little distance first."

"So we're just going to drive?"

"Yes, for now."

"You haven't even asked me why my husband is trying to..." What word did she want to use? *Kidnap? Murder?* "Hurt me."

"Do *you* even know?" he asked.

"No," she said. "Not really. That's almost the worst part of all of this. I think he's...I don't even know exactly what he is. He seems to have some kind of sexual fetish. He said something in his sleep, and then I found something on his computer. When I confronted him on it, he flipped out. Shoved me against the wall. *Choked* me."

Black didn't seem fazed by the information. "Has he ever done anything like that before? Anything violent?"

"No. Never. It came out of nowhere."

"Maybe he's worried about you divorcing him and taking half of his money."

This couldn't be about Dallin wanting to avoid a costly divorce. It had to be about something else.

She said, "When we met at the hotel, he wrote something down on a piece of paper. He wrote 'I'm doing this for you.' He showed it to me for just a second and then took the paper away. After that, the other guy came in and things went bad quickly. But that keeps sticking with me. Dallin was trying to tell me something."

"What do you think he was trying to tell you?"

"I don't know," she said. "The night he had the dream, before he spoke in his sleep, he told me he was sorry, and I didn't know what for. I asked but he didn't answer. It's like there are little pieces of the Dallin I used to know still in him, trying to connect with me. But other than that, it's like he's a different person." Then she shook her head. "It's not just that. He *is* a different person."

"People change," Black said. "Especially when they become successful."

"Not like this," she said. She looked over and glanced at his ringless fingers. "I'm guessing you aren't married?"

"No." His stare was fixed straight ahead, and he squinted against dull sunlight. "I was once," he added.

"Did you leave her or did she leave you?"

He glanced away from her. "She left me."

"How long were you married?"

"She died the day after our fourth anniversary."

It wasn't the answer Hannah expected. "God, I'm sorry." She knew better than to ask what happened, though she was curious. Black was no older than forty, she guessed. So his wife had died young. An early case of cancer? Or was it something sudden and tragic? Maybe something violent relating to Black's line of work?

Black continued. "Your next question is how I would have reacted if my wife, the one person I knew the most, suddenly tried to have me killed. Is that it?"

"I just don't know how to relate to anyone what it feels like."

"And no one could ever understand unless they were going through it themselves. But I can tell you this: I've worked with dozens of people in your situation. Mostly women, though not always. And I can tell you if you looked back, really looked back on the last few years, there will be clues. Signs, subtle ones, usually, that will point to the true nature of who your husband is. There are very few reasons for this type of behavior to come out of nowhere."

"Such as?"

Black seemed not to be expecting the question.

"Actually, off the top of my head I can't think of any reason."

"So you're saying I should have seen this coming?"

"I'm saying what your husband is doing is extreme, but I would guess there were behavioral clues in your past that suggested he was capable of violence."

That feel good, cunt? I want you to tell me what it's like to bleed out. Tell me everything...

Hannah felt her stomach tighten as Dallin's words came back to her. But that was just last week. What were the clues from the past year? The past five years? She hated the thought of obvious signs to which she had been oblivious. Moreover, she hated the idea she should have been looking for signs of distrust in someone she loved so deeply. She had been on edge her entire childhood. In Dallin, she thought she had found someone she could lose herself in. Instead, she realized he was no better than Billy.

Black opened the center console. Hannah immediately saw the butt of a handgun and her body tensed as Black reached in. His fingers moved past the gun and he pulled out a cell phone and handed it to Hannah. The phone was tiny and had only the requisite parts to make a phone call, and nothing else.

"Prepaid cell, untrackable," he said, handing it to her. "I always have one nearby, usually for a client. That one is now yours. Use it to call your sister, but keep your conversation short. Don't tell her about me. Do tell her to remain vigilant."

"*She* should go to the police," Hannah said. "She could tell them what I told her. About Dallin."

Black shrugged, which was the most indecisive thing Hannah had seen him do. "It probably won't help."

"You really don't like cops."

"I'm sure there are some good ones," he said. "You just have no idea which ones those are."

"That sounds a little dramatic."

"Look, I've been doing what I do for a long time, and in that time I've learned many things, usually the hard way. I've learned never to trust someone who has nothing to lose. I've learned the value of prepaid cell phones. I've recently learned never to take someone else's car unless you know it's free of any tracking devices. And I've learned that the chances the police will help someone in a complex situation like yours are lower than the chances they will either hurt you or just fuck things up worse than they already are. These rules are not absolute and don't always apply. But they are *my* rules, and if I were you, I wouldn't go to the police, nor would I recommend it to your sister. Now, there are several things I would advise, so call your sister and then we can go over your options."

"I think that's the most you've ever said to me."

"I'm not the chatty type." He nodded at the phone in her hands. "Keep it under a minute."

She dialed and Justine picked up on the third ring. Hearing her voice made everything suddenly seem so real. It was both comforting and terrifying.

"Justine, it's me."

"Oh my God, Hannah. I got your message. Where the hell are you?"

She felt an impulse to blurt out everything, despite being told less than a few seconds ago not to.

"I'm fine, that's all I can really say right now. I can't tell you more. It's...not safe."

"Hannah, Dallin came here. To my house. *With the police.*"

"What?"

Black shot her a look.

"What did he want?" Hannah asked.

"He didn't talk much. The cops were looking for you."

"Was he under arrest or something? Did they know what he did to me?"

"I don't think so. I think they were looking for you for some other reason. Dallin said his company was missing a lot of money and you disappeared right after it happened."

Embezzlement. "Did you tell them what he did?"

There were a few moments of silence before Justine answered. "I...they were in and out so fast. I didn't know what to say. And some reporters came by as well. Hannah, what the hell is happening?"

Black nodded at her. *Get off the phone.*

"Justine, listen to me. I need to hang up soon, but you need to know Dallin is...he's trying to kill me. I can't believe I actually just said those words. I'm safe now, but that's why I'm not coming home. Not yet."

"Hannah, what are you talking—"

"Please, Justine. Just be careful. I don't even know what that means. But protect yourself and your boys. Take Zoo to Cynthia, across the hall from my place. You know her, right?" Justine said she did. "Good, she'll take care of him. Maybe you and the boys should get out of town for a few days. I'll pay for everything when this is all over, okay? Take a nice vacation somewhere."

"Hannah, what happened? *Where are you?*"

"I have to go."

She disconnected the call before she could second-guess herself, and then filled Black in on what her sister had said.

He had no questions. He nodded twice but otherwise didn't react to Justine's side of the conversation.

After five minutes of silence, he pulled the car over in the parking lot of Walmart, parking in the back of the lot.

"What size are you?" he asked.

"Size? Size for what?"

"Clothes. Pants. Shirts. Bra. You need to go underground for a while. That requires a few supplies."

CHAPTER TWENTY

Hannah fidgeted as she waited in the car. She watched the shoppers enter and exit the store, none smiling. An overweight woman in hot pink sweats—the word *LOVE* stretched to the limit of the fabric along the width of her ass—barked at her daughter, then reinforced her message with a palm to the back of the little girl's head. The girl just looked down and frowned, accepting the punishment as she probably so often did.

Twenty minutes later Black exited the store and loaded at least ten plastic bags of purchases into the back. Hannah figured most of what he bought were clothes and toiletries, but the one item not bagged was a black suitcase, its American Tourister tag flapping as Black loaded it into the back of the car.

As they drove, the radio dribbled out soulless songs from the 90s, and the increasingly fading reception heralded their proximity to no-man's land. Black didn't say more than a few words until at least ten songs in, at which point he reached in front of Hannah and opened the glove compartment. He pulled out a long piece of red silk. At first she thought it was a handkerchief, but then she realized it was a blindfold.

"We need to go to my place," he said. "It's the safest place to hide out for a while. I know this sounds extreme, but I don't want you seeing how to get there, so I need you to put this on. That's more for your protection than mine."

"You keep a red blindfold in your car?"

"I'm a magician with many pockets," he said, offering nothing else.

The Hannah of yesterday, or even just a couple of hours ago, might have had further questions about this. A protest, perhaps.

But the moment she chose to get back into Black's car, she decided to listen to him. She wasn't so stubborn or proud she couldn't admit she needed help, and though it was a risk to trust this man, she felt she had little other choice. So Hannah took the soft piece of silk, wrapped it around her eyes, then tied it once behind her head. Despite its red shade, the blindfold bled no color through to her eyes. There was just a deep, satisfying darkness.

The comfort of black.

A few minutes later the songs on the radio finally succumbed to static and Black turned it off. In her darkness, Hannah surrendered to the sounds of the road, the rhythm of her breathing, and the rush of the wind on the car. Together, the sounds lulled her into a sleep she didn't expect nor would have thought possible given all she couldn't stop thinking about.

For the minutes she actually slept, Hannah dreamed of Billy. It wasn't the Thanksgiving dream, and she could barely consider it a dream at all, for it was little more than a jagged collection of images, a slideshow that had no timeline or purpose. Some of the images were based on reality, some just flashes of an alternative history. Billy in his swimsuit at the dingy neighborhood pool, his muscles lean and taut, tensed as if he might have to throw a punch at any moment. Billy smoking in his bed, remote in his hand, the once-white bed sheet covering him a dirty gray from being washed with hard water year after year. Billy grabbing his wife's ass as she walked past him in the living room, his leer carnivorous, her expression a mixture of exhaustion and resignation. And, Billy on fire, the flames licking his face like a faithful dog. In this last image Billy grinned and welcomed the heat as the fire peeled back his skin, rendering him nothing more than a skeleton, the butt of a Pall Mall still squeezed between the exposed phalanges of his left hand.

You can't burn me, Hannie. Don't you get that? Some things just don't catch fire.

"We're here."

Hannah jolted awake and removed the blindfold.

Black was looking over from the driver's seat, and as he came into view, she felt an odd relief at the sight of him. He brushed a thumb against her forehead, drawing off a thin film of sweat, a small gesture that felt powerfully intimate.

"You were dreaming," he said.

Hannah looked through the windshield and saw a driveway of what looked to be a very normal house. She turned her head around and scanned the street, which was lined with similar houses, a collection of tan and brown, of gray shingles and stucco siding, simple lawns well cared for, and identical mailboxes standing like sentries every fifty feet, black and rigid.

"*This* is your house?"

"Yes."

"I thought it would be some remote castle somewhere. Thought we'd be entering through a cave or something."

"That's my other place." Black clicked the button of a remote and the garage door opened. As he pulled the car forward, Hannah saw the garage was entirely empty save a stepladder and a blue tarp folded in the back corner.

"I assume you live here alone?"

"I do everything alone."

He closed the garage door, and the darkness again fell over them. "Come on," he said.

Hannah followed him into the house, which was only slightly more decorated than the cabin in the woods. There was art, but it was generic art, the stylish prints found in an upscale office of a law firm. The furniture was modern and appeared barely used, no creases or wrinkles in the leather sofa, no scratches on the surface of the glossy dining room table.

"This doesn't seem like a place where you would live."

"Why? You don't even know me."

"I know enough. And of everything you might be, you're not boring. This place is boring."

He looked around the room, and Hannah thought she saw a ripple of sadness flutter over his face. It was gone in a second.

"Yes, boring. Plain. It's one home in a sea of identical ones, and as far as anyone knows, I'm just like everyone else. Pay my bills, keep my lawn trimmed. Pay my taxes."

"Why the need for secrecy? You help other people disappear, you told me. Why do *you* need to hide?"

His mouth tightened. At first she didn't think he was going to answer. Finally he said, "Because I was my first client."

She didn't know why, but the idea that Black was on the run felt exciting to her. "Now that's interesting," she said.

"Nine years ago I had to make a choice," Black said. "I chose freedom. So when I'm giving you advice about disappearing, it's not just because it's what I do for a living. It's my life."

"You're a criminal?"

"In the eyes of the law, yes. In my opinion, I've already paid the price for my past mistakes."

"So your name isn't Black?" she asked.

"Does it matter?"

"Yes," she said.

"I'm Black to you. That's what matters."

"Why did you have to disappear?"

This time he smiled, a gentle smile that bordered on patronizing. "Did you want something to drink?"

"So no answer?"

"I have water, beer, wine, coffee..."

"Okay, I get it. You get to know everything about me, but you get to remain a mystery. The man in the mask."

"Hannah, I barely know you at all."

"But you at least know my real name."

Another smile. "I also have bourbon, which I'm going to pour for myself."

It was barely past morning. The idea of not drinking alone was nearly as powerful as the lure of the alcohol itself.

"Bourbon sounds perfect."

CHAPTER TWENTY-ONE

Alcohol and Hannah were sometimes friends, sometimes enemies, and usually both within a span of several hours. She didn't like to admit that, for the past two years, she had grown more dependent on her nightly wine, or bourbon, or tequila, or whatever was available. She enjoyed the steady nighttime buzz as much as she disliked the molasses brain in the morning, and the two sensations battled with such equilibrium that the routine became a consistent, seemingly unalterable cycle. Wash. Rinse. Repeat.

Hannah grazed her thumb along the glass tumbler containing two fingers of Maker's Mark and two ice cubes. The glaze of the liquid was a smooth caramel, and she craved it like a child lured by a candied apple gleaming in a polished-glass display.

The bourbon slid down her throat in one gulp, leaving behind a pleasurable burn. She put the glass down and poured some more.

"You might want to slow down," Black said. "You hardly had anything to eat today."

"I might be small, but I can hold my liquor."

"I don't doubt it."

Black lifted his glass, emptied it, then also poured more.

Hannah straightened in her chair. The sunlight streaming through the kitchen window warmed her neck, while the bourbon warmed everything below it. "I'm going to get you drunk enough to tell me your real name," she said.

"You'd have to get me *really* drunk. And then I'd have to kill you."

Hannah sipped this time. "Well, that would save you the headache of what to do with me otherwise."

Black stood and walked over to the plastic bags on the counter. He pulled out a box of hair coloring. "Hope you like black, because that provides the greatest contrast to what it is now. It would be helpful, but unless you can do it yourself there's only me to do it, and you definitely don't want that."

Hannah had never dyed her hair in her life. The idea of changing it to black made her nervous but also excited. A chance to hide in the shadows.

"What else did you buy?"

"Clothes, mostly. Toiletries. Some food. Another cell phone. A cheap tablet, so you can at least go online if you need to. A few other things. Most of the things I need to help you are here in the house."

"Things like what?"

Black spoke as he piled the contents of the bags on the granite countertop. "Tools for making new IDs for you. The more difficult work needs to be done on the phone and online. If you're going to disappear, it's not just a matter of changing your name and hoping for the best. We need to change your past. Erase old footprints. Create false trails."

"Is that what you did for yourself? Create false trails?"

"I continue to do it." Black walked over to her, and she swiveled her tall counter stool to face him. She had the sudden impulse to simply open her legs and let him walk into her, his body pressing against hers. She could reach around his waist and pull him harder against her stomach, her thighs. She hadn't felt that way about another man in a long time.

"Listen," he said. He stopped short of where her knees would touch his legs. He placed a hand on the counter and leaned in close to her. "If you disappear, if you *really* disappear, it will be your full-time job. It's impossible to disappear completely, and there will always be traces of you out there, popping up from time to time. Pings of your existence. If someone is looking for you, and if they know what they're doing and have the patience to keep at it, they *will* find you the moment you let your guard down. And it doesn't take much." He looked around the kitchen. "This house? I've been here eight months. It's the longest I've ever stayed anywhere, and I won't be here much longer. So don't be fooled. If you want to erase your existence, you are going to have to work really hard at it."

"But I don't want to disappear. Not...not like you have. I have a whole life that I've built. A *good* life. I mean, aside from the obvious situation."

"Nobody wants to. Who would? It's a matter of the other options available. I don't know if you need to disappear forever, but if you go back now, the consequences would be severe."

Disappear forever. Hannah struggled to grasp the concept. She would never see her sister again, or her beautiful nephews, one of whom would never remember her and the other having perhaps a vague recollection of *Auntie Hannie*. And what about Zoo? Would she not even be able to take her dog with her? How would she even live, and where? And what about all the money, all the wealth she and Dallin had built together? Would she just be forfeiting that, leaving it all to him?

Then there were her friends, those daily points of human contact that gave every person's life a routine, a structure. Though she had many social connections, she had to admit most of her friends were little more than acquaintances. Many of them she knew more about from their Facebook posts rather than actual conversations with them.

A sudden realization struck her, one both enlightening and depressing. *If I disappeared, how much am I really leaving behind? How many people and things in my current life do I actually, truly care about?*

It was too heavy a thought to ponder, so she dropped it. "The news," she said.

"What?" asked Black.

"Can we turn on the news? I want to see what they're saying about the shooting this morning. Shouldn't we see if my name is being mentioned at all?"

"If you want," was his response, seemingly indifferent to the idea. To Hannah, it seemed like a natural thing to do. Scour the news, the Internet, see what's being reported. So much had happened. Something had to be on the news, hadn't it?

He handed her the remote control, and she aimed it at the flat screen mounted to the wall.

"I'm making lunch," Black said. "Sandwiches okay?"

Hannah would have been happy just drinking her lunch, but she knew she had to eat something. "Perfect." Hannah first found CNN Headline News and lingered there for a few minutes, expecting to see something about the shooting earlier this morning. *Black shot a cop—real or not—in downtown Seattle. That must be a big story.* But the headlines of the day were political ones, which meant it was a pretty slow news day.

Hannah turned to the local networks and found soap operas instead of local news. She checked the time on the TV receiver: just after one in the afternoon. There would be no local news airing at this time, unless the networks broke into the regular programming with a big story. But nothing interrupted the fake tears and the dramatic music of the soaps today.

Hannah turned the TV off and took another sip of her bourbon, which was now starting to taste more like an enemy than a friend. How quickly it turned, she thought. How difficult to maintain that perfect balance of pleasant numbness. She rinsed out her glass and replaced the liquor with tap water, gulped a full glass down, then filled it up again.

Black handed her a plate containing a very simple-looking sandwich and apple slices. "Believe or not, I'm a good cook. Don't let this jade your opinion, but it should do for now."

"This looks great," she said. "But if you need to prove yourself, you can cook me a nice dinner." Hannah consumed her meal faster than he did, caring not at all if she appeared like a feral cat greedily devouring its prey. He wasn't even halfway done when she looked up from her empty plate.

"Want more?" he asked.

She shook her head. "I want to get online. Check the news."

"Not now," he said.

"There's got to be something about me. About all of this."

"What are you hoping to find?"

"Anything to give me a clue what to do next. I mean, Justine said Dallin was talking about missing money that I took. I want to know what that's about."

"Later," Black said.

Hannah felt the angry little girl in her well up. "Why?"

"Because you're not going anywhere for a few days. You're safe here, and feasting on a news cycle will overload your brain, which is close to that point anyway. I can see it. You need to sleep, even for just a few hours."

"I don't *want* to sleep."

"You've had one adrenaline spike after another. You need your brain to relax."

"I slept in the car."

"But not enough. There's a guest bedroom you can crash in. Don't worry, I won't let you sleep all day. We have work to do."

Hannah didn't want to sleep but knew he was right. She spun around and started going through the bags from the store. She found the hair dye and pulled it out.

"Show me where the guest bedroom is," she said. "I'll dye my hair and then rest a bit."

Black walked her down the hallway and around a corner.

"Staying hidden must be exhausting," she said.

"It is. But it's better than being dead or in prison. Besides, you learn to adapt. Your body adjusts. It becomes normal."

Hannah never felt she knew a normal life, so she had a hard time thinking anything would become that way in the future. Her gaze followed him until he disappeared around the corner. Then Hannah shut the bedroom door and turned the small lock that, she knew, wouldn't stop anyone who really wanted to get in.

CHAPTER TWENTY-TWO

She woke in a dark room; sunlight no longer spilled through the edges of cellular shades as it had when she'd first pulled the covers over her. After dying her hair she slept deeply, her wet hair still wrapped in a towel, and after awakening she opened her eyes, reached up and felt the thick, damp cotton. Moments passed before she remembered where she was, and then a few more seconds before recalling her hair was no longer blond but raven black. She walked to the bathroom where the light was on as she had left it, the sink splattered in streaks of black, watery dye. Hannah removed the towel, unwrapping it with hesitation, as if this was the first unveiling of a face after reconstructive surgery.

Her newly black hair fell around her face and shoulders in wet, clumped strands. It was such an unnatural color for her, as if someone had cut the mane off a bay horse and fashioned a wig from it. The color changed her. Such an easy thing, to dye one's hair. But she seemed truly another person in the mirror, and as she stared at herself she wondered if it was merely the hair that made her different.

Her eyes seemed lighter in contrast to her hair, her face more pale. She reached up, and in the mirror saw her fingers stroke an outline of her cheeks, one of which bore the fresh cut from what seemed like a lifetime ago. She leaned in and looked more closely in the mirror, but that didn't answer the question of what it was that suddenly seemed both so different and familiar to her. She stepped back a few feet and saw herself from a distance, and then it hit her.

I look just like him.

The truth was, Hannah and Billy shared no physical traits. Justine was the one who had inherited her father's washed-blue eyes and pointed jawline. But in the mirror Hannah saw the beauty on the outside and the rage within, just like with Billy. Despite the ugliness of his character, Billy had been a strikingly handsome man, and as a young man probably could have been a model if he'd had the chance. Wiry and muscular, with smooth, tanned skin and casual facial stubble. He hadn't even had to work at it. He had just woken every morning, usually hungover or even still drunk, yet he was striking in his looks. Which is why his rage was all the more horrifying. Rage from something appealing is always jarring, like a fluffy housecat ripping apart a bird in the backyard, the cat's normally cottony white facial fur matted in drying blood and tufts of feather.

But she *wasn't* her father, and if she was going to deal with whatever was happening to her life, she couldn't keep hiding behind the blame and hatred so easily directed at Billy. Her life was hers alone, and it was time for Hannah to regain some control of it.

Hannah left the bathroom and unlocked her bedroom door. The house was lit against the night. She had no idea if it was seven at night or three in the morning. Then she saw Black.

He was sitting on a stool leaning over the angled top of a desk. An architect's desk, she thought. A light attached to the back of the desk arced up and over the top, bent to shine a focused beam directly on the part of the surface where he was working. In his left hand he held an X-Acto blade, working it delicately over something pressed against the top of the desk.

He heard her and turned.

"Wow," he said.

"Wow?"

"Your hair."

She reached up and touched it.

"It looks great," he said.

She took another step forward. "I've never dyed it before."

"It suits you. I don't think you even need to cut it. Add some glasses and you'll be a new person."

She moved closer, feeling energy well up within her, spreading from her core, through her chest, pulsing outwards, making her fingertips flush with the heat of her blood.

"I'm working on some documents for you," he continued. He nodded to the top of the desk. "Won't be done tonight, but tomorrow for sure. Then we need to go over several more things before finding you a place to start. When I say start, what I'm referring to is—"

He stopped talking when she walked close enough to be within a foot of him. He looked up at her, his eyes almost level with hers, as she reached and cupped the sides of his face with her hands.

Black said nothing.

Hannah didn't hesitate. She leaned in and kissed him, her eyes closing a second before feeling his lips on hers. Just like that. Over eight years since another man's lips had touched hers, and Hannah wore Black's taste as she did her black hair. New. Different. *Necessary.* He tasted almost oaky, perhaps the lingering bourbon on his lips, the taste of something aged just the right amount of time. She felt her nipples harden under her shirt as she held his face tighter in her hands. Then she pulled back and looked at him.

"I need this right now," she said.

She expected him to say something. Agreement. *I want you, too.* Protest. *Hannah, I can't. I don't sleep with clients.* Reason. *Doing this won't get back at your husband. Your judgment is clouded.* She expected *something.* But Black said nothing, as if he was in perfect sync with her thoughts, as if he knew why she needed to be in control of something right now, even if it was just sex. Or maybe he simply wasn't going to argue with a beautiful woman pressing her mouth against his.

Black rose from his stool and reached out with his fingers, grabbing the bottom of her shirt. He pulled up, lifting the shirt over her arms, then let it fall to the floor. He then reached behind and unhooked her bra, and Hannah felt the excitement at baring herself in front of this man. Before Dallin, there had been four other men, the first when she was seventeen, the last one two months before she met her husband. Then eight years of Dallin. Hannah never imagined herself with any other man, but a lot of things had happened she hadn't ever imagined. Despite her sudden lust for Black, Hannah knew this was a defense mechanism. As crude and mechanical as it sounded, she needed to fuck Black to maintain composure. To keep control.

Black sat back in his stool and bent forward to her bare breasts, his tongue finding one of her nipples. Her body stiffened in pleasure as he tasted her, and it seemed every nerve ending abandoned its location to the exact spot where his tongue touched her. His mouth left a burning trace across her skin as he explored her.

He paused, and when he did, she removed his shirt and ran her hands along his shoulders, around his back, his neck. She kissed him again, letting her tongue touch his for a moment. She again tasted bourbon and wanted some for herself.

But not now.

Hannah reached for the top of her jeans and unbuttoned them. She pulled the zipper down and slid the denim over the tops of her thighs. The jeans fell to the ground, and she stepped out of them, keeping her mouth on his neck as she did. Then Black slid a hand around the small of her back and the pressure of his fingers aroused her even more than the kissing. He pulled her into him.

Hannah climbed on top of him. The stool swiveled, but he kept her tight against him, his arms wrapped around her, her legs around him.

She felt him grow hard through his pants as she rocked her hips against him. They remained that way, her mouth exploring his, the heat from his skin building a sweat she felt through her entire body, until he finally stood, lifting her with ease, and carried her into his bedroom. He put her on the bed, not throwing her down, but not gently either. He climbed up over her, supporting his weight on hands placed on either side of her shoulders. He leaned in and drew his tongue along the base of her throat, moving from one side to another.

She squeezed the back of his neck and brought her nails down the length of his back. Then she wrapped her legs around his waist and pushed him to the side, rolling him over on his back. He looked up at her as she straddled him, his eyes registering something that bordered on surprise.

"Tonight," she said, "I'm the one in charge."

CHAPTER TWENTY-THREE

"Everything you do leaves a trace." Black reached over the table and poured her more wine. As sparse as his belongings were, Hannah noticed there was no lack of alcohol, and their first bottle of Malbec was nearing the dregs. "So, erasing your identity is nearly impossible. All you can do is cover your steps the best you can, and, more importantly, create false leads for those who are chasing you to follow. Did you ever see *The Shining*?"

"I read the book," she said. It was one of the few horror books Hannah read as a teenager. She had little use for literary horror when she had enough real fear just sitting through dinner each night.

"It's like the end when Jack is chasing Danny through the snow. The boy gets just enough ahead and then retraces his steps backwards in the snow before jumping off the path. He left a false trail, and he got away. His father ended up freezing to death in the snow."

"That must have been the movie version," Hannah said. "In the book, Jack bashes his own face in with a croquet mallet, and then the hotel's boiler explodes and kills him. Plus, the boy had supernatural abilities, which helped him escape."

Black moved another slice of pizza onto his plate. He had made good in his promise to cook for her, though it consisted of nothing more than taking a frozen DiGiorno pizza out of its cardboard box and sliding it into the oven. "Well, I guess I'll stop using that analogy with my clients," he said. "My point is, if you really want to disappear, you have to abandon any path you were taking before. You have to avoid everything you once knew."

Black spoke casually as he chewed his food, as if they hadn't just been naked and wrapped around each other thirty minutes earlier. But Hannah knew better. She had been distant to him as soon as their clothes were back on, and he must have sensed this. Sensed her need for space. She didn't regret what had happened, but she hadn't fully processed it either.

"But I don't want to disappear forever," she said. "I don't want to just leave everything."

"Most of my potential clients say the same thing. They think they'll be fine. They end up going back to their regular lives."

"What happens to them?"

Black shrugged and reached for his wine glass. "If they're not my client, I don't have any need to keep track of them."

"So maybe they're fine," she said.

"Doubtful." He wiped his mouth. "I know a few who died. Saw it in the news. But most of the people who come to me aren't as high profile, so if they end up getting killed I really wouldn't have cause to know about it." He pushed the pizza toward her and she grabbed a slice. "But you're naive to think your husband would just decide to give up on what he started. In my opinion, the only way that happens is if he dies or goes to jail. And even jail doesn't stop a lot of people."

"Maybe I can lay low for a few days, maybe a week."

"No matter how long you want to remain hidden, you need to prepare as if you're leaving forever. It's the only way."

"But I need money. How do I do anything without money?"

"I have some I can loan you for now. Ideally, we can get you access to your accounts, though I'm sure your husband has been able to block your access to your money by now. But there are a few different things we can try. I assume you have decent liquidity. The more we can access, the easier all of this will be."

A chill ghosted her arms. She had been looking at the table most of the meal, but now she brought her gaze up directly to his face.

"If we can get access, how much do you suggest I take out?" she asked.

He stopped chewing. "How much do you have?"

"A lot." She sipped her wine. "What I'm asking is how much is your fee? I assume you're not doing this *pro bono*."

He hesitated. "Depends on how long you need to disappear for. But fifty thousand is a typical starting fee."

"What if I don't agree?"

He nodded at the front door. "I'm not holding you here, Hannah. You're free to leave, and I can take you somewhere where you can call a cab. I'm not trying to take advantage of you," he said. "I truly believe this is the best course of action, but I do charge for my services. It's a lot of work. And risk. If I'm helping you that means my trace becomes easier to pick up. That risk comes for a fee, and my fees start at fifty thousand."

"Even after nine years...or however long you've been hiding? You're still worried about being found? What did you do?"

Black didn't answer.

"Tell me your real name," she said.

"No."

"Then tell me why you needed to disappear."

"I don't tell people details about my life. If you want to be off the grid, you don't talk about your past."

"So you get to know everything about me but I don't get to know anything about you?"

"That's pretty much it."

"Bullshit," Hannah said. "If you want me to trust you, you have to tell me something...*anything* about the real you."

"Like I said, Hannah, you're free to go at any time."

"It's a Mexican standoff. I'll know something about you, you know everything about me. We'll be forced to trust each other, if no other reason than for fear of exposure."

"Hannah, just listen—"

She reached out and grabbed his wrist. "Black, will you please understand? I just need something that's the truth. That's real. Hell, you can even lie as long as you do a good job. Just tell me something I can *believe*. Tell me why you needed to disappear."

He searched her eyes for several seconds, assessing, and Hannah pictured his mind whirling with calculations of risk versus return. Finally, he put down a pizza crust on his plate, lining it up with two others, and pushed the plate a few inches away from him.

"Nine years ago I broke out of prison," he said. "And I've remained hidden, which is an exceptionally difficult thing to do."

"I thought you were a cop."

"I was."

Hannah felt herself straighten in her chair, both elbows resting on the tabletop. "What did you do?"

Black now stopped moving and looked directly at her.

"I killed someone."

She pushed back in her chair, but she knew it was more out of reflex than any kind of flight response. *If he wanted you dead, Hannah, you'd be long gone by now.*

"Who?"

"The guy who smashed his car head-on into my wife's. He was drunk, and he killed her." His voice was level as he spoke, but Hannah saw his right hand quivering. He seemed to notice this and moved his hand under the table. "I was on duty that night. I wasn't the one who responded to the call, but I got called in to the hospital. They took both of them there. My wife and...and the other driver."

He paused and Hannah said nothing. She wanted to say *It's okay, you don't have to tell me.* But that was bullshit. She wanted to know everything.

"I lost my mind," he said. "I was in the room when she died. She never woke up. I didn't even see the EKG machine go flat. There was a beeping from one of the monitors, and the doctor looked up at me and told me she was gone. It was the day after our fourth anniversary, and suddenly she was just...gone. The doctor...Jesus, he couldn't have been over thirty. I remember how young he looked. Looked like he couldn't grow facial hair with a month to do it, you know? Anyway, the doctor asks me if I wanted to see a grief counselor. I told him no. Then I walked out of the hospital room and found my partner there. Kyle. Kyle and I had been on the force together four years, and he knew me better than anyone except my wife. So I saw Kyle there, and he looks at me, and he just knows. Knows she's gone. And I can see in his eyes the fear. The loss. The look of, *holy shit, what if it had been my wife?*"

Black poured more wine even though his glass wasn't empty. "I see that on his face, and I realize at that moment he would do anything for me. He was my brother. And I asked him what happened to the other driver. He tells me he's in a room three doors down. I ask if he's okay. Kyle doesn't know. I ask him to show me the room. Kyle looks at me and hesitates just for a moment. The kind of moment where, in the movies, he wouldn't have told me. He would have taken me home, and stayed with me all night. Done anything to prevent me from going into that other hospital room. But this wasn't a movie, this was real life, and Kyle was my brother. So he looks at me a few more seconds and then nods behind me. 'Two seventeen,' he whispers. Either he was crazy as I was, or he didn't really think I would do it. Maybe he thought that, being a cop, I would somehow keep it together, grieve some other way. Get counseling."

Another pause. Another gulp of wine. Hannah remained silent as Black set his glass down. "So I walk into room two seventeen," he continued. "There's a doctor and two nurses there, which tells me this fucker is still alive. Hell, my wife only had one doctor in the room because they knew she didn't have a chance. But this guy, this guy has all the attention in the world on him. He's got blood on his face, and I can see a laceration on his forehead, stitched up and swollen. And he's awake, rolling his head back and forth, sputtering some babble I couldn't at first understand, but then a few seconds pass and I hear him asking for a drink. He wants a fucking drink. And he's not in pain, the guy is laughing. A drunk's laugh. Happy delirium."

Hannah felt her fingers squeeze her wine glass, and she momentarily looked over at the half-empty bottle of bourbon on the counter.

Black continued. "The doctor looks up at me. Now, it's not too unusual for a uniformed cop to enter a room like that. Maybe I want to talk to a suspect, get some information. So this doctor doesn't tell me to get out, he just looks at me for a moment and tells me the guy can't talk now because they need to take him to surgery. *Surgery.* They're going to spend tens of thousands of dollars to make sure he lives."

Black pushed back in his chair and stood. He walked to the back of the kitchen and grabbed the bottle of Maker's Mark, seeming to know, like Hannah, the moment when something stronger was necessary. He grabbed his dirty glass from earlier, filled it, and took a swallow.

He came back to the table with the bottle and the glass, then poured more and pushed the glass toward her. "I feel better when I don't drink alone, which is almost never."

Hannah picked up the glass and swallowed, then slid it back toward him. He refilled it and kept it for himself.

"I said nothing to the doctor," he said. "I just stood there and looked at the guy in the bed, rolling his head and smiling. The doctor tells me again I can't talk to the guy. I walk in the room a little further, and I sense someone enter the room behind me. Found out later it was Kyle. Then one of the nurses gives me the widest eyes I've ever seen and she rushes over and whispers something in the doctor's ear. See, she knows who I am at this point. She saw me with my wife, and now she sees me here in the room of the guy who killed her. She *knows* this isn't a good scene. So she tells the doctor, who looks a little freaked after the nurse tells him who I am. Then he comes over to me and says, 'You can't be here.' I look at him for a moment. He was just a distraction, a fly on a horse's ear. He was a large guy. Tall. Looked like he could throw down if he had to. Confidence, you know? But I didn't care. I didn't care about anything at this point. I'm in the blackness now.

"Then I hear Kyle behind me. Says, 'C'mon man, let's go.' Guess that was his conscience coming into play. But that was his only effort to stop me, to do something sensible, and I figured that's about as much as I would have made if it were him instead of me. Because deep down, he wanted what I wanted. He just didn't want to see me get into trouble. But I knew he was thinking, *Do it. Do it, man*. Because that's just who we were. All of us. We were all able to hold it together long enough until something finally unraveled inside, and then we turned into our primitive selves."

Hannah suddenly saw words in her head. Typeface on a page. *Kill the pig. Cut her throat. Spill her blood.*

Black sipped and then wiped his mouth with the back of his hand. "And you know what?" he said. "I almost listened to him. There was a moment—I remember it so clearly—a second where I came back from the darkness and knew where I was and what was happening. Knew the right choice to make. I remember shifting my weight, about to turn around. Leave the room."

Black leaned forward over the table, his shoulders pointing toward her.

"And then the guy in the bed says something. He looks at me and his eyes scrunch up and his mouth twists up, and I see a tooth sticking out, barely attached, like piece of food left on his face. He's got this shit-eating grin, like he's going to burst out laughing any second. And in a slurred voice he says to me, 'Hey, officer, did you arrest that cunt who hit me?'"

Hannah felt the bourbon burn in her gut. She said nothing.

Black leaned back. "I don't remember any of what happened next," he said. "But I've been told, because there were plenty of witnesses, including Kyle, who apparently tried to stop me but wasn't fast enough." A long exhale. "Apparently I walked up to the side of the guy's bed, pulled my service revolver out, and blew his head apart."

"Wow."

"Yeah, wow."

"I mean...shit. Wow."

"Yeah. Shit wow." Black rubbed his hands together. "I never... never tell anyone this. I haven't talked about this since my first day in prison."

"How does it feel to talk about it?"

"I hate it. But, like you said, you know nothing about me. You deserve to know something, and I'm not telling you my name."

"So you went to jail," she said.

"No, I went to *prison*. Jail is for small stuff, or for temporary holding. Prison is where you go to turn into a different person. And even though I was a cop, even though I had some sympathy on my side, and even though I pled temporary insanity, I still got twenty years. Twenty fucking years in state prison. You know what kind of fun a cop-turned-convict has in state prison? Not much."

"How long after you went to prison did you escape?"

"Two years. Two years of the worst hell I've ever known. Two of us got out together. I'm still free. He isn't."

"The other guy got caught?"

Black nodded. "He was sloppy. He lasted three months, better than most. But he got a little lazy, which is all it takes. He went back. I stayed out."

"How do you know he was caught?"

"Because we remained together until a few days before he was re-arrested. Which is another thing I've learned. You have to be alone. No matter how lonely you get, once you stop being alone, you're vulnerable. He knew too much about me." Black looked distantly beyond her. "Still does."

Something started ringing. Hannah looked around and saw nothing.

"Excuse me," he said. Black walked into the next room, toward the sound of the tone. She heard him answer a phone and then mumble, his words clipped and guarded. He was silent, and then spoke. Silent, then more words. His voice grew.

"No," she heard. "No. Jesus, *what?*"

His voice trailed as he moved further away. She heard a door close and then more angry words muffled by wood and sheetrock.

Silence.

Another door slamming.

Minutes later, Black walked back into the kitchen, his posture rigid.

"What's wrong?" she asked.

"Nothing. I need to do some work upstairs. The house is locked. Keep your shades in your bedroom down."

"Who was on the phone?"

"It's nothing to concern you."

"What's going on?"

"There are things I need to do."

That was the end of the conversation. Black shut down after finally having opened up, stinging Hannah with his silence. He walked out of the kitchen and turned off the light, leaving Hannah in the dark. He caught himself a moment later and flicked the switch back on.

"Reflex," he said. "I'm used to being alone."

CHAPTER TWENTY-FOUR

Day 7

"Where are we going?"

"Someplace safe."

"I thought we *were* safe."

Black kept staring straight ahead as he drove.

"I thought so, too."

"What changed? I thought we were staying at your house for a few days."

The morning sunlight hit the side of Hannah's face through the car window which meant they were driving north.

"Plan changed."

"Why?"

The only sound was the asphalt treadmilling beneath the car wheels and the rush of the air against the windshield. Black said nothing.

"You know, more than a two-word answer would be nice," she said. "I mean, we had sex. Then we had dinner, where you told me things you supposedly never said to anyone else. Then you get some call and turn cold on me, then wake me up in a rush first thing in the morning and tell me to pack my stuff because we're leaving." She rolled a hair tie off her wrist and put her hair back in a ponytail. "I deserve a little more than 'plan changed.'"

He stole a glance at her and snapped his attention back to the road the moment their eyes met. His jaw was tight, she noticed, and his hair genuinely out of place, rather than just a sculpted version of disheveled. But it was more than just that. He looked harried, uncertain. Unprepared, which is something she guessed Black hardly ever was.

"Did you even sleep last night?" she asked.

He didn't answer.

Hannah let out an exasperated sigh at his silence then kept looking out the window, out at the pine trees whipping by the side of the road.

Then a thought hit her.

"Why didn't you blindfold me?" she asked.

Nothing.

"You blindfolded me going to your house. But this morning we just drove away, and I saw exactly where you live. All of a sudden you're not concerned?"

"Like you said last night," he said. "Mexican standoff."

The answer contained as much explanation as his previous one. *Plan changed.* Might as well say *Shut the fuck up and do what you're told.* Nothing rang true.

"Are we headed to the border?" she asked.

His only answer to that question was taking the next exit off the highway and then silently navigating a series of roads, each one lonelier than the previous, until nearly a half-hour later they were on a simple dirt road flanked by a panoramic view of evergreens. It wouldn't be long before snow coated the endless sea of spiny needles.

Black stopped the car. The road was too small to pull over to the side, but no other cars were anywhere to be seen.

"Where are we?" Hannah asked.

"The middle of nowhere."

"This is the change of plans?"

"It's a start."

Hannah looked out the windshield and saw the expanse of forest before her. The curving land sloped into a narrow valley in the distance, a strip of blue-gray river snaking along its floor. In happier times, Hannah would have considered all of this beautiful. Now she found it desperately lonely.

Black turned his shoulders toward her. He unfastened his seatbelt, allowing him to fully turn and face her.

"I have some things to tell you," he said.

Hannah kept her own seatbelt on. She briefly glanced at her door, checking that it was unlocked, before moving her gaze to him.

"What?"

"You're in danger. *Real* danger."

"No shit," she said.

"You don't understand, because...because there are things I haven't been truthful about."

She felt her leg muscles stiffen, pushing her body straighter in her seat.

"What are you talking about?"

"You need to disappear. For real. It wasn't safe back at my house. Everything's been compromised."

"Why do you keep saying 'for real'?"

Black reached for a plastic water bottle nestled in the driver's side door. He twisted the cap and took a sip so small Hannah thought the gesture intended more to buy time rather than quench thirst. He spoke again, but this time he looked straight ahead rather than at her.

"I'm working for someone," he said. "This person wants you to disappear, and he hired me to do it. Everything that's happened...it's all been staged to make you believe your life was in danger. To make you want to run away. I was waiting for you in the coffee shop that day."

His words drilled into her, into her core, squeezing her gut. Hannah pushed the button releasing her seatbelt, which spooled back into its harness. She had heard him, but didn't know what to do next. Was he even telling the truth? Other questions flooded her brain in fragments, overlapping each other so the only words that seemed to resonate were *what, who* and *why*. She felt herself recoiling against the car seat.

Then she said, "Dallin hired you to do all of this?"

"Let me finish," Black said. "I got a call last night. Things changed because...because something happened."

"What? What happened?"

He shook his head as if trying to erase the reality of what he had to say. Then he paused, looked at her directly, and said, "They killed your psychologist."

"*What?*"

"Madeline Britel, that's her, right?"

"Yes...I mean..." Dr. Britel's face flashed in Hannah's mind. Always sitting in the same chair, the same bonsai tree on the floor next to her. The smell of leather in the office. Books. A faint aroma of her perfume. Long black hair, a few streaks of gray that the doctor did nothing to conceal. Stern face, hard eyes, but the occasional smile that could warm her expression entirely. She heard the last words Dr. Britel said to her:

Do you feel safe?

"Please tell me what the hell you're talking about," she said. "Tell me this is all a lie."

Black shook his head. "My...my business partner called me last night and confirmed it."

"Who's your business partner? I thought you worked alone."

"Later," he said. "He said it's on the news. That's what I was doing last night. Confirming it. She was shot outside her building. Her office ransacked. Staged to make it look like a robbery, I'm sure, to throw off the scent. They knew you spoke to your psychologist about what happened with your husband, at least his talking in his sleep. That would have been in her notes. If the police were ever able to subpoena those notes, which is difficult but not impossible—"

"Are you saying my husband murdered my therapist?"

Black held his hand up. "There's more. The client told all this to my partner last night as a means to show their seriousness. They had a change in plans, and I think killing your doctor was about more than cleaning up a loose end. They want to try to scare me into doing something that wasn't part of the original plan."

Hannah started to speak, her mouth so dry it seemed a wool sock had been shoved inside it for hours.

"What's...what's the new plan?"

He leaned in just enough to be either comforting or threatening, depending on the words he spoke next.

"They want me to kill you."

Hannah knew what he was going to say a second before the words came out. As he spoke the words, she grabbed for the handle of the center console, pulling it open. Yesterday there had been a gun in there, and that was her only hope.

She saw the dull black handle of the weapon.

Hannah snatched the gun and fumbled with it for a split second—almost dropping it—before wrapping both hands tightly around the grip and pointing the barrel directly into Black's face.

Besides a solitary blink, Black made no other movement. He kept his focus on Hannah's eyes, not on the gun in front of his face.

Hannah saw her hands shaking and wished she could hold the gun steady, with power and authority. The weapon had a weight to it greater than she expected.

"Okay, take it easy, Hannah. I didn't say I'm going to kill you. I said my client *wanted* me to kill you. I'm *not* going to hurt you. That's why we're out here. That's why—"

"Stop talking," she said. "Just shut up."

"Hannah—"

She straightened her arms. The gun was almost touching his face. She watched the tip of the barrel waver from one eye to another as her hands shook, wondering if she could really do it.

"Shut up. Goddammit. *Nothing* is real. *You are not real.* I trusted you, despite all my instincts not to. I *trusted* you. It was the only choice I had, and even that was wrong."

"If I was going to kill you, I would have done it while you were sleeping. I'm trying to help you. Just let me explain."

"*Stop talking.*"

"Hannah, I could just swat the gun out of your hands. You're not going to shoot. So just put it down and let's talk."

The shaking of Hannah's hands moved up into her arms, and the harder she squeezed the gun, the more she trembled. She licked her lips, tasting the salty sweat beading on her upper lip. She pulled the gun back away from his face to try to steady her grip. But her arms still shook with the adrenaline surging through her body.

Black leaned back, putting more distance between his gun and his face.

"It isn't even loaded," he said. "I keep the bullets in—"

Hannah closed her eyes and pulled the trigger.

CHAPTER TWENTY-FIVE

The shot was deafening in the tight confines of the car, and when she opened her eyes the first thing she noticed was the shattered glass of the driver's window. Black's hands were in front of his face, and Hannah winced as she expected to see blood pouring from between his fingers.

He removed his hands. His face was fully intact. Hannah had missed, the combination of shaking hands and closed eyes dooming her aim, even at such a short distance.

"Jesus Christ," he said. "I can't believe you really pulled the trigger." He pushed himself back against the car door as Hannah quickly brought the gun back up.

I can't believe it either, she thought. She wanted to think she missed on purpose, but she hadn't. Just for the fact that she couldn't hold her weapon steady was the only reason he was alive. Or maybe it was some kind of divine intervention.

"Get out of the car," she said. "Just get out of the fucking car."

"Fine, Hannah." He kept his hands up. "Let's both get out of the car and we can talk, okay?"

"I'm done with talking," she said. "And I'm done with trusting."

"Hannah, you can't just leave me out here."

She kept the gun pointed at him, and now her hands seemed steadier. "I'm going to tell you one more time to get out of the car, and then I'm going to shoot again. Next time my eyes will be wide open, and I won't miss."

Black opened the door and got out, leaving the door open. Hannah kept the gun trained on him from the passenger seat of the car.

"Dallin is your client," she said. "But you said 'they.' Who else hired you?"

"Does it matter?"

"Who are your clients?"

"Will you not just abandon me if I tell you?"

Hannah aimed the gun just to the left of Black and pulled the trigger again. Black jumped as the bullet screamed past him. The sound of the blast echoed inside her head, but this time it felt good. The gun felt less heavy. A sense of power and control surged through her.

"Will you stop doing that?" he said.

"Tell me. Or the next one's going into you."

Black ran one hand through his hair, smoothing it back for a second before long strands fell again over his forehead.

"Yes, Dallin," he said. "Dallin's my main client. He was the one who initially contacted me."

"Was he the one who told you to kill me?"

"No, the call last night was from my partner. He'd been given the instruction to...the change of plans."

"Who's your partner?"

Black sighed.

"Tell me," she said.

"You know him as Peter."

Hannah saw the man in her mind. The huge hands, the deep stare. She could smell the chemical on the rag he used to send her into unconsciousness.

My job is to mitigate risk.

"The thug from Echo?"

"He doesn't work for Echo," Black said. "He works for me. I knew him in prison."

Another falsehood. Another deception.

"Tell me everything right now," she said. "Goddammit, tell me everything, and if I think you're lying I swear to God I'll—"

"Hannah, there's so much you don't know. I don't know everything. In fact, I'm thinking I know a lot less than I suspected.

Let's get back in the car, drive away from here, and I promise I'll tell you everything I know. That's what I was trying to do anyway before you pulled the gun on me. I was driving you away from danger. Just take it easy, okay?"

"Let me tell you what *I* know," she said. "I know if you tell me to take it easy one more time, I'm shooting you in the face. Right the fuck in that beautiful face of yours, Black. And then you won't be able to tell any more lies. You won't have to run away from anyone again."

She barely felt anything, any emotion, any sensation at all. She simply observed what this tiny woman with the gun and cheap hair dye was saying.

"*Hannah,*" he said.

"You need to tell me everything. Who the other clients are. And why all the pretense? Why not just kill me earlier?"

Black didn't seem to hear her. He was distracted by something else.

"*Hannah,*" he barked. "We've got company."

She felt her mouth say the word "*What?*"

"Look."

Hannah turned her head and looked through the rear window of Black's car.

She saw a white pickup, battered and rusted, the war scars of hard use. It pulled to a stop fifty yards away, and Hannah hadn't even heard it approaching. A man stepped out of the truck and started walking towards their car. There were many things about this man that screamed caution to Hannah, but none more so than the shotgun he carried.

CHAPTER TWENTY-SIX

Black whispered with enough force for it to be a hiss.

"Give me the gun, Hannah."

"The hell I will."

"I'm not going to hurt you," he said. "Goddammit, I wish you would just believe that. This guy looks like a problem."

Hannah turned her head again. *If someone was ever to film a version of* Deliverance *in the Pacific Northwest*, Hannah thought, *this guy would be in it.* The first thing she noticed was the man was broad and thick, carrying the kind of extra weight that suggested power rather than fat, like a linebacker. His beard was almost as long as the hair on his head, all of which appeared to have avoided the bite of a comb in weeks, maybe months. His small, dark eyes were set back behind high, puffy cheeks. The flannel and denim encasing him had faded into monochromatic shades.

He's a bear, Hannah thought. *Grizzly*.

"Is he working for you, too?" she asked. Her grip on the gun did not loosen.

Black seemed to want to argue more but must have thought better of it. He called out to the man.

"Morning," Black said.

The man kept walking without responding. As he got closer, he shifted the shotgun so he held it with both hands. It wasn't pointing at them. Yet.

"Can I help you?" Black said.

Black took a firm stance on the dirt road, right leg back, knee slightly bent.

Grizzly finally stopped walking as he reached the back of the car. His voice was soft, but Hannah could still make out his words through the open car door next to Black.

"Heard shots," he said. "Gunfire."

Hannah saw Grizzly's breath fog in the cold air, frothy vapor that dissipated as it rose past his meaty face.

"We're okay," Black said. "Appreciate you checking, but everything's okay."

Grizzly turned his head and saw Hannah in the car. She held up the gun, making sure he saw it, but pointed the barrel up. Grizzly gave her the slightest of nods.

Then he nodded at the broken window and the glass in the dirt.

"Don't suppose everything's okay at all." With the calm of a hunter approaching his kill, Grizzly lowered the shotgun until the barrel pointed directly at Black.

Black held his hands up in the universal gesture of *take it easy, man.*

"It was an accident," Black said. "We came out here so she could learn to use a gun. It accidentally went off."

Grizzly smiled. What teeth he had left were the yellow of century-old newspaper.

"Inside a car? Mister, either you lying to me, or you the worst fuckin' teacher ever existed."

Black leaned into the car. Hannah saw real concern on his face, and if this was all just another part of the storyline, then Black missed his calling as an actor. "Tell him everything's cool," he told her.

"Stay lookin' at me, pretty boy."

Black straightened back and faced him.

"She'll tell you. Honey, come on out of the car."

Hannah did as she was told, but only because it would buy her a few more seconds to figure out what to do. She stood outside the passenger side opposite Grizzly and Black, leaving the door open. She looked down through the car window and eyed the keys dangling in the ignition. She had to do something, any-thing, to get out of here, and maybe Grizzly was her chance.

"This man was trying to hurt me," she said.

Black snapped his head to her from his side of the car, his eyes wide. "What are you doing?"

"Keep your hands up." Grizzly now held up his shotgun. Tight. Controlled. Prey in sight.

"Look," Hannah told Grizzly. "I just want to get out of here. This is my car. I just met this man last night, and...and I made a mistake. A big mistake." She glanced over and Black shot her a look that scared her more than the blackness in Grizzly's eyes. "This morning I woke up with a gun in my face, and he drove me out here. I don't know what he was planning to do."

The man grumbled. "'Cept you're the one with the gun."

"I was able to grab it from him when...when he stopped the car and tried to touch me."

"Hannah, *what the hell*?" Black said. He half-turned toward her.

"I'm not gonna ask you again." The man brought his shot-gun up to eye level and took another step toward Black. "Stay fac-ing me."

Black spun back toward Grizzly. "Would you just let us talk for a minute?"

Grizzly then strolled casually up to Black and flipped the shotgun around, holding the butt of weapon in his right hand. Black seemed to realize at the last moment what was happen-ing and swung at Grizzly, but his fist was ducked by a speed that Hannah wouldn't have afforded the large man. Black lost his bal-ance and Grizzly struck, slamming the stock of the shotgun into Black's forehead.

Black crumpled to the ground.

"There," the man said. "Problem solved."

Hannah cringed at the sound of the impact and heard herself yelp.

"Little faggot," Grizzly said to Black's motionless body.

"Don't know much about fighting, do you? Only know about talking. Real men fight back, not fall to the ground." Grizzly laughed and then spit on the ground next to Black.

The words *real men* raised the hairs on Hannah's arms.

Hannah struggled to keep her cool despite knowing she'd been the cause for what just happened. *But wasn't this what you wanted?*

"Well, thank you," she said, wanting nothing more than to get in the car and drive away. But Grizzly was standing next to the driver-side door, looking directly at her over the car's rooftop. "What's your plan with him?"

"With him? Don't have a plan at all. Figured he'll wake up at some point, probably stumble along enough to find a ride somewhere."

"Is he okay?" she asked.

"Do you care?"

Do you, Hannah?

"I guess not," she said. "We went together to a party last night. If he's found dead, I was the last person he was seen with."

Grizzly squinted at her for a moment as if trying to run her words through a lie detector. Then he bent down out of view for a few seconds before reappearing.

"He's breathing. Just gonna have a bitch of a headache when he comes around."

Hannah hesitated before making the decision that it was okay to leave Black there. If he was alive, he'd be fine. *Not that you really care, do you, Hannah? You may have slept with him, but that was about control. Maybe a little comfort. You don't owe him anything, especially not after what he told you today. Even if he was telling the truth, even if he wasn't planning to kill you, he's still working for Dallin, and that's enough to leave him passed out on a cold dirt road.*

"I need to go now," she said.

Grizzly chuckled, which sounded almost like a growl.

"So, you a party girl, huh?"

Hannah felt for the trigger with her finger.

"I'm going to leave now," she said. To get to the driver's seat, she'd either have to walk around to where Grizzly was standing or climb across from the passenger side.

Grizzly started to walk around the back of the car. Hannah counteracted his motion, side-stepping around the front of the car.

"You're not going anywhere," he said. "But you can certainly thank me. In fact, I have a few ideas of how you can do that."

Hannah lifted the gun.

"Stay away from me."

"Seems to me you were trying to shoot your boyfriend at close range and missed. Don't suppose your aim is gonna be much better at this length." Grizzly lifted his shotgun and aimed it at her. "Now, I don't have that problem," he said. "I'm a fine shot, and even if I wasn't, this shotgun just sprays buckshot all over the goddamn place. Hard to miss. From this distance I'm quite sure that pretty face of yours would end up in little bits and pieces on the ground."

"I swear I'll shoot," Hannah said.

"Go ahead. You shoot first." She could see the smile peering at her from behind the stock of his gun. "If you miss, then it's my turn, okay? Or, you could put the gun down, we go back to my place for a little fun, then I'll bring you back to your car. No worse for the wear." He laughed. "Okay, maybe a little worse, 'cause I got a big dick, honey. And you're gonna have to take all of it. But least you'll be alive. Least that face will still be nice and smooth. Least you'll have—"

Hannah fired the gun.

It kicked in her hands, but she held firm and had lined up Grizzly in the sight while he'd been talking. She'd aimed for the chest but wasn't sure where the bullet had hit him.

But it definitely hit him.

Grizzly spun and dropped to the ground, first on one knee, then both, then rolling onto his back. He left his shotgun on the road where he'd dropped it, and used his hands to grab at his stomach. He made a horrible sound, a horrid mixture of retching, wheezing, and moaning, the sound of a TV zombie.

Hannah knew the first thing she had to do was move his shotgun out of reach, and as little as she wanted to get anywhere near Grizzly she ran around the front of the car, around Black's still body, until she reached Grizzly's weapon. She picked it up and threw it as far as she could, realizing as it was in mid-air that it might fire and kill her as it landed. But it crashed to the dirt fifteen feet away with no more than a soft thud.

Grizzly didn't even seem to notice her. He was on his back, focused on the hole in his stomach and the spreading pool of blood gurgling up through his dirty flannel shirt. Hannah took a few steps back, keeping her gun aimed at him the entire time.

"You...you fuggin' shot me." His voice was strained and he did a half-crunch, attempting to look at his wound, but the pain overtook him and his head collapsed back onto the hard dirt with a thud.

Hannah felt nothing for him. Felt nothing for what she had done. Maybe it was shock, but she didn't think so. This man just took the punishment for everyone who had fucked up her life in the last week. And even though her body shook with adrenaline and fear, she didn't feel guilty. In fact, she even felt a little good.

She looked up and down the dirt road, which twisted out of view not too far in the distance in both directions. She didn't get the sense the road was traveled much, but who knew? Grizzly had heard the gunshots, so he couldn't have been too far away. Was he hunting? Was there a house or cabin close by?

Black was still passed out and Grizzly writhed in the dirt, his moans morphing into agonizing, gurgling howls. Blood now spilled up and over his massive gut and into the dirt, rendering it into a red clay. She had to get the hell out of there, but what did she leave behind? Did she leave Black? Did she leave Grizzly wounded but alive?

Fuggin' cunt whore, she heard. Hannah looked down at the man she'd shot. Blood bubbled from his nose, streaking the brown and white bush of his wildly ungroomed moustache. He wheezed as he spoke, each word sounding like it caused more pain than the previous one, making what he had to say seemingly the most important thing he'd ever uttered. "I'll cut your god-damn tits off."

A scene unfolded in Hannah's mind. She saw herself leaving in Black's car, leaving the two men on the road. Someone comes along soon after—most likely one of Grizzly's kind. Maybe even a relative. A brother, perhaps. Grizzly is still alive, and his brother loads his kin and Black into his truck. The brother ties up Black while he takes Grizzly to the hospital. They call the gunshot an accident, but the truth is they don't involve the police because they want to take care of things their way. Mountain justice. Back at their ramshackle cabin, the two brothers decide the best way to hunt down Hannah is through Black. They take turns on him, taking not hours but days. They slowly destroy his hands, his feet, his teeth, ears, maybe even an eye. Piece by piece, until Black tells them everything he knows about Hannah. Finally they put him out of his misery, slicing his throat as they would a wild pig. They dump Black's mutilated body deep into the woods before setting out in their truck. They have a new purpose in their shitty lives. Finding this woman named Hannah. And when they do...

Two things were very clear as Hannah decided what to do next. One, she had to take Black with her.

Two, Grizzly had to die.

CHAPTER TWENTY-SEVEN

Hannah walked closer to Grizzly, cautiously, using the kind of slow, small steps associated with someone approaching a closet door in a horror movie. But she needed to be closer to him. She needed to do this right. One shot. Like putting a deer hit by a car out of misery.

She tried to steady her hand as she pointed the gun at his head. Grizzly looked up at her—eyes squinting beneath squirrel-tail eyebrows—and jerked his head from side to side. Hannah knew she could not close her eyes this time. Shooting at Black was a reaction. Shooting this man now was something different. It was an execution, and if she was going to do it she would not close her eyes. She would not squirm as if stepping on a spider. She would aim, pull the trigger, and make sure he died. He would have raped her. He probably would have killed her afterwards. If she let him live, he might be able to find her. So now he was going to die, and even though the man was deserving of it, she was going to respect his life enough to keep her eyes open as the bullet shattered his skull.

Hannah sucked in a breath and wiped sweat from her forehead with her arm. The wind kicked up just a touch, enough to swirl a few strands of her black hair around her face. She raised the gun a few inches, lining up his skull through the notch of the sight.

"No," he said. It seemed the only thing he could say through the pain, and he repeated it over and over. *No. No. No.*

Her finger tickled the trigger. *Just pull it, Hannah. Pull the trigger and get the hell out of there.*

"No..." Head thrashing. Body twitching. He first tried to push back, his heels digging into the dirt and then slipping, but he was unable to move more than a couple inches.

Then he did the only other thing anyone in that situation could do to avoid death. Hannah should have seen it coming. She should have remembered how fast this man was, but she assumed his wound had incapacitated him.

Grizzly attacked.

Hannah saw his arm swipe toward her, and what she thought was his attempt to use momentum to push away from her instead became a python grip on her ankle. He squeezed like a monster grabbing a child's ankle from beneath a bed. And before she could shoot, Grizzly yanked her leg hard enough to topple her over.

Hannah fell hard, her tailbone slamming into the cold dirt. Tears welled in her eyes, the instantaneous reaction to searing physical pain. Her legs fell over his stomach, and she brought her left heel down onto his wound, not so much as a defensive move but a simple attempt to try to get up.

Grizzly howled and finally rolled to his side, toward her, pushing her legs back into her chest. And then he was on top of her. Just like that, with the same speed and agility he had shown in hitting Black. His weight pushed the air from her lungs and, as she looked up at him, she knew she was in trouble. This wasn't a man attacking her. He truly was a wounded bear, filled with the strength of every chemical flooding his body begging him to survive. His face was contorted with rage, spit hanging from his lower lip, a reddish white ooze threatening to fall in her eye.

Hannah tried to point the gun at him, managing to bring her arm up only a few inches before Grizzly slammed his massive fist into the left side of her face.

With the impact, nothing seemed to work anymore. Not her arms, her legs, not even her ability to move any part of her or make any sound. The only thing that worked in her body was her nerve endings, which filled her brain with the notion of unbelievable pain. Her right cheek dull and flat against the ground, her left cheek on fire, a vision of a dirt road and trees in the distance. She heard him above her, grunting, growling. His weight crushed her, and as she tried to wriggle out from beneath him he pushed his palms into her shoulders, grinding her into the soil.

She felt wetness on the left side of her face, the side that seemed to have collapsed into itself, the side with the eye that would not open. Either it was her own blood or Grizzly's spit.

"If I'm gonna die," he said, "I'm taking you with me."

Suddenly the bulk of his weight was off her, though the pressure around her hips suggested he was straddling her waist.

This was how she was going to die. Hannah hoped it would be quick. Hoped his wound was too debilitating for him to do anything else but smash a rock into her head, bringing her quickly to an end.

She felt her fingers twitching outwards, seeking the gun, like a spider in a sink searching for something to cling to. But there was nothing. Only tiny pebbles and the sensation of dirt packing up beneath her nails.

She gave one last burst of effort, one last struggle, but it didn't matter. It was as if she was trapped under a fallen tree. She swiped her arm up toward her assailant and her fist landed against his flannelled torso with a soft thud. He didn't make a sound as she hit him.

Then Hannah felt the weight of his hand on her face, grabbing, squeezing. The pain seared through the nerves damaged by his knuckles, and she felt her head turning in his meaty paw. *He's snapping my neck. He's going to twist my head right off.* Her neck tightened reflexively and a spike of nausea shot through her core. The idea of her head turning until her neck simply cracked was unimaginable, but now it was happening.

fuck fuck fuck oh God

But Grizzly wasn't breaking her neck. He was lifting her head off the ground so Hannah could look up at him.

She saw nothing out of her left eye. Out her right she saw Grizzly staring down at her, smiling for a moment before succumbing to a bloody, hacking cough. Tendrils of thick, red saliva wormed from his lower lip, one of them breaking off and dropping onto her chin. Now he didn't seem as much of a grizzly as a bulldog, wide jowls wet in anticipation of a kill.

"Need...need to look at me when I kill you," he said, struggling through his words. He straightened and grabbed his gut, grimaced through the pain. "Fuckin' cunt. *I'm gonna choke you out, and you're gonna smell my breath as you die.*"

"No," she said.

"Yes," he replied, and the smile was back. "*Hell* yes."

Hannah lifted her head and spat at his face. The small glob she could manage landed on his neck. "Then just fucking do it already," she said. "And then I hope you bleed out, you pig." She swiped at him again, and this time he caught her wrist and squeezed.

Kill the pig. Slice her throat.

"Crazy bitch," he said. He took her wrist and pinned it beneath his knee. Her only free limb was her left arm, and she landed a feeble punch on the side of his head as he leaned forward. He smiled as he put his fingers around her throat, his yellowed teeth crooked like tombstones in a ghost-town cemetery. The pressure from his hands increased, but slowly, a pound at a time. He wasn't strangling her with hate, but with studied practice. He peered down at her and stared into her face with wonder. Hannah could still breathe, but she was only a few exhales away from not being able to inhale again.

"Keep your eyes open," he said. "I want to see them turn."

She *could* smell his breath, just as he had promised. Rotten breath, the smell of tangy decay. If only he could smother instead of choke her, Hannah could at least escape this one last humiliation.

"Fuck you," she managed, before she could no longer breathe. She was now underwater with the surface just out of reach. *Close*

*your eyes, Hannah. Close your eyes and let go. Be at peace. Don't feel
the pain, but anticipate what's next.*

Hannah closed her eyes, but instead of peace she only heard
Billy, who haunted her even in her moment of death. The one
moment that she should truly own for herself, he was there.

*Ain't nothin' waiting for you after death, Hannie. Don't be stu-
pid. What was you before you were born? Not a thing. That's how
death is. Not a thing. In fact, that pretty much sums you up, don't it?
You're not a thing. Not at all.*

All she could do was try to shut out his voice and hope for it
to be over quickly. She felt her body temperature rise as her pulse
quickened. Panic set in with every second she didn't breathe,
which made her body fight for breath more violently. Her body
spasmed. Muscles shuddered. Adrenaline surged. Reflexes took
over. She heard herself gagging, felt the pressure on her neck,
the sense her throat was going to simply cave in on itself. Liquid
squeezed through her closed eyelids, either tears or blood. *Seconds,* she thought. *A few more seconds, and then peace. Just a few
more...*

A brightness flashed beneath the lids of her eyes, a scream
tore through her brain, and then there was a sudden lifting. A
sense of comfort, of lessening pain. The pain was still there, but
the immediacy of it was gone.

No more pressure on her throat. No more stench of animal
breath. Yet still the weight on her hips and thighs.

Hannah felt air rush down her windpipe, cold and thin, filling her empty lungs. She gasped at the suddenness of it all, almost
gagging. The gasping turned to coughing, which in turn flared
the pain on the left side of her face.

If I'm dead, this fucking sucks.

Hannah opened her eyes. Grizzly remained straddled on top
of her but he was now sitting upright, his hands held loosely in
the air, fingers arched toward the sky. He was staring at the barrel of a shotgun that was leveled directly over Hannah's head. The
end of the barrel was less than a foot away from Grizzly's face.

Black's hands were tightly wrapped around the stock of the shotgun, his finger on the trigger. He remained on his knees, wobbling slightly, as if the world were trying to twist beneath him. A massive, red welt—the distinct outline of the butt of the shotgun visible—covered most of his forehead.

"Take it easy there, hero," Grizzly wheezed.

Black pulled the trigger.

The shotgun roared and Grizzly's face exploded like a water balloon, bursting into a wet, red mist. His body rose from the impact of the buckshot, lifting off Hannah and collapsing on the dirt in front of her feet. Hannah pushed herself up to her elbows and stared at what was left of the man who almost killed her. She felt bile rise in her throat at the sight of bits of gray matter and skull scattered along the road. She turned to Black.

"You..." Her throat burned. "You could have hit me," she rasped.

Black struggled to his feet. "Again, a 'thank you' would be nice."

She rubbed her neck, which felt like it had just been released from a noose. "I didn't need to be..." *Jesus, Hannah, really? You didn't need saving?* She looked at the ground. "Thank you."

"And I made sure the gun was close enough to him so the blast didn't hit you. Sometimes I do know what I'm doing." He rubbed his head, wincing when his fingers reached the welt. "Though I underestimated him."

Hannah stood, and when she was upright a new wave of pain rolled over the left side of her face. Black walked up to her and reached out to her face. She pulled away.

"Let me see," he said.

She turned her head a few degrees toward him but kept her gaze to the ground.

"Can you see out of that eye?" he asked. "It's pretty swollen."

"A little," she said.

Black turned from her, stumbled a few steps, and picked his gun up from the ground. He tucked it in the waist of his jeans.

"Now do you believe I'm not going to kill you?" he asked.

Hannah looked back at the corpse. For everything Black had told her was fake, the dead man was real. The missing face, the bloodied shreds of skin, the scattering of yellowed teeth among pebbles and dirt. All real.

"I don't know what to believe," she said. "Every time I believe something, I'm wrong."

"Okay, I'll make it easy for you," he said. "I'm holding both guns now, so I get to make the rules." He glanced up and down the road. "That guy might have friends or family up around here somewhere."

"He mentioned going back to his place."

"And it's probably not too far away. We have to get the hell out of here."

"Can you drive?"

"I'm pretty wobbly," he said. "Concussion, probably. How do you feel?"

"Horrible," she said. She nodded back at the body. "But I'm clear. I can drive."

"Okay, good."

"What about him?" she asked. "Are we just going to leave him like that?"

"No time for a funeral," Black said.

"That's not what I meant. I mean, he was clearly murdered. Aren't you worried about an evidence trail?"

"Of course I am," he said. "But our prints aren't on anything we're leaving behind. If we had more time we could—"

"Burn him," she said.

"What?"

"We can burn him. Him and his truck."

"Jesus, that just popped right into your mind, didn't it?"

"He was on top of me," she said. "Maybe one of my hairs came off on him. And..." She replayed the horrible seconds back through her mind. "I spit on him."

"Fuck." He looked around the ground. "Dirt is pretty soft," he said. "You can see footprints, car tracks, but they're pretty undefinable. No use in torching his truck. It's going to be obvious he was killed over here."

"You have a lighter?" she asked.

"Yeah. The problem is accelerant. I don't have a tube to siphon gas with." He stumbled over to Grizzly's truck, then pulled the sleeves of his shirt over his hands to use as gloves as he opened the trunk.

"Here we go," he said. Black removed a gallon-sized metal gas can and held it up to her.

"Lighter?"

"Glove compartment."

Hannah went back to the car and fished in the glove compartment. Seeing nothing, she unzipped a small black case, something she'd expect to house an iPod. She found a pack of Marlboro Lights and a translucent green lighter.

"You smoke?"

Black had removed his jacket and shirt, and was using his shirt to hold the metal can as he doused gasoline over the body.

"Keep them there for clients."

Hannah felt herself freeze, found her mind searching for realism in a decidedly surreal moment. Black was naked from the waist up, the muscles rippling from the side of his ribcage as he shook the last drops of gas on Grizzly's remains. Black's breath swirled in the cold air around his face, his hair falling forward over brows of furrowed purpose and a swollen forehead. When he finished, he set the gas can on top of Grizzly's bloodied belly and slid back into his shirt and jacket.

"Give me the lighter," he said.

Hannah shook her head. She was part of this surreal world, and she had to own it. She could not run anymore. She couldn't try to hide. Couldn't do what she had done as a child, scurry away, hands over her face, telling herself that everything was okay, and that her mother was going to be *just fine*. Because all of this was just an extension, perhaps a natural conclusion, to what Hannah had experienced her whole life. She had tried to do something about it once and failed. Not anymore.

"No," she said. "I'm going to do it."

He looked like he wanted to protest, but ended up saying, "Well, get over here and do it. We have to go."

Hannah walked over to the body and looked down. Grizzly was no longer a man. He was a prop in a theme-park haunted house, a collection of gore you sidestepped around, wondering if the actor disguised as a prop would lunge at any second.

Black pointed to a small river of wet dirt extending a few feet from Grizzly's arm. "I left a trail of gas. Light that and then get the hell out of the way. Keep the lighter—don't leave it behind. I'm going to pull the car around." He tugged her arm lightly until she looked at him. "Okay?" he asked.

Hannah continued to stare at the body, and the thought of setting the flesh on fire brought her back to a time almost twenty years earlier. Black left her side and Hannah squatted next to the body. She no longer saw Grizzly. She saw Billy, passed out in his favorite chair, the shitty green one that smelled of mold and cigarettes. Thanksgiving night, 1995.

Hannah flicked the lighter. Once. Twice. On the third try the flame shot up from her thumb. And with no other thought, she touched the flame to the dirt, stood, and backed away. The fire rose as it snaked along the dirt, hungry, looking to feast. Seconds later it found its meal in Grizzly's body, engulfing it completely. Hannah watched long enough to feel the heat on her face and witness the flannel on Grizzly's torso fuse onto the skin beneath it. She turned when Black pulled the car alongside her.

He slid to the passenger side and Hannah climbed into the driver's seat. She shut the door and pulled the car into gear.

"You okay?" he asked.

She could smell the acrid smoke and the remains carried within it. She tried to hold her breath against it.

Then she pulled the car forward without answering Black, back the way they came, away from the valley of the trees, away from Grizzly's abandoned truck, and away from the plume of black-and-gray smoke that carried with it memories of something she should have done decades ago.

PART III

SMOOTH

CHAPTER TWENTY-EIGHT

They stopped south of the Canadian border, pulling off the interstate and winding along a two-lane strip that hugged the curves of a small river. Hannah drove where Black instructed. The blow to the head left him off balance and disoriented, and he made Hannah pull over once so he could vomit onto the dirt shoulder.

The only words exchanged between them were commands. *Take this exit here. Keep on this road. Left at the gas station.* Hannah was thankful for the silence so they didn't have to talk about the body they had set on fire. In her mind she saw Grizzly die over and over again. She saw the inside of his skull, his brain. Fragments of bone. The initial spray of blood, and then just the oozing pool, black red on cool dirt.

She didn't feel guilt. Perhaps that would come later. But she felt an unbearable weight, the oppressiveness of an event that could never be taken back, the knowledge of something that would forever be part of her, an unwashable stain.

And there were still so many questions unanswered. Black had certainly only told her a fraction of what was going on.

As she drove, Hannah stole glances of herself in the rearview mirror. Her face looked as bad as it felt. The fire in her cheek had abated only slightly as the bloody bruise spread slowly over her face like a virus.

She brought her speed down to the posted thirty-five as they passed a green metal sign welcoming them to Silverson, population just over three thousand. The sign was old, rusted on the edges, the lettering faded from time. *The population count hasn't been updated in decades*, Hannah thought. She looked around at the stillness of the town around her. *If anything, it's probably decreased.*

"Couple of miles ahead there's a motel," Black said.

"We're staying in this town?"

"For a little while."

"Don't you think we'll stick out?" she asked. "Two strangers who look like they just crawled out of a bar fight?"

"I'm not a stranger here," he said. He looked out the window. Hannah couldn't tell if he viewed the streets of tiny Silverson with comfort or gloom. "We're just south of the border. I usually bring clients here for the last few days before we cross. It's a small town and some people know me, but I'm still anonymous. Everyone here is. It's the kind of place where people looking to hide stay for just a little while and then they move on, usually up into Canada. No one here has a past. It's only the future here."

A stray-looking dog with tight, wiry fur stopped and watched Black's sedan roll by. The animal's eyes were cloudy and wide, its tongue lolled to one side, as if it was simply too much effort to contain it otherwise.

"If this is the future, then we're fucked," she said.

"It's safe here, and that's all that matters right now. Up on the right." He pointed to a small building sitting by itself a hundred yards down. "That's the motel."

Hannah saw yet another rusted and faded sign, this one announcing the entrance to the creatively named Silverson Inn. The massive sign swooshed like the Nike logo and was covered in cracked, white plastic, with light bulbs dotting its perimeter in a flashy Vegas fashion. Half the bulbs were broken, and Hannah guessed the other half hadn't lit the sign for years, the owners giving in to apathy after realizing Silverson was no Vegas, and they'd wasted way too much money on the damn sign.

The motel was single story, a stretch of identical doors and brick walls, the hue some shade of brown mixed with despair. There were maybe ten rooms showing on the front side.

"Who the hell stays here?" Hannah asked.

"We do," he said. "It's not so bad. Free breakfast, which means bagels and coffee. And if we're lucky, the sheets will be clean."

Hannah felt herself shudder, thinking back to the sleek angles and glimmering style of the Four Seasons. Still, better here with Black than at a luxury hotel with Dallin.

She pulled into the parking lot, an unnecessarily large expanse populated with weeds, cracks, and faded white stripes. She parked near a *Reception* sign and Black got out of the car.

"Wait here," he told her. A few minutes later he returned carrying two keys—actual metal keys attached to small pieces of what looked like driftwood—and told her she could keep the car parked where it was. The rooms were right next to the reception.

"You got two rooms?" she asked.

"You wanted only one?"

"I didn't say that."

He tossed her a key. "Well, we have two rooms. That doesn't mean we have to use both."

Black took his bags from the car and led them to their rooms, which were adjacent and identical in their ancient, monochromatic décor.

"What now?" she asked.

Black unzipped a large black duffel on his bed and started rooting through the contents. After a minute he pulled out a prescription bottle. "Vicodin," he said. "One each, and that should at least help with the pain." He shook the bottle, and the little pills rattling inside sounded comforting to Hannah.

"You carry Vicodin with you?"

"When we left the house this morning, I didn't plan on ever going back. I took the important stuff with me."

"Everything that's important to you is in that duffel bag?"

He nodded. "That and the backpack. Yes."

Hannah wondered what size bag she would need to contain everything important to her. A week earlier, she wouldn't think any bag would work. Now, she wondered if she even needed a bag at all. She'd take Zoo, of course. *Did Justine ever give Zoo to her neighbor?* And she would grab some photos, old ones. And—

"We need money," she said. "My money. I...I just can't leave and let Dallin have everything. I'll need money to live on."

"I know. I'm planning on that. I have some cash with me for now, and we can tap into my accounts as necessary. Any chance you know your account numbers?"

She nodded. "I know my checking and savings account. Not the investment accounts."

"How much in your checking and savings?"

"Maybe a hundred thousand."

He started rooting through the bag again. "That's a start, though I'm guessing you no longer have access to those accounts. The key will be accessing your investment accounts."

He gave up on the bag with a sigh, as if acknowledging he hadn't succeeded in cramming all his treasures into one small place, and there were things he was already regretting leaving behind.

She took the bottle of Vicodin and unwrapped a plastic cup next to the sink. The cup would be clean, but God only knew what shape the tap water would be in. She filled the cup half-way—the water seemed clear—and washed the pill down. She had never had Vicodin before, but Hannah figured the worst reaction possible would still be an upgrade to her present condition.

"You haven't asked more about Dallin," he said.

She handed him the pill bottle and the remaining water in the cup. He poured two pills into his palm, stared at them a moment, and dumped one back in. He swallowed the other.

"I'm not ready," she said.

"No, you're not. You need some rest first, and then we need to assess your injury." He reached up and drew his finger along the hair hanging in front of her swollen eye, which had returned enough to normal for her to at least see out of it. "Don't think your cheekbone is broken."

"I'm fine," she said, wanting to believe it. "You're the one with a concussion."

"The Vicodin will help. And some rest. And not thinking too much, which will be the hard part."

She took a step towards him. "When I say I'm not ready to hear about Dallin," she said, "it doesn't mean I can't handle whatever the truth is. I just don't want to know right now. Maybe I will in a few hours, maybe over drinks in some dumpy bar tonight. Maybe not until tomorrow, or the next day. But you're going to tell me everything, and I'm guessing it's not going to be good. But I'll be able to handle it, because I pretty much feel like I can handle everything now."

"Yes. You can."

Another step forward. Hannah stood in front of him, and she could smell him. The smell of Black, the smell of his body from last night. The smell of dirt from the road. The smell of sweat, of skin recently spiked with adrenaline. She traced a fingertip very lightly over the contusion on his forehead.

"I've made a decision in the last hour," she said. "Since we got back in your car. Since...since you killed him." She reached up to his shirt with one hand and flicked open the top button. "I've decided to trust you. For better or for worse, I know I can't do this alone, so I'm going to trust you. Don't make me regret that, okay?"

He looked from her fingers back to her face. "I won't."

Hannah reached down and unbuttoned the rest of his shirt, then slid it off his body.

CHAPTER TWENTY-NINE

Cigarette smoke ghosted the stale air of the bar, creating a thin, ethereal mist that hung below the can lights spotting the ceiling. Half the bulbs had burned out and the darkness suited Hannah. The bar was named Yorick's. In case there was any confusion as to the reference, a bleached skull rested on the top of the bar, a half-consumed cigarette clamped between its yellowed front teeth.

"Thought you couldn't smoke in bars anymore," Hannah said. Black led her to a booth in the back, one beneath a broken light, and Hannah couldn't tell if the seat's cracked vinyl was red or brown.

"No one in Silverson cares about laws like that," Black said. "And anyone who does care doesn't come to Silverson."

He slid into one side of the booth and she sat opposite him. Her hand touched something sticky on the laminate tabletop, and she wiped her palm on her pants.

Hannah looked around, and it took her only a moment to count the five other patrons, all of whom sat at the bar, perched like seals at a zoo, leaning from the edge of the water toward the trainer dangling fish before their snouts. They were all men, and they were all silent. The skinny bartender rested his tattooed forearms on the bar top, his thumbs playing a silent symphony on his iPhone.

A Neil Diamond song floated from tinny speakers in the corners of the room.

Hitchin' on a twilight train
Ain't nothing here that I care to take along

"Well, hey there, Black."

Hannah looked up at the waitress who seemed to appear from nowhere. What she actually saw was mostly her silhouette, since she was backlit by one of the few bright bulbs in the whole place. Her hair spilled over broad shoulders, which in turn narrowed to the kind of waist wasted on twenty-year-olds. Tight jeans hugged bowling-pin thighs. Her arm held up a tray, and from it the waitress took two waters and set them in front of Hannah and Black. The woman's perfume wafted into Hannah's nostrils, the scent attacking like some kind of warning shot, a cannonball lobbed across the bow.

"Been a while," the waitress said.

The woman took a half-step closer and that was enough for the light to fall on her face. The face was familiar in a vague way for a few seconds, and then complete recognition slammed into Hannah.

"Holy shit," Hannah said.

The woman turned her attention directly to Hannah, and Hannah felt she was looking at the screen of Dallin's laptop again. That was where she had last seen this woman.

"Oh, hell," Black said. "I...I didn't even think about it. Look, Hannah, I'm sorry. But I guess it was something I was going to tell you anyway."

Rebecca, the web slut who had promised Dallin both discretion and a good time.

"What is it, sweetie?" the woman asked.

"You're the whore from the computer," Hannah said.

"*Excuse* me?"

Black held up a hand and tried to say something, but the waitress cut him off.

"Wait," she said. "Is *she* the reason I made that video?"

Black opened his mouth, seemed to think better of it, then simply nodded.

The waitress turned back to Hannah. "Look, honey, I'm sorry. But they paid me a lot of money for ten minutes in front of the camera, and you can guess the tips in this dump don't quite pay my rent."

Black looked resigned. "This is Jill," he said to Hannah. He didn't introduce Hannah, nor did Jill seem to expect an introduction.

Jill offered Hannah a pointed smack of her gum in lieu of a handshake. "Pleasure," she said.

"Not so much," Hannah said.

Jill shrugged and offered the slightest smile, as if she was beginning to like the idea she'd been part of Dallin's master plan.

Hannah turned to Black. "Does she know Dallin?"

"Look, I'm the one who hired her, okay? She's never met Dallin. The whole video was my idea."

"*Your* idea?"

He leaned across the table and whispered to her. "You made a decision to trust me. I'll tell you everything in time. Let's just get a drink first, okay?"

He leaned back.

Jill's gaze pivoted from Hannah to Black. "What happened to you two? Lover's spat?"

"Car accident," Black said.

Jill put a hand on her hip and scanned the two of them like a general surveying a battlefield before an attack. "Never see you with the same person, Black. You come here, few days at a time, always with a different person, then you disappear again. Why you even come to this place I'll never understand."

"I come here because this is a place where people don't ask questions."

"I know," she said. "It's what makes it so goddamn boring. Okay, I get it. What are you drinking?"

"Bourbon," he said. "Neat."

Hannah said, "Jack and Coke."

Jill turned and walked away, the sway in her hips set to full volume.

"Some fling of yours?" Hannah asked. "And part-time actress for hire?"

"Like I said, I like it here because no one asks questions."

"How much did you pay her to rip my heart out?"

"Three hundred bucks."

"*Three hundred bucks?*"

Black changed the subject. "You still woozy from the Vicodin?"

Hannah stared at him for a while, wanting to let her anger take over. Black had hired that bitch to pretend to be fucking her husband. The moment *Rebecca's* face appeared on that computer screen had been a cold knife in Hannah's stomach, and it was all just part of some plan where actors were paid to spiral Hannah's existence out of control.

But now wasn't the time to hate. She would listen to what Black had to say, and she would focus her anger on the one person responsible for everything: Dallin.

"A little," she finally answered. "The nap helped."

"How's your face?"

"Hurts. But I'll live. How's your head?"

"More of a dull ache. No more nausea, though, so that's progress."

Hannah put her elbows on the table and clasped her hands, squeezing them together then letting go. Squeezing, then letting go. An image of Black flashed in her mind as she stared at him, an image of him on top of her, the sweat on his forehead, the definition of his shoulders, the veins in his neck. Their time together in the motel room was an escape, just like the nap that had followed. But that was only a temporary reprieve from the reality she now had to confront again.

"So are you going to tell me the story? The real story?"

"Earlier you said you weren't ready," Black said. "Are you now?"

"It would be easier if my drink were here."

Black scanned the bar, and moments later Jill swept around it and walked toward them with their drinks. She set them down and asked them if they wanted food, which Hannah did, but not as much as she wanted Jill to walk away, so she shook her head.

Jill left, and Hannah lifted her drink to her lips and sipped. The pour was generous.

"Is she really dead?" Hannah asked. "My psychologist. Madeline."

"I'm sorry, Hannah."

Hannah looked over and stared at the dirty wall next to the booth. "I saw her for over five years. Jesus." It was strange, she thought. Madeline was a friend. She knew every last detail of Hannah's life. Yet Hannah didn't feel like crying over her death. Would that come later, or not at all? Right now it just seemed like another fact to absorb. A piece of information to file away in someplace she could access later.

"Why?" she asked.

"I can think of a few reasons," Black responded. "Mainly that she was a liability. But I think also as a warning to me. To let me know the plan had definitely changed, and I'd better be on board."

"Tell me everything," she said.

Black swirled the bourbon in his glass. "I have a feeling I don't know *everything*. But I know what I know. Where do you want me to start?"

"From the moment Dallin first contacted you. I want to know what he said to you, how much he's paying you...and how the hell he even found you."

Black made half his drink disappear in one swallow. "Dallin wasn't the one who contacted me initially."

Hannah remembered Black talking about his *clients*. Plural. That Dallin wasn't alone in the plan.

"Who contacted you?"

"Someone I knew in prison. We called him Smooth."

"Smooth? I don't know anyone called that. Why would he hire you to do this to me?"

Black set his glass down. "You do know him. You just know him by another name."

And then Hannah knew. How had she not seen it before? Even the prison nickname made sense. Smooth. Just like his face. A smooth surface concealing the storm just beneath.

"Billy."

CHAPTER THIRTY

"We didn't share a cell, but we both worked in the laundry together. For two years, day in, day out." Black kept his gaze on the table. "Nothing to do but talk while you were working. I was happy remaining quiet, because in prison staying quiet was usually the smartest thing to do. Most guys get into trouble first with their mouths, and I learned quickly to shut up and fly under the radar. But Smooth liked to talk. Loved to talk about things he was going to do when he got out."

"You were in prison with Billy?"

"Like I said, two years. He'd already been there for a while, and kept causing problems, so they kept increasing his sentence."

"But you escaped," Hannah said.

"Actually, we both did. He got caught. I didn't."

"How did you break out?"

Black shook his head. "It wasn't as hard as you'd think," he said after a long silence. "Hard part is staying out." He circled the rim of his drink with his forefinger, as if he could coax the glass to sing. "We were out about a month," he said. "To be honest, I never thought we would make it that long. But we were careful, and after a month I started to believe we could really do it. Live off the grid. Be invisible. But when you don't have someone like me to help you, you have to rely on friends or scrupulous strangers. That's when you become vulnerable. We were sharing a dingy apartment when the cops found us. I narrowly escaped. Your dad didn't."

"Billy," she said.

"That's right."

"I mean I never refer to him as my dad. Just Billy. Or Smooth. That name fits him, in a way."

"Well, after he was caught, Smooth became my greatest vulnerability. He knew everything about the persona I took on after getting out. And, while I changed it again, there was just too much he could tell the police about me." Black shrugged. "He knew all the details. Bank accounts we'd set up. E-mail addresses and online identities we were using. Names of people who we'd paid to help us. That kind of thing."

"Couldn't you just change all that?"

"I did, but there was still a hell of a trace. I knew they would be leaning on him hard about me. Adding extra time to his sentence for escaping, then offering to reduce it for some nuggets of information about me. Hard not to be tempted by that. So I figured he was talking his head off, and I was in a panic trying to scrub my trail and build a new identity." Black looked up at her and Hannah saw the welt on his forehead outlined in the dim light of the bar. "But the thing of it is," he continued, "Smooth never talked. Never said a word about me. We weren't even great friends, and though we escaped together, I never felt comfortable trusting him. In fact, I was weak and probably trusted him too much. But he never said a word."

That almost sounded noble. But Hannah knew Billy was anything but that.

"How did you know?"

"Peter," he said. "The guy who works for me."

"Yeah, you mentioned him," she said. "The asshole who drugged me and stuffed me into a trunk."

Black sighed. "He's the one. Well, Peter was with us in prison. We were close, probably the only real friend I had in there. He was doing a stint for securities fraud. Guy is smart as hell, by the way. Anyway, I told him about our plan to escape, but he didn't want any part of it. Didn't have much time left on his sentence, so it wasn't worth the risk to him. When he finally got out, I tracked him down to see if he wanted some contract work. My client list was growing, and I needed someone who was good with overseas bank accounts, electronic transfers, that kind of thing. It was Peter who told me Smooth had been quiet the whole time. Hadn't said a word about me."

Then it made sense to Hannah. "He was saving up for something. He needed you."

Black nodded. "As it turns out."

"When did he contact you?"

"When he got out. Few years ago."

Hannah thought about her father being out of prison. Just... loose. She had assumed he was out by now, but now she finally had confirmation. She pictured him as a feral dog, roaming the land, looking for scraps. Fighting. Surviving.

"He wanted to get back in business with me," Black continued. "It was never my plan to partner up with him. We escaped together, and we had a plan to stay on the run together for a little while. But I didn't want it to be that way for too long. The business was my idea, and I know I talked to Smooth about it before he was recaptured. But I never wanted him as a part of it. Smooth was bad news. I knew he'd be a repeat offender. He'd had his sentence extended many times for fights. Smuggling things in. Being bad is just in his blood, and it didn't take an ex-cop to see that."

Hannah felt herself nodding. Remembering.

"Your dad—sorry, *Smooth*—found me through Peter. I didn't want anything to do with him, but..."

"But you didn't want to piss him off," Hannah said.

"No, I didn't. I was pissed off at Peter for bringing him to me, but what was done was done. Fact was, Smooth was back in my life, and if I told him to fuck off, I'd have to go and change my identity all over again, which is a major operation. I trust Peter. Smooth, not so much. But I was stupid. I should have just bolted the second he came back into my life."

"But you didn't."

"I didn't. I got lazy. I didn't think I was, but I was. You let your guard down for an instant, and the people looking for you will find you. Trust me."

"So Billy works for you?"

"*Worked.* He did a few jobs. Some minor contract work that I overpaid him for. Setting up safe houses for clients. Helping with IDs. That kind of thing."

The jukebox shifted to Guns N' Roses. *Sweet Child o' Mine.*

"I have to say," Black said. "He was good at it. Had a knack for helping people disappear. I mean, he only did some of the smaller things, but he was good. I just didn't trust him. Just knew one day he'd be a problem. Guy is so wound up. Just always waiting to explode. No sense of the world around him, you know?"

"Yes," Hannah replied. "I know. It was like...like he was surrounded by ghosts all the time. Tormenting him. All he could do was lash out blindly, and his fists always found something to connect with."

Black swallowed the rest of his drink and set the glass down. "Did he hit you?"

Hannah was so shocked she nearly laughed. "You don't know?"

"No."

"You were with him two years in prison, together for a month when you escaped, and then you worked together. He never mentioned me?"

Black shook his head. "Never. Yapping all day long and never said one word about you. He talked about his wife and one daughter. Justine."

One daughter.

That pissed Hannah off, as if somehow the idea of Billy disowning Hannah should matter. But it did. It mattered like the way in a dream where your lover cheated on you, *in front of you,* and wondered why you were so upset. He was *not* allowed to disregard her existence. She could be hated, but she would not be ignored. After all, Billy went to prison because of what he did to Hannah. Not Justine.

She took a long sip of her drink that she wished she could freeze in time.

She asked, "Did he tell you why he was sent to prison in the first place?"

"He only just said he was innocent. That's the battle cry of the guilty, of course. But no. He never told me the initial charge. I assumed it was a domestic."

Hannah gulped the rest of her drink and slammed the glass against the lacquered wood of the table. The noise was loud enough to stop the mumbled conversation of the bar's remaining soldiers. The ensuing silence let them all hear Hannah's declaration.

"I tried to set him on fire," she said.

Black held up his hand. "Keep it down," he told her.

Hannah turned and saw Jill standing by the bar, frozen in place like a mannequin, looking at both of them. Hannah raised her glass and shook it between her fingers. *Bring me another, bitch.*

Hannah no longer cared who heard her, but she lowered her voice anyway. Now was not the time to make things difficult.

"One Thanksgiving night he beat my mom for the millionth time, and I couldn't sit and watch any more. He fell asleep in his favorite chair, and I poured gasoline on his feet. I had the lighter in my hand." She looked up at Black, whose face remained unmoved but his eyes had grown just the slightest bit wider. "I was going to set him on fire," she continued. "The whole house. I would have done it, and I would have watched him burn to death. Then I would have run away with my mom and sister and we never would have looked back."

Black's expression was one of sudden clarity, as if he just understood why it was important to her that she be the one to light Grizzly on fire.

"But you didn't do it," Black said. "Smooth didn't have any burns on him, least none I ever saw."

"He woke up. Woke up and smiled at me. Told me, 'Better

finish what you started, Hannie. You light me up, or I'm gonna come and kill you.'"

"Jesus."

Hannah was silent as Jill approached and set another drink in front of her. And she was silent as she walked away, suddenly not wanting to jump right back into a story she had rarely talked about with anyone. But since there was little left to tell, she took a gulp of her drink—more Jack and less Coke this time, as if the bartender just *knew*—and finished.

"I tried to do it," she said. "I brought the flame to the gas, but he was too fast. He stomped on my hand, and the flame went out. And that was it for me."

This time Black was silent as she paused.

"It was the first time he had laid his hands on me. It had only ever been my mother, though with her he'd always used an open hand. Not with me. I got his fists. I was fifteen. My mother finally called the police, something she never did when she'd been the victim. When they arrived, I was on the floor near his feet, unconscious. He was sitting back in his favorite chair. Smoking a cigarette, so I'm told. Watching TV." Another swallow, and then she began to feel the dulling of her brain, the glorious dampening of her senses that a second drink offered when it was made strong enough. "*That's* why Billy went to jail. Because he liked to beat up women and girls."

Black stared at her awhile longer, then dropped his gaze when she kept staring back.

"How bad?" he asked.

"Bad enough."

"You healed well."

"I was lucky." But there was nothing truly lucky about five stitches above her eye, or multiple contusions to the chest, shoulders, and left cheek. She hadn't been killed, and hadn't had any permanent damage. So, yeah, if that was lucky, so be it.

"No wonder he never said anything," Black said. "He did have a temper. Got into a lot of fights. He was usually on the losing side of them."

"He wasn't used to people hitting back." Seconds later she swallowed the contents of her glass, the second drink disappearing so much faster than her first.

Black pointed at her empty glass.

"Want another?" he asked.

"I'm getting drunk tonight, so, yes."

He nodded in somber acceptance of this, not seeming to endorse her idea, nor dissuading her from it. Black held up two fingers for Jill.

"Where did you go after that? Did you stay in the house?"

"That's the best part of the story," Hannah said. She tilted her glass and one last syrupy drop slid along her tongue, teasing her. "My mother became a wreck without Billy. She was so fucking dependent on him—and his beatings—that she didn't know how to survive without him. Much less take care of two girls. She claimed disability, though her only real disability was coping with life. For three years after Billy went to prison Justine and I took care of everything, taking the government checks and adding it to the income from the minimum-wage jobs I rotated through each afternoon after school. We barely scraped by, and there was no other family member willing to help us out. By the time my mom killed herself three years later, it was almost a relief. Drank herself to death." Hannah looked at the empty glass on the table and offered a short, bitter laugh at it.

"There was a little insurance money, and that's when Justine and I moved out to Seattle. She was still a minor, but the courts gave me guardianship of my sister. I feel like I saved her, but sometimes I think Justine blames me for everything. As if that fucked-up life we had in Kansas gave her some kind of comfort. Structure."

"Did he ever hit your sister?"

"No, never. He treated her the best of all of us. Though that means he just basically ignored her."

He saved the verbal abuse for me and the physical abuse for Mom, Hannah thought. *Justine always just watched. Watched and then hid. Billy never even seemed to notice her, yet she's the one he mentioned in prison. His one daughter Justine. I suppose his other daughter was dead to him at that point. Well, fine by me.*

"So you fired him?" Hannah asked. "You said he didn't work for you anymore."

Black patted the welt on his forehead as if checking it was still there.

"We were about to part company," he said. "He kept asking for more and more responsibility, more pay. I just didn't trust him. I knew I made a mistake in hiring him, despite his work. Peter and I were planning on moving on, taking what money we'd saved up and going somewhere else, establishing new identities, rebuilding our business."

"But something happened," Hannah said. She knew the answer before he responded.

"Yeah," he said. "*You* happened."

CHAPTER THIRTY-ONE

Black ordered food and waited until Jill walked away before he told Hannah anything else.

"It was the first I heard of you," he said. "I hadn't seen Smooth in over a month. Didn't have any new work for him, and was starting to roll up my operation, getting ready to relocate. Peter was setting up new accounts for us. Truth was, I had a nice amount of cash saved up by that point, but not enough to be without work for an extended period of time. I wanted enough to retire, disappear forever. Europe. There's a little town on a lake in Italy I've had my eye on."

"How much did you need to retire?" Hannah asked.

"A lot more than I had, and my lack of patience made me vulnerable. Smooth was a liability to me, but the money was coming in. Stupid. I should have disappeared the moment he came back in my life."

"So it was his idea," Hannah said. "He's the one who approached you about me?"

Black nodded. "Called me one day and said he had a job. A big one. I asked who the client was and he told me he was."

"Not Dallin?"

"As far as I could tell, Dallin was just the bankroll for the job. But he wasn't the brains behind it."

"So, why would Dallin do it?"

"I can't answer that for you."

"You never asked?"

Black folded his arms on top of the table. "Hannah, I'm not noble. I'm a criminal. I murdered someone, then escaped from prison. I didn't ask questions because Smooth, through your husband, offered me a fee that I couldn't turn down."

"How much?"

"A half-million up front. Another half-million once the plan worked, meaning you disappeared. I agreed once they proved to me they had that kind of money, and once I was assured you weren't going to be hurt. But they didn't want you dead." A fluorescent light above them buzzed and then finally died, dropping a shadow over half of his face. "They wanted you scared badly enough to want to disappear. Why? I don't know. They never told me. I figured it was something to do with wanting to avoid a costly divorce, and your husband was going to pay off Smooth as part of the plan. Now, based on what you told me, it seems part of the motivation was based on Smooth getting revenge."

A million bucks, Hannah thought. Dallin was willing to pay a million dollars to make me disappear. But what was the point of any of it?

"But...but why not just kill me from the outset?"

"Hard to say for sure. But murder isn't an easy thing to pull off," he said. "Especially the murder of a pretty white woman, particularly a rich one. The police would be all over it. If your marriage was bad, Dallin would be a suspect. The plan was for me to stay with you for at least six months, and then to always know where you were. That way, if Dallin or Billy were ever implicated in your murder, we could always produce you. Show you were actually alive. The plan would have failed by that point, but there wouldn't be a murder charge."

Hannah fell back against the hard, cracked vinyl of the booth. "This is so fucked up." She crossed her arms. "So everything about me being in danger was faked?"

"Yes. My job was to orchestrate everything."

"Dallin speaking in his sleep was an acting job? Him shoving me against a wall and choking me?"

"Yes."

Hannah stole a glance over to the bar where Jill leaned on the countertop and chatted with the bartender.

"Yes," Black said. "Her, too. All an act."

"And our chance meeting at the coffee shop?"

"Arranged," Black said. "I was pretty certain you would stop there before meeting with Dallin. If not, I would have 'bumped' into you in the street, just so you might remember me later."

"And the guy shooting at us at your cabin?"

"Real bullets, but purposefully bad aim. If that shooter was for real, we'd have been killed instantly."

"And the 'cop' you shot?"

"Peter's brother," Black said. "Remember when we were downtown, walking to my car, and then I went into that store? You saw me on the phone. I was communicating our position to Peter's brother, so he knew how to find us. Everything was set up. All the bullets were fake."

Hannah thought back to the cop's body doubled over in the alley. The terror she felt in that moment.

"And what was that talk of embezzlement? That I stole money from Echo?"

"Part of the plan," Black replied. "That was actually Smooth's idea and Peter's execution. They actually did siphon eight million dollars from one of Echo's cash accounts and left your electronic trace on it. If you went back to Seattle, you'd have a hard time proving you didn't steal that money. The idea was to put enough pressure on you to feel you had no choice but to disappear. I'd like to know what they actually did with that eight million."

"You thought of everything, didn't you?" she asked.

"I was highly paid to do a good job. I'm not going to lie to you, Hannah. I knew your life was being ruined, and I'm sorry to say I was okay with it. But that changed last night. When they changed the plan."

"What about you fucking me? Was that part of the plan?"

He leaned forward. "You fucked *me*, remember. And no, that wasn't part of the plan."

She leaned across the table and changed her voice from a shout to an angry hiss.

"And they never asked you to kill me?"

"Not until last night. Peter called and told me Smooth had killed Dr. Britel, that she was a liability because no one knew what you might have told her about Dallin. Then he said Smooth ordered me to kill you."

"And why would Billy think you'd agree?"

"Because there was another million dollars in it for us if I did."

Hannah felt a rush of cold air run over her arms, coolness that didn't exist in the bar, but in her blood.

"That's a lot of money," she said.

"It is."

"And yet I'm still alive."

Black scowled. "I'm not a monster, Hannah."

"So what did you tell Peter?"

"I told him to stall. Buy a little time, even if he had to pretend we were on board. But we need to run. There are two bodies now, your shrink and that redneck back in the woods. There's no wiggle room for us here. It's time for you, me, and Peter to disappear."

"Or maybe this is just another part of the plan," Hannah said. "Keep layering more and more pressure until I agree to disappear forever."

Black jerked a thumb to point behind him. "You saw that man's brains today, yes? How his skull opened up and spilled everything out? You think that was part of some plan?"

Hannah couldn't keep the image of the gore from her mind, but she let it in only a few seconds before she was able to shut it back out.

"Yes," she said. "I saw it."

"I can get you Internet access. Then you can read about Dr. Britel's murder as well."

"Maybe her murder was always part of the plan."

"No, too complicated. They would have simply killed you, like you said earlier."

"I just don't know who—"

Black held up his palm to her. "Hannah. I'm going to disappear soon, and when I do, no one will be able to find me. I'm not going to pretend I don't care about you, because I do. More than I'm going to let you know. But I need to take care of me first. Do I want you to come with me? Yes. Am I going to *force* you to come? No. You have to make your own decision, but I'm not going to put myself at more risk for you. They murdered someone, Hannah, and now we're tied up in that, whether we had something to do with it or not. This thing is out of control, and I never should have taken the job. I don't want to go back to prison. I can start over with a new identity, but it needs to happen soon. With or without you."

He leaned back, held his drink to his lips for a few moments, and then closed his eyes as he drank. That seemed to be all he had left to say, and he was right. Hannah *did* have to make her own decision. Her life was so tattered and unrecognizable that all she could rely on was her own instinct. Logic couldn't apply anymore, because logic had been twisted into lies layered on more lies.

"And Peter? Is he supposed to come with us?"

Black smiled. "No. Peter has his own plans. He's a very smart man, and he's also a bit of a loner. In prison, he talked about buying a small vineyard in Argentina. That's all he wants to do. Live alone in Mendoza and make wine. He's already bought the vineyard under the name of a dummy corporation, and he has a small staff running it. The only reason he hasn't left already is he wants to make sure we get away first."

"I have a hard time picturing him as a good guy," Hannah said. "After all, he drugged me."

Black shook his head. "He hated doing that. Truth is, he's the only man I truly trust. Trust him with my life. He actually reminds me of the partner I had when I was a cop, back when my wife was killed. Strange to think about. My best friends were my partners, the first when we were law enforcers and the second when we were law-breakers. I'm going to miss Peter."

"But you could stay," she said. "We could all stay. We don't have to run."

"Yes. We do."

"So I'm just supposed to let them win?" she asked.

"Would you rather be dead? Don't be fooled, Hannah. Things have changed. I think Smooth has gone rogue. He killed your shrink, and I'm guessing he thinks it's worth the risk to kill you as well. Maybe he planned this all along, maybe he always wanted to see you dead. But somehow he's convinced Dallin it's easier now to have you dead than hidden. Once they find out I'm not doing the job, they'll do everything they can to do it themselves."

The alcohol made it so much easier to rage and to cry, and the latter took over. "Why are they doing this to me?" she said. Hot tears spilled over her cheek. "Why would anyone do this? I haven't done anything. I...I'm a *good* wife, goddammit. Not perfect, but good. Why would Dallin *do* this? If he hated me so much, why not just divorce me?"

Black reached out and stroked her forearm. "I don't know," he said. "But I don't think it was Dallin's idea to have you killed. I think that was all Smooth."

"I just need to know the truth," she said, wiping her cheek with one hand. "Can we at least get that? Before I make any decision, can we at least find out the truth?"

His fingertips brushed lightly, back and forth, over her skin. "How do we do that?"

"I want to talk to him. To Dallin."

She expected a terse *no* from him, but it didn't come. Instead, he said, "If we could get him talking, we could get access to the money. They did something with that eight million they took from Echo. Peter set up the account for them, but we don't have access anymore. Having that cash would make things a whole lot easier for us."

"What do you propose?"

He swirled the last of his drink in his glass. "We need a little time to make preparations. We can stay here, lay low. It has to be done right."

"How much time?"

"Two, three weeks."

Hannah sighed. "In this place?"

"It's no resort," he admitted. "But it's anonymous."

Hannah wasn't even sure what the plan was exactly, but there was a plan now, wasn't there? She felt a little more in control, but that didn't stop the tears. They kept coming, tears of exhaustion, of desperation, of the pain of betrayal by her husband, and, in a small part, tears of gratitude she wasn't in this alone.

She needed to cry, so Black finished his drink as she wept, looking down at the table, giving her as much privacy as someone could in so small a space.

After a few minutes of neither of them speaking, Jill came over to check in on them. Hannah looked up at her and saw the expression on Jill's face change from reserved haughtiness to something approaching concern.

"You okay, sweetie?" Jill asked.

Hannah thought about that for a moment and decided there was no easy way to answer. So she simply said, "Men fucking suck."

Jill looked over and scowled at Black.

"Amen to that," Jill said. "Next round's on me."

CHAPTER THIRTY-TWO

Three weeks passed, and the tiny hamlet of Silverson morphed from a depressing shithole to a depressing shithole with a few Christmas wreaths hung on rusted lampposts. Twice it snowed, just enough to cover the ground and trees in a thin blanket of white, each time lasting only a few days before succumbing to the occasional bursts from the early-December sun.

Thanksgiving came and went with little fanfare. Hannah hadn't wanted to acknowledge the holiday at all. This year she and Dallin had planned on hosting dinner in their condo, inviting Justine, her nephews, and a small group of friends. For years after the Thanksgiving that she'd last seen Billy, Hannah had ignored the holiday altogether, but in her twenties she'd realized it truly was a time to be thankful; Hannah knew her life was blessed because Billy was no longer a part of it. So she began embracing Thanksgiving once again. Thanksgiving was a good time, a time to be reminded of how things were much better than they could have been.

What did Dallin do for Thanksgiving? she wondered. *Did he still get together with Justine, cursing Hannah, blaming her for embezzling money and disappearing? Would Justine believe his words at all, remembering the voice mail Hannah had left? And what did Justine do with that message? Did she share it with the police?*

Black had insisted on a Thanksgiving dinner, even if that dinner consisted of a rubbery chicken platter at Yorick's. Hannah had poked at her meal as she got stupendously drunk, so much so

Black had to carry her from the bar to the motel. Hannah vaguely remembered tickles of falling snow on the back of her neck as she was draped over Black's shoulder. He had put her to bed, and, for a change, had gone back to his own room to sleep. Hannah awoke the next morning, alone, head throbbing, stomach lurching.

So became Thanksgiving.

The last few days Hannah felt more in control, driven largely by a sudden lack of taste for alcohol. The urge was still there, the compulsion, but beer now tasted flat, and wine acidic. She took it as a sign and consumed less. Yesterday she didn't have a single drink, which was the first time in as long as she could remember. What followed was a fitful sleep, but she woke up proud.

Their new documents were complete. New accounts set up with a modest amount of cash in them. Cover stories created, memorized, every detail of a new past rehearsed for hours a day. And once he could stall Billy no longer, Peter went underground, waiting to hear from Black the time and place to eventually meet up.

Now all Hannah wanted was to hear Dallin tell her everything. And she wanted the money. If she was going to run, he didn't get to keep everything. If she was going to disappear, so was the eight million dollars from Echo.

* * *

Hannah sat on her motel-room bed, legs crossed, using Black's laptop to surf the net, as she had obsessively since he'd agreed to let her use it a few days ago. There had been reports of a shooting of a police officer in downtown Seattle, but subsequent stories claimed it wasn't real and was all part of some reality show.

The official embezzlement report stood at $8.2 million, all of which Hannah allegedly had siphoned from one of Echo's cash accounts. Details were vague, most provided at a brief press conference led by an Echo's corporate attorney. Hannah heard the recorded segment on CNBC's archives, her anger rising as he spoke.

Echo is fully cooperating with the local police and federal authorities in finding Ms. Parks and bringing her in for questioning.

Dallin granted interviews to no one.

Also sickening to Hannah were the reports related to the murder of Madeline Britel, Hannah's psychologist, shot in the chest outside her office as she was leaving work for the evening. Office tossed, computer and iPad stolen. Hannah knew she died because Hannah told her what Dallin said in his sleep.

But the most discomforting interview was Justine's. A local station had done an exposé on Hannah and the central question focused on why, if Hannah was already rich, would she steal money and disappear? They interviewed Justine, whose answer was the last Hannah expected to hear.

Hannah was wealthy, but she wasn't happy. Lately she'd been acting...I don't know...weird, I suppose. I think maybe there was some discord in her marriage. She...she has issues with men, which comes from our father. Sometimes her answer is to run away. And...God, I hate to say this, you know? Because I don't even know. But maybe there's someone else. Another man. I don't know. I just know Dallin is devastated and misses her dearly, even after what she's done. I just want her to come home.

Footsteps in the hallway, the creaking of floorboards beneath mildewed carpet. The sound of metal against a doorknob. *Her* doorknob. A violation of the *Do Not Disturb* hanging outside the door. Black had gone to Seattle two days ago to reconnoiter Dallin's movements, and she didn't know when he would be back. Hannah reached under the pillow of the bed and grabbed the gun Black had left for her.

She was almost certain it was Black on the other side of the door, but the idea of certainty no longer existed for her.

She held the gun up and pointed it at the door.

The knob twisted, and the door opened faster than she expected. She felt her finger twitch against the trigger, almost pull back involuntarily. But she held fast as her heart pounded.

Black appeared in the doorway, and Hannah sighed in relief.

"I almost shot you," she said, lowering the gun.

Black's gaze swept over the bedroom and then rested back on her face. She saw something there. Sadness? Pity? Frustration?

"No, you didn't," he said.

"You have misplaced confidence in me, then."

"No," he answered, taking the gun from her hand. "The safety is on. What are you doing?"

Hannah sighed. "Looking at things online that I'm immediately trying to forget."

Black removed a backpack that appeared fuller than it was when he'd left. He dropped it to the bed. "I saw your father," he said.

The words punched Hannah in the chest.

"He's in Seattle?"

"I saw him meet with Dallin in a parking garage. Risky move, actually. With all the press, Dallin's been pretty good about laying low. But if he was seen with your father, the press would certainly have more than a few questions."

"How...how did he look?"

His eyebrows lifted just a bit.

"Smooth or Dallin?"

Hannah didn't know why she asked the question, and she didn't have a real answer. Who *was* she talking about?

"I...I guess Smoo—Billy."

"Smooth looked like Smooth. A little older than I last saw him."

"What about Dallin?"

"Dallin looked stressed. Nervous."

"What did they say?"

"I don't know. I couldn't get that close."

"You get photos?"

"No, nothing. I couldn't stay."

The thought of her father and her husband meeting face to face seemed as unreal as anything else that had happened. The men were so different, though now perhaps not as different as she had once thought.

For the millionth time the question flashed in her mind: was the plan Dallin's or Billy's? If Dallin wanted to get rid of Hannah, why would he need Billy? Hannah had barely discussed Billy in all their years together. Perhaps Dallin needed someone from the criminal world to put the plan together, but that seemed unlikely. Dallin had a swarm of people and nearly endless funds at his disposal. A cretin like Billy would add little to the equation.

More likely, Billy sought out Dallin. Getting out of prison, Billy would need money, and Hannah could only imagine the thoughts going through Billy's head when he learned his oldest daughter was wealthy.

That little bitch? Never expected her to amount to shit. Guess her face finally healed, she grew a pair of fine tits, and fucked her way into fortune. And, seeing she got her good looks from her daddy, seems only fair she pays me a royalty fee.

Then Billy probably hatched the plan after working for Black, seeing what he did, learning the craft of making people disappear. Probably thought, *well, damn, this is a pretty cool trick. Maybe I can make Hannie disappear, and take some of that money in the process. Wouldn't that be sweet?*

It made sense to Hannah, up until the point when Billy actually approached Dallin. Dallin knew what Billy had done to Hannah, and Hannah couldn't imagine any other reaction from her husband except the one where Dallin beat the shit out of Billy.

But that hadn't happened, had it? No, the two had met, and rather than Dallin crushing her father, he chose to conspire with him. Conspired to get rid of his wife, first agreeing to an elaborate plan to make her want to disappear, then changing that plan to actually having her killed.

Why?

It was the question Hannah wanted answered most. She burned to hear Dallin's answer, to see his face as he tried to come up with any reasonable explanation he could tell her, and finding none, telling the truth, whatever that possibly was.

"So I think we can do it," Black said. He turned and sat on the edge of the bed, next to her, the long-abused mattress sagging like the back of an old plow horse.

She turned to him. "When?"

"Tomorrow. It's not a great plan, but I've had worse. And it's the only way, if this is what you want."

She looked at his face, his day-old stubble that had turned into three, the ridges around his eyes, the few stray black hairs that swooped across his forehead. But most of what she saw were his eyes, because, when they looked at her, they were piercing.

"It's what I want," she said. "I have to talk to Dallin."

"And we need his money," Black said.

"We need *my* money."

"Yes, sorry. Your money." He let out a slight sigh, one sounding like fatigue rather than concern. "I'd go fifty-fifty on our chances."

"In your line of work, are those good odds?"

Black lay flat on the bed.

"Nope."

CHAPTER THIRTY-THREE

DAY 29

When Hannah saw Dallin, she was flooded with thoughts and emotions, mostly negative ones, questioning ones, feelings of confusion, anger. But, rising up from within her swell of emotion, the same sentence kept looping in her mind, a thought that had started as a raindrop and gradually built into a river over the past three days. She couldn't control when the words would pop into her head, and the moment she finally saw her husband it came suddenly and louder than ever.

I should have had my period by now.

"Get down," Black said. "It's time."

Hannah bent forward in the back of the car Black had rented with a fake driver's license and credit card. They'd arrived in Seattle before dawn, before the sun painted the heavy rainclouds with a dull orange, and before Dallin left the apartment for work. In the days Black spent trailing him, he noticed that, while Dallin was never far from security during the day, he always drove to work alone.

"Stay down until I tell you," Black said. "I don't want him to see you. It's starting to rain. That's going to help us."

Hannah had only seen the side of Dallin's face, briefly, looking north down the street as he was preparing to turn in that direction. She saw the familiar sweep of his hair, the line of his nose which crooked just enough to give him an aristocratic air. She saw the BMW he had bought her as a gift but usually drove himself. All of this in a few seconds but it was enough to attack her senses, quicken her pulse, and fill her with both fear and surging anger. Yet the words were still there.

I should have had my period by now.

Not that she was so regular with her period you could wind your watch to her cycle. Even as a teen she could be off by a few days, and the more she worked out, the more irregular she became. But in the last couple of months, ever since Dallin finally agreed it was time to start a family, Hannah had been particularly cognizant of her cycle. The last time she had sex with him—the last time they would probably ever have sex, she thought distantly—she'd been a week into her cycle.

Of course, Dallin wasn't the only man she'd had sex with since then. The first few times she and Black were together he'd pulled out, and then in the motel they had used condoms. Well, most of the time.

"We've just a short window here," Black said as he drove. "It takes him about twenty minutes to get to work, but once he's on the highway there's nothing we can do. So it needs to be within the next few blocks."

Stop focusing on your body, she told herself. *Now's not the time.*

"Okay, he's turning now. Soon."

The sound of rain pelting the car became suddenly heavy and loud, like they were driving through a swarm of locusts.

"Hold on," Black said. "Right behind him. Light coming up."

Hannah wrapped her arms around her legs, assuming a crash position.

"Get ready..."

She squeezed her legs and wondered if the seatbelt, which she still had around her, did any good in this position.

"Now."

Two seconds of silence and then a jolt as the car rolled into the back of Dallin's—*Hannah's*—BMW. The impact was light, really just a rolling bump, but Hannah felt the jolt through her whole body.

"Here we go. Keep low."

She pictured Dallin in the BMW, annoyed but resigned to the fact he had to deal with someone rear-ending him. In the rain.

She felt Black accelerate for a few seconds and then pull to the right, slow down, and then finally stop. Black said nothing else as he got out of the car, and the sound of rain filled Hannah's ears in the brief moments the car door was open.

Dallin would stay in his car, Hannah thought. He would roll down the window and make the guilty party come to him. He would want to stay dry as they exchanged insurance information. If he was lucky, he'd be back on his way to work in five minutes.

Cars blared their horns as they passed by.

Hannah used every ounce of her will not to sit up and look. Right about now Black would be leaning into Dallin's car, removing the keys from the ignition, and subtly brandishing his gun.

You're coming with me, or you're going to die here on the street.

Would Dallin resist?

Seconds stretched into a least a minute, a minute that felt like an hour. Still bent forward, Hannah's rapid breaths warmed the skin on her legs. The police could show up at any time. Another motorist could see Black's gun—which Black wouldn't actually take out unless he had to—and decide to interfere. Their car could get rear-ended by someone not paying attention, a possibility compounded by the driving rain. A million different ways for it all to go wrong and only one way for it to go right.

Finally a car door opened. Passenger side. Hannah tensed but remained low. She heard weight settle into the passenger seat, directly in front of her.

Then she smelled him. He smelled like Dallin, the Dallin who used the same soap every day, the same shampoo, the same Ralph Lauren *eau de toilette*. In the midst of his plan to have his wife killed, in the midst of keeping up an appearance of concern for her, Dallin had still sprayed the two or three little bursts of that fucking cologne on his neck every morning, as if everything was the same as it was last month.

Hannah had once loved his smell, but now his scent seemed like rot to her. Decaying flesh sloughing off bones.

A moment later the driver's-side door opened.

The seat pushed back as Black settled into the car.

Hannah grabbed the gun that had been resting on the floor of the car. Back near the motel, in the woods, Black had shown her how to use it. The handle, cool at first, quickly warmed from the heat of her hand.

The car lurched to the left and a blaring horn shot through her brain. She heard the tires squeal on the wet pavement as Black accelerated down the street.

"What about my car?"

Dallin. It was the first time she heard his voice since the Four Seasons, since he told Hannah how sorry he was and told Peter she had mace in her purse.

"You don't need your car," Black said.

"Where is she?" Dallin asked. His voice was shaky, even desperate sounding.

Where Hannah was—directly behind him, crouched on the floor inches away but perfectly hidden behind the passenger seat.

Black remained silent for a moment. Hannah tensed even more as she felt the car turn right and then accelerate. On-ramp to the highway, she guessed.

"Just stay quiet and stay still," Black answered. "If you can't do that, it's going to be a problem."

But Dallin couldn't remain silent.

"Did...did you do it? You just disappeared on us. Is she gone?"

She could almost hear Black smile.

"Now what do you think?" Black asked. "That was a lot of money you offered me to kill her. Think I'd turn that down?"

Before Dallin answered, Hannah sat up and leveled the gun at her husband's face, who had just turned at the movement.

If she could replace the honeymoon photo Dallin broke when he slammed Hannah against the wall, she would replace it with a picture of his face in this exact moment.

Hannah smiled. "Hi, honey."

CHAPTER THIRTY-FOUR

How easy it would be to pull the trigger. Just a few pounds of pressure. His face was less than six inches from the nose of the gun. If she fired, the nine-millimeter bullet would smash into the bridge of his nose, rendering it to pulp on its journey through skull and brain. Instant death. Blood and brain matter all over the front seat, the windshield, the dashboard.

Hannah didn't fantasize about seeing that happen, yet neither did the thought upset her. A month ago she wanted a baby with this man. Now the thought of his head spread across a car interior made her sad only in a detached way, like reading an article about an atrocity in a country two oceans away.

"Hannah," he gasped. "Oh, thank God you're okay." Dallin's eyes remained wide as he looked at her, smiling, the kind of smile she normally would have believed meant he was truly happy to see her. But she had learned the depth of his acting ability.

He reached out to touch her but she yanked her head back.

"What happened to you?" he asked. "Your face. It's all bruised. Hannah, what happened?"

She didn't answer, the silence felt wonderful. Hannah looked forward and saw Black flash his gaze at her in the rearview mirror. His eyes shone in the yellow morning light. He gave her a look of assurance, a look of his belief in her. They had a plan, and they would stick with it.

"Baby, they *made* me do it. I didn't have a choice." Dallin twisted in his seat to face fully.

"Keep your eyes forward," Black said.

"I'm just—"

"You're just doing exactly everything I tell you to do. Face forward and shut the fuck up. She's not going to say a word to you, not now, at least. Her job is to keep the gun trained on your head while I drive, and if you think she's going to have a problem pulling the trigger, you're an idiot. I've seen her shoot a man before. Killing you would just be gravy."

"Shoot a man before?" Dallin snapped his head back to her. "What's he talking about?"

"Eyes forward!"

Dallin did as he was told. Hannah kept the gun level and stared at the back of the head she knew better than anyone's.

"They made me do it," Dallin repeated.

"No more talking now," Black said. "But you're in luck. The reason we are here is because Hannah wants answers. I told her it would be safer to just disappear, but she wants to hear the real story, plus I think she has a few things to say to you as well." Black moved the car to the right lane on the highway. Their exit was coming up soon. They weren't taking Dallin far from home, but no one would find him. "And you're also going to get us some money," Black continued. "You answer some questions and get us some money, and then we disappear." He turned to Dallin. "You don't do those things, and then *you* disappear. You understand? You can answer now."

Dallin remained silent and immobile.

"Hannah, I don't think he understands."

Hannah pushed the tip of the gun up against her husband's left earlobe. It was the place he would close his eyes and offer a pleasured shiver at the flick of her tongue. With the cold metal of a weapon touching it, his body recoiled.

"I understand," Dallin said.

"Good, now just stay calm, sit back, try to relax. Just a few more minutes. Again, I don't want any more talking, no unnecessary movements. Got it?"

Dallin nodded. Hannah pulled the gun back but kept it

aimed at him. She remembered holding the gun on Grizzly, how it seemed to increase in weight every second she held it. Now she felt more confident with it in her hand, more assured.

A familiar ringing. Black looked over at Dallin.

"My phone," Dallin said.

"Let it go," Black said.

It rang four more times, the ringtone the same one he always used, so familiar to Hannah, at times an annoyance, usually someone from work, an update, an emergency, guidance needed. Dallin always answered his phone, and Hannah could see the muscles in his neck tighten at his inability to answer it now. *Especially* now.

Seconds later another chime, the announcement of a voice mail.

"Hand me the phone," Hannah told her husband.

Black turned as he exited the highway. "Why?"

"We should check the voice mail. If they're already looking for him, it would be good to know."

Black thought about this for a moment and then gave a nod. Dallin didn't move.

Hannah pushed the gun up under his ear again. "Darling? Please give me your phone. I'm not going to ask again."

Dallin slid his hand inside his jacket pocket, and Black eyed him as he slowly pulled out his phone. Black reached over with his right hand and patted Dallin's chest and hips.

"You think I have a gun?" Dallin asked.

"No," Black said. "I don't think you would know what to do with a gun. Then again, I would have said the same thing about her, but now she can put a bullet through a Coke can from fifty yards."

It wasn't true, Hannah knew, but it sure sounded good. She was confident she could at least put a bullet through a head at fifteen inches.

Dallin reached back with his hand and handed Hannah the phone. Their fingers touched briefly during the exchange, and his index finger extended, stroking her finger slightly, as if he could communicate some kind of passion and love in the split second chance he had. To Hannah it felt as comforting as a meaty spider crawling up her finger.

"He made me do it," he repeated. "I was protecting you. I did it for you."

"*Quiet*," Black said.

She yanked her hand back then navigated the screen of his phone to his call log. She was surprised when she saw the name attached to the recent call.

Justine.

Why was Justine calling him?

Hannah touched the voice mail icon and launched the app. It showed all of Dallin's voice mails visually, grouped like e-mails. She sucked in her breath at the list. *Justine, Justine, work, work, unknown, work, Justine, Justine.*

Hannah repositioned the gun and stared at the back of Dallin's head as she selected the most recent voice mail.

Her hand began to shake as Justine's voice filled her head.

Hey, baby, it's me. Just checking in, seeing if you've heard anything yet.

The words weren't real. Couldn't be. It was another part of the plan, an elaborate hoax, all perfectly timed and orchestrated to elicit a reaction from her, a reaction that somehow, *somehow*, played into their needs. Hannah almost couldn't bear to keep listening to the last few seconds of the message. But she did.

I just want this to be over, you know? I need to be with you. I miss you. Connor misses you. He needs you, too. A boy needs his daddy...

CHAPTER THIRTY-FIVE

She looked up and saw Black staring at her in the mirror. Deep, quizzical eyes, concern blended with confusion. *What?* he mouthed.

Hannah shook her head. "It's not true," she said.

"What's not true?"

Dallin began turning his head to her, and Hannah saw something fly at him from the left. It caught her so much by surprise she didn't register until a moment later it was Black's hand, palm open, striking the side of Dallin's face. Flesh cracked like lightning.

"*Keep your eyes forward,*" Black said. "You have a bad habit of thinking rules don't apply to you."

Dallin reached up and rubbed the cheek Black had struck. Slowly, Dallin turned his head back around, and once again he stared through the windshield, silently, his body rigid.

"What is it?" Black asked Hannah.

She dropped the phone over Dallin's shoulder and onto his lap. She didn't want it. Didn't want to dissect the meaning of it all. She didn't want to be a part of the joke anymore.

Dallin picked up the phone and replayed the message. Hannah watched his face fall.

"It's not true," Hannah repeated.

This time, Dallin didn't need a reminder to stay silent. Hannah didn't know if he was scared of Black or scared to give Hannah an answer. Maybe both.

Before Black said anything else, he reached over and took the phone from Dallin, then pried the backing off with one hand. He turned the phone over and rapped it against the steering wheel until the battery fell onto the floor of the car. "There's no more using this phone," he said. "We don't want anyone tracing his signal. Now, Hannah, tell me what the hell's going on."

Hannah leveled the gun at her husband.

"It was a message...from my sister."

"Justine?"

"She...called him *baby*. She also told him that Connor—her youngest—that Connor needs his daddy. It's bullshit." The gun shook in her hand. "It's all just more lies."

Dallin's head now faced downward and shook slightly from side to side. He brought up his hand and squeezed his forehead.

"Is it true?" Black asked him.

"Of course it's not true," Hannah said. "Everything is a lie. Another calculated lie. Perfectly timed." Despite her denials, Hannah felt her mind fighting against the math, not wanting to do the calculations. If she didn't think about it logically, then the story would remain merely a lie. It was a battle she couldn't win. *Connor is almost a year old. Dallin's been distant for nearly, what, two years?*

"The timing doesn't make sense," Black said. "I mean, they had no idea we'd be intercepting him today, so she couldn't have left that message knowing you would see it."

Hannah shook her head. "No, somehow they knew. Don't you see? It's all part of it."

Yeah, Hannah, and what's the point of all that? Why would Dallin pretend to have an affair with your sister, an affair that resulted in your nephew? Did Dallin start pulling away from you two years ago as part of this intricate plan? C'mon, Hannah, you're not that stupid, are you?

Dallin said nothing. Now he looked to his right, out the window, the pale sunlight washing over his ashen cheeks. Hannah trained the gun on that perfectly smooth right cheek, but he paid her no attention. He was looking out, past the streets, the houses, the storefronts peppered with sun-faded plastic signs, and far into the distance, his gaze pointed on nothing but another choice, as if by seeing a better decision he could actually go there. It was the grim look of acceptance of a path ill-chosen, with no possibility of return.

Her hand shook as she fought to steady the gun, which suddenly felt a thousand times its normal weight, just as it had before she shot Grizzly.

"We're here," Black said.

Hannah looked to her left at the motel where they had rented a room. An anonymous place for anonymous deeds.

"Let's just get inside," Black said. "Focus, Hannah." He swerved the car into a parking space outlined by jagged fault lines ripping through the asphalt.

Black got out and opened the door for Dallin, who walked slowly across the parking lot with Black close behind. Hannah looked around at the lot and saw it mostly empty, just a scattering of cars, two of which looked abandoned. She brought up the rear, no longer needing to keep her gun trained on her husband since Black was also armed and would make sure Dallin didn't make a run for it. Her own gun was in the pocket of her coat, and she kept her fingers on the grip as she walked.

Black opened the door to Room 24, a first-floor room facing the parking lot. He ushered Dallin inside and quickly followed, allowing the faded, brown door to swing closed behind both of them. She knew what Dallin would be seeing right now: a chair with two rolls of duct tape next to it. Would he panic at the sight of those things? Or would Dallin do as asked, sit there and let Black snake the tape around his torso and limbs, binding him tightly to the chair?

Part of Hannah wanted Dallin to resist, wanted him to refuse to cooperate, just so she had an excuse.

You don't need any more of an excuse, she told herself. *The last two years apparently contained enough excuse to execute him a hundred times over.*

The heels of her boots clicked on the asphalt, steady beats in rhythm with a confident step. This was no longer the woman scared of her husband, worried about what he was thinking or how he might react to her. Worried that he would smell the alcohol on her breath. That woman was gone. What remained was Billy's blood, which coursed through her veins, filling Hannah's every nerve with anger, rational or not, and a sweet desire to destroy, even though she knew that destruction would not ultimately satisfy. Yet she couldn't feel any other way.

Hannah took a deep breath as she approached the door to Room 24. She took one last sweep of the building with her gaze, finding something different this time. A dash of pink in a window above. Hannah slowed her approach and focused on the figure in the window of Room 37, up and to the right of Room 24. A little girl—no more than five, Hannah guessed—looked down on Hannah with empty eyes and long kinked hair that fell over half her face. She clutched a naked doll to her chest, suffocating it against her own body, perhaps as an act of compassion.

Hannah finally stopped walking and just kept staring at the girl. She wondered what her story was. Were her parents in the room? Was the family passing through town, maybe looking for better work somewhere? Or was the little girl alone with her mom, hiding from an abusive husband and father, one who would do bad things if he found them. *Shut that curtain*, the mother would say. *Can't afford to be seen.*

Hannah offered a wave using the hand not gripping the gun.

The little girl just stared back and wrapped her arms tighter around the doll. Then she took a step back and the curtain closed, and the girl's room once again became the same as all the others surrounding it, just a place to keep the stories locked inside.

CHAPTER THIRTY-SIX

Dull sunlight struggled to fight its way through the thick, ancient curtains of the motel room, and the small amount achieving its goal barely illuminated the shape of Hannah's husband, strapped to the chair from chest to waist with silver duct tape, motionless except for the anxious gaze flicking back and forth between Hannah and Black. Black turned on the single lamp in the room, its shade stained from some unknown brownish liquid, perhaps coffee. The smell of mildew hit Hannah, and the overall feeling of suffocation within the tiny room made her long for the decrepit Silverson Inn.

Black sat on the edge of the single bed and placed the gun next to him. He lowered his head into his hands and rested there, his hair spilling through his fingers.

"Lock the door," he said.

Hannah turned and twisted the lock.

Black waited a few moments longer and then lifted up his head. He looked first at Dallin, who returned the stare for a second before finding the floor.

"She has questions for you," Black said. "I can't imagine it's going to be an easy conversation, but I strongly encourage you to tell the truth."

"You won't shoot me in here," Dallin said.

"You think anyone in this shit motel isn't used to hearing the random gunshot? You think anyone here is going to say a word? I assure you no one cares. No one wants to get involved."

"You won't shoot me," Dallin repeated, though the conviction left his voice. Dallin tried to squirm in his chair, but the tape held him fast.

Black continued. "Before she asks you whatever she wants to ask you, we need something. That eight million taken from Echo? You're going to give it to us."

Dallin turned to Hannah. She saw the contorted face of desperation he so rarely displayed, but had on occasion revealed to her. Forehead rippled by worry lines, eyes drawn into tight circles, focus drilling on her. Pleading.

"He'll kill you," Dallin said to her.

Hannah didn't know which *he* Dallin was referring to. Billy? Black? The idea she was at a point in her life where death threats against her needed greater specificity nearly made her laugh. Nearly.

"No, you're talking to me now," Black said. "You're going to tell us how, *exactly* how, we access that money. It's planned for Billy, isn't it? Have you given it to him yet?"

Dallin wouldn't look at him. He kept staring at Hannah with desperate, defeated eyes, rendered gray by the contrast of the dull-red slap mark on his cheek.

"It wasn't supposed to end up like this," he said. "Hannah, I'm telling you, you were supposed to be fine."

"Fine?" she said. "How do you define *fine?*"

"Dallin," Black said, "I'm losing my patience."

Dallin ignored him and strained against the tape. Hannah didn't think he was trying to escape. *He wants to touch me. Put his hands on my arms, tell me "the truth." If he could only touch me, he might be able to control me. And his lack of control is driving him mad.*

"Hannah," he said, "you have to believe me. They made me do this. They...Billy...he knew about—"

Black got up from the bed and smacked the back of Dallin's head. "Dallin! We're talking about the money. We're not talking about anything else right now."

Dallin turned, spitting as he yelled back. "You can have the fucking money! I don't care. I'll tell you how to get it. Now give me a *goddamn minute* with my wife." Dallin's body shook in the chair, and his forehead had the wet, sickly glaze of someone stricken with the flu. His next words were more controlled, steadied. "Please, just let me talk to her. Alone."

Hannah looked at Black when she heard the word *alone*.

"No," said Black.

"Yes," said Hannah.

"*Hannah.*"

"It's okay," she said. "I don't need your help. I don't need protection. He's taped to the chair and I have a gun, for God's sake."

"But it's not necessary," Black said.

Hannah's gaze moved from Black to Dallin. "You've been married before. You understand the need for a husband and wife to talk, don't you?"

"Hannah..."

"It's okay, Black. If you're worried I'm going to do something stupid, you don't need to be." She kept looking at Dallin as she spoke, and the room felt suddenly a little cooler, a little larger. "I'm in control now." She took one step closer to her husband. "I'm in control."

Black moved over next to her, leaned in, and whispered in her ear. "We need that money, Hannah. It's the only way this works. It's the only way to leave for good."

Hannah nodded, understanding the words but hardly hearing them. Black stood next to her a few moments longer, as if his mere presence, his body near hers, would somehow get her to change her mind. When it didn't, he told her, "I'll be right outside."

And then he left, the breeze from the closing motel room door stirring up a new swarm of dust motes, which swirled and danced in the incandescent light.

And then it was quiet.

Hannah was alone with her husband.

She wanted to kill him.

CHAPTER THIRTY-SEVEN

I know what you see, Hannie. You see me in that chair, don't you? You see the man who wronged you, and now you want to do something about it. You can now. You can do what you couldn't do when you were just a kid. You can light that fire this time. He ain't going anywhere. You can watch him burn.

"Fuck you," she said, her words directed to both her husband and her father. "I'm not like you."

But you are and you know it. Stop trying to hide the moldy cake beneath the icing. You're no better than me. When you shot that redneck...you tell yourself he woulda done bad things to you, but you liked it, didn't you?

Hannah closed her eyes and slowed her breath. She stilled her mind, neither repelling nor inviting any further thoughts. She didn't speak, at least not at first. It wasn't that she didn't have anything to say. Rather, she had too much. Too many questions, and she had to be ready for the answers. This was perhaps the last time she would ever see Dallin, and whatever he said in this shitty, dark motel room would stay with her forever.

Hannah sat on the corner of the bed and rested her hands on her knees, the hard edges of the gun pressing from inside her coat pocket against the side of her leg. She wasn't holding it, but it would take only a second to grab it and fire. Her gaze swept over Dallin's torso and arms, which appeared securely strapped to the chair. But she wasn't stupid. Hannah knew, if he wanted, Dallin could half-stand in the chair and try to slam into her. Or into the wall, and try to break the chair apart. But he wouldn't get far. She would shoot him first.

She wouldn't hesitate. There was no question in her mind.

He seemed to understand this, for he sat motionless in his chair, a schoolboy freshly chastised. He didn't take his gaze off her, and Hannah considered how much the look of confidence had changed since she'd first met him in the lobby of the hotel all those years ago. The cocky boy who told her he'd just got funding for his company, he was moving to Seattle, and he was taking her out to dinner. The colorful light in his eyes back then was pure, full of the future in wait, coated in a perfect blend of confidence and naiveté.

Now that color was replaced by a dull haze, cataracts of bad decisions, and any hope left was not for the distant future but simply for the next few minutes.

Dallin broke the lengthy silence first. "I love you."

"Give me the account information," she said.

"*Hannah.*"

"Black is right about the money. And since I have no idea how the rest of this conversation is going to go, I had better get the money now."

"If I give you the information, you won't have any need for me," he said.

"I have no need for you at all," she said. "This is about your needs, Dallin. If you feel a need not to bleed to death on this dirty motel carpet, you'll give me the account information." She pulled the gun out of her coat pocket and placed it on the bed next to her. "Now."

His gaze shifted from the gun to her face. "It's in an account. Offshore. I haven't given...given Billy access to it yet. Everything changed when he...when he said to...you know. With the change of plan."

"You mean when he said to have me killed?" Hannah said.

Dallin slowly nodded.

"Give me the information."

"I can access it on my phone."

"We're not turning your phone on. Try again."

"It's a file. On the SD card."

"Give me the file name and password. Now."

Dallin did, no longer resisting. Hannah opened the motel-room door and relayed the details to Black, who still had Dallin's phone. She hoped Black could use the SD card in his own phone, which was cut off from any GPS tracking.

When she closed the door again, Dallin said, "Your father is not going to stop looking for you."

"I'm willing to bet I can run faster than he can," she said.

The next few minutes were spent mostly in silence. Hannah sat on the edge of the bed and stared blankly at the wall. Dallin twice attempted to talk to her, but she wouldn't answer him.

A knock at the door. Hannah got up and answered.

Black had a smile on his face.

"It's there," he said. "All of it. I contacted Peter and gave him the info, and he transferred it to our account."

Hannah nodded. She didn't even feel happy or relieved.

"Don't kill him, Hannah," he said. "You're not like that."

Hannah blinked and looked up at him. "Everyone thinks they know me," was all she said. Then she closed the door, leaving Black to the sunlight.

CHAPTER THIRTY-EIGHT

"Is it true?" she asked.

Dallin didn't answer at first, and then he mumbled, "Is what true?" But it wasn't really a question, because he knew exactly what she was talking about. He was just trying to buy time, and Hannah remained silent, letting him. She had all the time in the world.

A yell came from the neighboring room, the muffled shriek of a child's excitement, a sound of being discovered during hide-and-seek. The thin plaster motel wall separated a child's happiness and a man's life untethering.

Dallin remained silent for another minute, and, as if seeing no other way to get beyond the place they were now, he looked up and said:

"Yes."

The urge to throw up welled through Hannah, making her hands clammy and her mouth water. She pushed it down.

"You've been fucking my sister," she said. "And Connor—my nephew. He's your *son*."

"I wasn't simply..." Dallin stopped himself, likely knowing there was no explanation that would make it any better. "Yes," he said.

"How long?" she asked.

"Two years." Pause. Then he added, "A little longer."

The image of Justine's television interview flashed through her mind. Justine, all made up, just the right touch of concern on her face. Justine, suggesting Hannah perhaps found another man...

"Cunt," she said.

Dallin let out a long, slow exhale, as if he knew it would perhaps be his last.

"All those nights at work. Weekends. The whole time you were with her?"

"Not all the time," he said.

"I'm such a fucking idiot," she said. "I didn't see any of it."

"Because you became a drunk," he said simply. "And that's something I should have seen earlier. You had everything, Hannah. You had a husband who loved you. You had money. Friends. And you just kept drinking more and more."

"Don't you put this on me," she said. "Don't you fucking dare."

But he continued. "I tried getting through to you, but you always kept it in control just enough. You drank just enough to keep you short of needing rehab but past the point where you stopped giving a shit about me."

"*That's...not...true.*"

"It is true, Hannah. It's true and you know it."

"Well, I'm not drinking anymore." She didn't know why she bothered telling him this. What did she want, his respect?

"That's good, Hannah."

Hannah eyed the gun on the bed. How easy it would be to make him pay for everything. One flash. One bang. Over.

No, I came here for answers. I don't have to like them.

"So you figured Justine—a younger, sober version of me—would make you happy?"

Dallin stifled a sob. Hannah had perhaps seen her husband cry a handful of times in all their years together.

"I...I didn't mean for it to start, and I take full responsibility for everything. But now I realize...I know she planned it all along. She wanted to take me from you. She wanted the life you had. She wanted the baby you weren't having with me."

The last sentence flipped Hannah's stomach to the point she had to sit on the bed.

"And I *was* happy with her," he continued. "For a while I truly was. And then she got pregnant. I freaked out. I wanted...I wanted her to get...to terminate it. She refused."

Hannah thought back to when Justine announced she was

pregnant. She said it was her boyfriend's, who quickly left the picture after that. It was in the spring, and for several months Dallin had been busier than ever. Traveling. Nights. Weekends. It had been a particularly bad time in their relationship.

"But I loved her, Hannah. I'm not going to lie. I loved her and wanted to be with her. Connor...Connor is the greatest thing in my life, and I couldn't even be honest about him. I'd have to make up an excuse with you just to sneak over there and see him. And when we went over to Justine's place together, I'd have to sit there and pretend to be an uncle. It ripped my heart out."

Hannah's voice was barely more than a whisper. "Don't try to make me feel sorry for you."

"I'm telling you the truth, Hannah. It's what you want, isn't it? I'm not going to hide anything else. Hell, if it wasn't for Connor, I wouldn't even care if you killed me."

"He deserves a better dad than you," she said. "And a better mother."

His eyes narrowed and a bead of sweat snaked from his forehead over the bridge of his nose.

"I'm a good father," he said.

Hannah finally picked up the gun and pointed it at his head. "You're not a good anything."

Dallin closed his eyes.

"Why not divorce me?" she asked. The gun quivered in her grip and she lowered it, not wanting him to see her hand shaking it. "If you love her, why not just end our marriage?"

His eyes remained closed as he spoke. "When Justine and I first...started...I thought that's what I wanted. We talked about it from time to time, but she was always telling me we had to take it slow. We had to be smart. But when she got pregnant, she changed."

"Changed how?"

"She became possessive. She demanded more of my time. Started telling me I had to leave you. And she...she started to become very hateful of you. Saying horrible things."

"What kind of things?" Hannah whispered.

He shook his head slightly. "Things about your past. About how you were the reason your father was always so angry. She... blamed you for his going to prison."

Hannah clenched her jaw. "He went to prison because he fucking *beat* me near death."

"I know. I know. But in her mind, despite the kind of man he was with your family, he kept a weird kind of stability. With him gone, your mom spiraled downward. Justine blames you for her death. I think a part of her always hated you for that. And then... then you both move out here. You became successful. She didn't."

These were all things Hannah knew, or at least suspected. But she never realized these feelings Justine had were so strong, so much in the forefront of her mind. How could Justine not see what a disease their father was? How weak their mother had been? If Hannah had carried Justine out of a burning home, would she have blamed Hannah for letting her stuffed animals burn?

"She changed," he repeated. "She changed and I started to pull away from her. I...I began doubting that I wanted to be with her. And the more I pulled away, the more she clung."

"You're such a weak man," Hannah said. "How did I never see how weak you really are?"

He kept shaking his head and looking down. He didn't seem to be denying what she said as much as he was putting himself into some kind of trance, forcing himself through the words, taking his mind into a place where he could free himself to tell her everything she wanted to know.

"After Connor was born," he said, "I fell in love with him. Even as I grew less attracted to Justine, I became more attached to my boy. I love Connor more than anything in this world, and I can't even tell anyone I'm his father. But...but every moment with him, I feel new. Different. *Better.*"

She squeezed the gun, which she held at her side. "I wouldn't know," Hannah said. "I'm not a parent."

Yet.

"I knew I had to divorce you," he said, ignoring her comment, forcing himself through the rest of the story. "I knew, for better or worse, the truth needed to come out. I had to be Connor's dad, and I couldn't do that behind all the lies. I was going to tell you everything. I knew you were going to hate me. I knew it would be a nasty divorce. But it had to be done."

Hannah thought back to the months after Connor was born. Were those months worse than any others in the last two years? Hell, she didn't even really remember. Had her drinking been so bad she couldn't even pick up on the turmoil her husband was bringing home every day?

"But you never said a single thing," Hannah said. "So what happened?"

Dallin finally opened his eyes and looked up at her. Even in the dim light, she could see the streaks of bloodshot against the whites.

"Justine had another idea," he said.

CHAPTER THIRTY-NINE

The door opened and Black peered in, his gaze sweeping the room, finally settling on the gun in Hannah's right hand.

"Everything okay?" he asked.

"Oh, yeah," Hannah said. "We're just getting to the good part."

"You need me in here?"

No," she said. "I'm good."

Black strode up to her and leaned into her ear.

"Killing him would be a problem," he said. "I would strongly advise against it." He didn't ask for the gun. He didn't even ask that she at least put it down. He just gave the one warning and walked back outside, closing the door behind him.

Hannah turned back to Dallin.

"What was Justine's plan?" She put the tip of the gun on his forehead, not because she thought he'd hold back on her. She did it because she wanted to see what it felt like. Did it make her feel strong? In control? Not really. She no longer needed the gun to control Dallin.

Dallin squirmed in the chair, inching for more comfort, but finally letting his body sag.

"It was a few months ago. I kept telling her I was about to tell you everything. She kept telling me *not yet*. That I'd get screwed in the divorce since I was the unfaithful one. She didn't want me losing all the money to you."

She lowered the gun. "*Bitch.*"

"She told me she'd been in touch with Billy. Before she and I ever...got together. I guess he'd gotten hold of her after he got out."

Hannah barely shook her head. "I can't believe she'd talk to him."

"She has a different opinion of him than you do."

"He was almost nice to her," Hannah said. "Because she never showed any ambition. Never cared about anything. I was the one who wanted a life. He hated me for wanting more than what we had."

"She told him about your wealth. *Our* wealth. It was all her idea. She figured a way to take our money and get rid of you. She roped in Billy, whose job it was to orchestrate everything with Black."

Hannah took a step back. "Wait, so she *planned* to seduce you? That was part of it?"

He nodded. "And to get pregnant. She told me she was on the pill, which I don't think she ever was. I think the original idea was to get me in a position where I had a financial responsibility to her. If she got pregnant, at the very least I would owe support. But that's nothing compared to the money she would get if I...if I left you and married her."

"And Billy would have the satisfaction knowing he helped destroy my marriage," she added. "But that's a lot of patience and planning. Any number of things could have gone wrong."

Dallin shrugged within the few centimeters the duct tape would allow. "But they didn't," he said. "You were in your own world," he said. "She and I...we had flirted before. She was confident I wouldn't say no to her, which I didn't. And once we started... it was just a matter of time before she got pregnant. I think the one thing she didn't account for was having feelings for me. And the closer she got to me, well, I think the more she hated you."

"I saved her," Hannah said. "I saved her from our home. I gave her a new start. I never did anything but help her."

"You had things she didn't," Dallin said. "You had dreams of something bigger. That's all it took."

"When did you find out they planned all this?"

"She told me a few months ago. Like I said, just as I got closer to telling you everything. She told me about Billy. She told me everything. How she wanted to be with me, how I was too good for you."

Hannah's skin tingled with heat, anger creating sweat.

He continued. "She must have thought I would be okay with the fact she'd been conspiring with Billy for all that time. That I would just agree to whatever they wanted. I think she thought I wanted to be with her as much as she wanted to be with me. Truth is, I just want to be with Connor. But there was no way of achieving that without Justine being involved. She said they came up with another plan, one that would get rid of you without risking all the money in a nasty divorce."

"Black," she said.

Dallin nodded. "Billy knew him. Knew he could make all the arrangements. I mean...I mean their plan was *crazy*. The things they wanted me to do. To pretend to be. Jesus, Hannah, believe me that I never wanted it. Our marriage may have fallen apart, but I never wanted to do this to you. I'm a fucking idiot. I *admit* it. But I was going to at least tell you the truth. You at least deserved that."

"But she changed your mind."

"I told her I wouldn't do it. By that point I really thought she was crazy. I was worried about Connor then. I was going to go to the police."

"Oh, please."

"Hannah, it's true. That's...that's when I met Billy." A cough, another strain against the tape. "Billy came to her house one night when I was there. I couldn't believe it. Here was the man I'd heard so much about. The man you...you tried to kill."

All she had to do was flick that lighter.

"He told me, 'Son, you're going to do what we say, and I'll tell you why.' He had Connor in his lap, stroking his hair. God, it was awful. Seeing Connor in the lap of the man who... Anyway, he said if I didn't do what they said, they'd kill you. Not only that, they would make sure all suspicion would be thrown on me. Husband having an affair with his wife's sister. A baby. A potentially ugly divorce. I would have lost everything, even if they couldn't prove it. You would have lost your life. And I'd never see my son again."

Hannah didn't know what to say. She tried to understand the position Dallin had been in, but all that stood out was he mentioned he would *lose everything* before mentioning Hannah would *lose her life*.

"Dallin, you *shoved* me. You *choked* me."

Then his face changed. The muscles keeping his cheeks and forehead taut went completely slack. His face fell, pulling his eyes open wider. The look on Dallin's face was one of true dismay, the realization that everything one believed in was definitely disproven in a lightning bolt of a moment. He seemed to choke, but the choke turned in to a hacking sob, and then to tears, flowing tears, unstoppable.

She said nothing as he cried. As his body shook and the waves of despondency gutted him. When the sobbing stopped, he looked to the floor for moments longer, and then lifted his head to her.

"I would take it all back if I could," he said.

"And yet you can't."

"You're right. I can't. I went along with it. I convinced myself they had me in a corner. But I could have stopped it. I have money. Power. I could have put an early end to it." She realized he was not just confessing to her, but to himself. "But I didn't. I got caught up in it. It seemed...tidy, somehow. Black had everything perfectly planned, and I could hide in the excuse that I had no choice. I had my role, which..." His eyes searched hers, but he was no longer Dallin. He was someone Hannah didn't know, perhaps the real Dallin. "I don't know," he said. "I hated it. But once I started I was...I was *into* it. I liked the aggression. The dominance. Maybe that's who I really am."

"You're a horrible person."

He nodded and his eyes welled again. "I know."

"You had my psychologist *killed*."

The nod turned to vehement shaking. "I had nothing to do with that. That's when it all turned. Billy acted alone on that. He thought she was a risk."

"He *murdered* her," Hannah said.

"I know. I swear to God nothing like that was supposed to happen."

"I don't give a shit who you swear to."

"Hannah...he changed the plan. I didn't want you killed."

Hannah switched the gun to her left hand. Then she walked up to him, balled her right hand, and smashed her fist across his face as hard as she could. The impact felt like a hammer blow to her knuckles and his head snapped to the right. She had never hit anyone in her life, and the impact shot blood lust through her body. She immediately wanted to do it again, but held back.

The motel room returned to silence.

"*Jesus,* Hannah." He lifted his head to her and she could see the welt blossoming next to his eye.

"In the car you asked where I was, as if you expected I was dead."

"But it wasn't what I *wanted,*" he said. "I had no idea what was going on. I would never want you dead."

"Wish I could say the same for you." Hannah switched the gun back to her right hand and held it against his head. Her breathing was fast, her heart beating like a rabbit's, and the sweat rising through her pores itched her skin. Dallin pulled his head as far away as he could, which was no more than a few inches.

As much as Hannah wanted to believe she wasn't capable of something like this—shooting someone who couldn't even defend himself—she couldn't escape the overriding desire in her mind.

She wanted to do it.

The door opened and Black walked back inside the room. The temporary shaft of sunlight perfectly illuminated Hannah's arm, outstretched, the gun in her hand pressed against Dallin's left temple.

"Take it easy, Hannah," he said.

Hannah kept her gaze focused on her husband. "Told you we needed a few minutes," she said.

"I gave you a few minutes. And I told you not to do anything stupid."

"Why? Seems to me everyone else gets to do stupid things. Dallin gets to fuck my sister. Even has a baby with her. That's pretty stupid. You get to plan my demise along with everyone else. So I figure, maybe just pulling this trigger gets to be my act of stupidity."

She saw Dallin look to Black with pleading eyes.

"So it's true?" Black asked. "About Justine?"

Dallin nodded.

"And you didn't know?" Hannah asked Black.

"No," Black said. "I didn't know she was a part of it. But it makes sense."

Hannah pushed the gun deeper into Dallin's temple, hoping it hurt. "And he says this plan, this whole plan, was Justine's idea. She conspired with Billy, who was out of prison. Told him how I was a rich girl now."

"Give me the gun, Hannah."

Hannah shook her head. "No."

Black was close, and he could have probably taken the weapon away from her if he wanted, but he didn't. He just said, "Okay, but if he's dead it makes things a lot more complicated."

"Why?" she asked. "We're disappearing anyway, aren't we? Might as well do anything we want. What's a murder charge anyway if we're gone for good?"

Black's voice was steady, his words slowly paced. "Because when you kill someone, they look a lot harder for you," he said. "But that's not why you shouldn't do it."

Her head throbbed with the blood pulsing through it.

"I killed a man who couldn't defend himself," Black said. "I murdered the man who took my wife from me. And you know what? In the moment, it felt good. It felt *right*." He took a step closer to her but didn't make a move for her weapon. "I felt justified in what I did, but it wasn't long before that went away. And it was replaced by a guilt that sits like a rock on my chest. Every day it's there, and I suspect it will be until I die. No matter what he did to me, I didn't have the right to take his life."

She felt her hand shaking. Dallin squeezed his eyes shut.

Hannah said, "You're a better person than me, then."

With his eyes closed, Dallin said, "Please, Hannah. I need...I need Connor. I need to be his father."

"Hannah," Black said. "Don't do this."

Visions attacked her, fragmented and momentary flashes of the past two years, memories of days with her sister, days of drinking, the birth of Connor, of nights alone, when Dallin was working, the second cell phone, the denials, the loneliness, his hands on her throat. There were simply too many thoughts in her head, horrid, impossible thoughts, none of which offered a way out, a proper explanation, anything to salve the wounds. Everything in her head was a deception, a mistake, a lie. So many thoughts, and suddenly Hannah felt she could not process any of them.

"When you shoved me," she whispered. "When you put your hands on my throat. I saw you. I *saw* you. That wasn't an act. That was real."

"It wasn't real," he said. "They were going to kill you if I didn't stick to the script. I tried to warn you."

More images. Dallin telling her *I'm so sorry.* And at the Four Seasons, the scribble on the paper: *They're making me do this.*

"Maybe you didn't want me dead," she said. "But you didn't want me around anymore. You could have gone to the police. You could have given him the money and he would have gone away. But instead, you went to these...insane lengths to get me to disappear. You did it because you want to be with her, and this was a way out."

"They were going to kill you," he said.

"Billy is nothing!" Hannah shouted. "A fucking *nobody*. And you...with all your resources. All our money. You could have stepped on him like a bug. Both him and Justine. But you let yourself believe you were trapped, because you *wanted me gone*."

Dallin remained silent. Eyes closed. A prisoner awaiting execution.

"Dallin," she said. "Do you want to be with her? Is that what you want?"

Very slowly, Dallin shook his head. "I want to be with my son. That's all I want."

Hannah kept the gun to his head a few more seconds, and then she finally lowered her arm and exhaled.

"Black's right," she said. "I probably *would* feel guilty if I shot you, and you're not worth occupying that much space in my mind."

She heard Black's voice behind her. "Once he realizes the eight million is gone, Dallin will have him to deal with."

"I'm sure he can get more," Hannah said, nodding at her husband. "I'm sure his mind is spinning with ideas now." She spoke directly to Dallin, "If you're lucky, maybe he'll go away, I'll go away, and you and Justine can live happily ever after. Is that it, Dallin? Is that your best-case scenario right now?"

Dallin continued his longing gaze at the decades-worn motel carpet, as if in it he could read the words that would somehow make sense. Then he repeated, "I just want my son."

A sudden urge came over Hannah, the familiar longing for a drink. Maybe a shot. Tequila. A couple. Something to dull her a little. Make her think more clearly, and push away the webs of confusion and hate. The rage kept creeping over her, consuming her from her toes upward, like a nest of spiders crawling up her body. She wanted to act out, to yell, to hurt, to pull the fucking trigger and watch her husband bleed, and her need for alcohol punctuated every negative feeling surging through her body. In this moment she never felt so much like her father. As much as she hated Billy, she understood him, and never in her life as much as now had she so desperately wanted to be nothing like him.

It was time to change. She would control the rage. And there would be no more alcohol, ever. She would focus on the future, whatever that held for her. But there was one gleaming light in the distance, and that would be her focus from now on. One thing that would define her from now on.

She said aloud the two words that would mark the beginning of her change.

"I'm pregnant."

CHAPTER FORTY

Hannah stood outside the motel room, arms crossed tightly across her waist, holding herself as if letting go would cause her insides to spill onto the ground. A moist breeze licked her neck, chilling her, causing her to squeeze even more tightly. Black stood a few feet away, and a full minute passed before either of them said anything.

"Are you sure?" Black asked.

She nodded. "I think so. Maybe the stress is making me late, but I don't think that's it. I've never been pregnant before, but I *feel* it."

Another pause, an unnecessary one since she knew the next question.

"Is it—"

"I don't know," she said. "Could be." Her stomach suddenly flipped, and she didn't know if this was due to nerves or the first signs of morning sickness. She steadied herself against it and willed it away, and the feeling gradually faded.

The only possibility the pregnancy was from Dallin came from the last time Hannah had sex with her husband, the night he spoke in his sleep. *Or pretended to speak in his sleep*, she thought. *The beginning of everything.* The idea she was pregnant from that night horrified her, as if she would deliver to the world some kind of demon spawn. Which was ridiculous, she knew. It would still be *her* baby.

The other possibility was Black was the father. Hannah couldn't even get her mind around that at all. A month ago, all she wanted was a baby with Dallin. More than anything else she ever wanted. And now the idea she could be pregnant from someone else came to her as...well, almost a *relief.*

She looked over at Black, who seemed a bit unsteady himself. "I don't know what to say," he said.

"Neither do I."

She stared at him, looking into his eyes, searching to see if the next question forming in his mind would be *Are you going to keep it?* But that question didn't come. Instead, he reached out and held each of her shoulders, leaning his face toward hers. "We need to go," he said. "We have the money, it's time to go."

"No," she said. She nodded back to the motel room door, behind which Dallin remained bound to the chair, his mind likely reeling from Hannah's declaration. "I'm not done with this."

She hadn't even given Dallin time to react to what she'd said. She'd said the words and then walked outside, trailed by Black. The first truth was, she didn't think it was her husband's. Not based on the timing of her cycle and the amount of times she and Black had had sex in the past month compared to the one time she and Dallin had. The second truth was she didn't care what his reaction was. The child was *hers*, despite who the father was. The third truth was she *wanted* the baby to be Black's.

"Hannah, eight million is a lot of money. I know it's not all you deserve, probably not even close, but it's enough to disappear for good. More than enough."

"No," she said. "I didn't do anything wrong. I can't just disappear and let the world think I stole all that money. And then, what, Dallin and Justine live their lives out together?" The image of Connor—Dallin's child—flashed in her mind and it was too much. Hannah doubled over and vomited onto the cracked cement of the sidewalk.

"Are you okay?" she heard him ask.

She wiped her mouth and waited for the next surge to hit her, but it didn't come. She slowly stood. "Fantastic," she said.

A faded gray El Camino with deeply tinted windows rolled into the parking lot and pulled in near the motel registration area.

"Hannah, do you even know what you want?" Black said.

Her first instinct was to say *I want things to be back to how they were*, but she wasn't convinced that was true. Because how things used to be was a lie, a dream pillowed into comfort by alcohol and money.

"I don't want them to win," she said.

"They haven't won."

"They destroyed me. My sister. My husband. Billy. They all plotted to get rid of me. They don't get to win." A man in dark sunglasses and slicked black hair got out of the El Camino and walked inside the motel. The hue of his leather jacket was a perfect match for his car. Hannah continued. "They had an affair for two years—*and a child*—and I didn't see any of it. I was too numbed by my drinking. Too complacent living in wealth, pretending I had become someone special. That I had moved on from who I really am."

"And who are you?"

The man in the leather jacket returned from the motel registration with a room key and opened the back door of his car. He leaned in and, after a moment, stood back up, holding a baby in his arms. He reached back in with one hand and grabbed a duffel bag, and then the man walked to a room a few doors down and disappeared inside to his own life, the baby quiet the entire time.

"I'm Billy's daughter," Hannah said.

"That's how you define yourself?"

"It's how I've been defined."

Black moved his hands up to her face. For a brief moment Hannah was conscious of just having been sick, how she must look, how she must smell, but the insecurities disappeared in the heat of his palms, as if absorbed from her through his skin.

"Who *are* you?" he repeated. It wasn't a question. It was a challenge. Once again, his voice low, he asked, "*Who are you?*"

The one question she could least answer was the one just asked of her. *Who are you, Hannah? What are the words to describe you?*

Are you a wife, a sister, a daughter? Are you a victim? A lover? Who are your friends, and are those friendships real? Are you a loner, an intellectual, philanthropist? An alcoholic? Are you rage, wrapped in skin, tight like leather dried in the desert sun?

Are you a mother?

Who are you, Hannah?

She closed her eyes and felt his fingers spread on her face.

"I can't let it go," she said. She wasn't even sure what she was referring to, but whatever "it" was, it clung to her, squeezed her, dared her to do something about it. "You can leave," she continued, her eyes remaining closed. "Set up an account for me, transfer half the money there. Take your half and disappear."

"You don't just get to make these decisions on your own," Black said. "If it's my child, I get some say. It's not just about you."

She hadn't expected that, hadn't even considered someone else could have claim about the baby inside her. But he was right. If it was Black's—and she was certain it was, in that undefinable way she even knew she was pregnant—she had to admit he had a right to be involved with her choices.

She couldn't argue. She could only repeat her wants.

"Black, I need to do this."

She heard him sigh. "If it's truly what you want, then I'm going with you," he said.

Hannah felt the tears come down her cheeks, and there was nothing she could do to stop them. "You don't need to protect me anymore."

She felt one of his hands lift from her face, and seconds later it was on her stomach.

"I said I'm going with you."

"Don't stay for the wrong reasons," she said. "I told you I don't even know if it's yours."

His was the voice of reason, she thought. Of absolute certainty. And of peace. "I know who *I* am, Hannah. And I know how I define myself. With that kind of clarity, there is never a wrong reason. Or a bad choice. There's only direction, and my direction will be yours. For now, maybe for a long time."

A few rooms down Hannah heard the cries of a baby, the little girl—*it was a girl, wasn't it?*—she'd just seen in the arms of her father. The cries lasted just a few seconds before fading, and Hannah envisioned the little girl being gently bounced into peacefulness by her father.

Hannah opened her eyes.

"Both of them. My sister and father. I want to see them before we leave."

"Just like you had to see Dallin," Black said.

"Yes."

"And what did you accomplish with him? Aside from the money, what did you get from seeing your husband today? Did you get closure? Did you get the answers you wanted?"

The words *your husband* seemed foreign to Hannah. "I don't know," she said. "I got answers. I'm not sure about closure."

"And now you risk everything by meeting with Billy and Justine. You know why they did what they did—Dallin told you everything. What are you going to do? What could you possibly accomplish?"

"Black, I'm not telling you it's a good idea. I'm telling you I have to do it."

"*Why?*"

"Because the same reason you would," she said. "If you hadn't killed that drunk driver, wouldn't you have gone to his trial? Wouldn't you have wanted to say something to him during his sentencing?"

Black stepped back, his face stunned. Hannah almost felt sorry for bringing it up, but not sorry enough to keep from driving her point deeper.

"That man destroyed your life, Black. Look at where you are—first prison, now constantly on the run. Everything you once knew as your life is gone, all because of that one person. If you had the chance, wouldn't you at least want to confront him? I'm not saying it would change anything. In fact, it probably wouldn't. But I'm not asking you to be logical about it. I'm asking you, *wouldn't you want that?*"

His face seemed to harden as he thought, his jaw tight, the lines in his forehead a bit deeper than before.

"Yes," he finally said. "Yes, I would want that. But understand something. There's no such thing as closure. I've chased it for years and have only found open wounds. When I stopped chasing, the pain lessened. But it doesn't ever go away. Nothing's ever closed, Hannah. You should know that."

"I need them to know they didn't win," Hannah said. "And that I'm not like them. Not truly."

"You're not. Of course you're not."

But his words didn't convince her. It was Billy's words she heard, the words he spoke to her as she stood in front of him years ago, gasoline splashed around his legs, the Bic lighter a lead weight in her hand.

With my last ounce of life I will make you suffer, baby. But you do what you gotta do, Hannie. This is your moment.

But Hannah had failed. Failed to rid the world of a monster, because for some, prison wasn't enough of a shackle to contain a blackness that would continue to spread. Billy had the blackness. And he was spreading.

She stepped forward into Black, and his arms folded around her. "Will you really help me?" she asked into his chest.

"Yes. But if we're going to do this, we need to get something else out of it. We can record the meeting and, if they say anything incriminating, we'll at least have some proof of innocence if we're ever found. I don't plan on getting found, but it would be a good thing to have. So whatever you feel like you have to say to them, get either of them to admit to what they did. Especially regarding Dallin's involvement."

"And then we can leave," she said. "I promise."

But Black said nothing, and to Hannah, it felt like a silent acknowledgment that nothing would turn out the way they were hoping.

In the room down the hall, the once-crying baby burst into an infant's fit of laughter.

CHAPTER FORTY-ONE

Day 30

Black snapped the handcuffs closed around Hannah's left wrist, cool metal squeezing against bone. She sat on the floor where he directed her, near the far corner of the cabin's only room other than the bedroom. It was the second time she had been there. The first time, she woke to the smell of bacon, dizzy and disoriented, and she had promptly escaped through the window at the sight of Black.

Now she was back, and this time, despite the handcuffs on her, she was in much more control. As she walked inside the cabin a few minutes earlier, she had seen the bullet holes in the frame of the front door, a reminder of the elaborate hoax all planned around her. Real bullets expertly fired expressly to narrowly miss killing her. Real bullets, real fear.

You're just a rube, Hannie.

Black unlocked the other end of the cuffs and handed her the key. "Here," he said. "You hold on to this."

She took the key and slipped it in the front pocket of her jeans and then pulled her gray sweatshirt down over her waist. Black then cuffed her to the old radiator next to the wall. The restraints were part of the stage setting: when Billy and Justine came inside the cabin, they needed to believe Hannah wasn't actually on Black's side. The cuffs might not be the thing to convince them, but they wouldn't hurt.

The heat from the radiator warmed the back of her hand.

"Want me to turn it off?"

"No," she said. "It feels good."

"Comfy?" he asked.

"Couldn't be more so," she replied.

"Good." He took a few steps over to the kitchen table and set his backpack on top of it. He unzipped it and removed two guns and a small digital video camera. He took the smaller gun, walked back, and handed it to her. She took it with her free hand.

"Slide it under the radiator," he said. "He won't be able to see it there."

She turned the gun over in her hand, re-familiarizing herself with it. Stock. Safety. Grip. Sight. The gun—a Beretta Nano 9mm—was one she'd used and been most proficient in at short-range shooting in her training with Black. The weapon felt solid, smooth, and light. A month ago she would have held a gun as she would a dead rat by the tail. Now it felt comfortable, and the mere graze of the stock against her palm gave her a sense of security. Power.

She slid it into the gap between the radiator and the hardwood floor, where it fit perfectly. Hannah brought her free hand back to her lap and then practiced reaching for the gun. She fumbled it at first, but on her second try she retrieved it in one quick and smooth motion.

"I'm going to tell you the same thing I told you with Dallin," Black said. "Killing them isn't going to make things any easier for us."

"I won't kill my sister," she said immediately. As much as the idea of causing Justine pain filled her with grim satisfaction, she couldn't do that to her kids.

"What about Smooth?" Black asked.

She mumbled to the floor. "One less person looking for us."

"Trust me, your father will never find us. He's smart, I suppose, but not to the level of picking up our trail."

Black waited for a response from her and, getting none, walked back to the kitchen table and picked up the video camera.

"Why won't you tell me what you're planning?" he asked.

"I told you, because I don't know."

"I don't believe you."

"That doesn't matter to me."

"But it matters to *me*," Black said. "This is dangerous, Hannah. For all of us. And pretty damn unnecessary."

Unnecessary was the last thing it was, Hannah thought. Nothing in the world felt more necessary than looking into Billy's eyes and telling him that he was a failure. All he had hoped for had gone away. If anything, he was setting Hannah free, free from a husband she didn't ever really know. Free from a poisonous family. Hannah had restarted life in Seattle, but she had never really known what kind of person she was. In the last month, she had discovered the real Hannah, but only after she'd been stripped of all she had known. The ultimate irony was that it took her assumption of a new identity to find out who the real Hannah truly was.

"I'll get them to say something incriminating," she said. "Then we can go."

"Just like that?" he asked.

"I don't know. Maybe."

Black studied her a moment longer and then turned away. He took the video camera and attached it to the lens embedded in one of the kitchen cabinet doors. He then plugged a cable from the top of the cabinet into the side of the camera.

"It's attached to mini microphones in the ceiling. And it's a fish-eye lens. It'll pick up anything that happens in this room."

"How long can it record for?"

"Couple hours. It's already going."

"Shouldn't need that long."

"God help us, no," Black said. He looked at this watch. "Any minute now."

Black walked to the front window, pulled back the drapes, and lifted the window. "We can hear outside better this way," he said. "Sorry if it gets cold in here." The early morning softened his face, illuminated his eyes. Hannah looked up at him from the floor and suddenly questioned the idea of all of this. Was it worth the risk? No matter what, there would be a confrontation.

Black had contacted Billy, telling him that while he wouldn't kill Hannah, he *would* turn her over for the same fee. He also told him he was holding Dallin somewhere as insurance that fee would be paid. *You and Justine meet me at the cabin*, he'd told him. *Bring the money, and I'll give you Hannah. When I'm safely on my way, I'll call you with Dallin's location. Then you can do with Hannah whatever you want. I'll be gone.*

That clearly wasn't going to happen, and when it didn't, Billy and Justine were going to be upset. Which is why both Hannah and Black each had a gun.

"I thought Peter was going to be here," Hannah said.

"He's supposed to be," Black mumbled to the window. He looked at his watch. "I told him to be here thirty minutes ago."

"Are you worried?"

"I'm always worried. That's part of being an escaped convict."

Hannah saw the thin cloth drapes wisp in the breeze coming through the window screen in front of Black. There was a cacophony of bird chatter outside.

"Is this stupid?" she asked. "Am I crazy for wanting this?"

"No, you're not crazy. But yes, it's stupid. It's a risk, although a calculated one."

"Just make sure Billy doesn't have a weapon. Or Justine, though I can't imagine. But will you do that? First thing?"

"You don't need to ask," he replied. "They aren't getting close to you with any kind of weapon. That was the part Peter was going to help with, but I can take care of it."

The cool air from the window spilled down to the floor and trickled over her, raising the hairs on her arms. She moved her cuffed hand an inch closer to the radiator.

"Something's wrong," Black said. "I'm calling Peter." He reached into the front pocket of his jeans and pulled out his disposable cell phone. He thumbed in a number and held it up to his ear, then turned to her as it rang. "There could have been traffic coming out of Seattle, but he should have—"

Then he stopped talking. His words cut off the same moment

Hannah heard the sound of something breaking, as if a very old and fragile tea cup had fallen to the floor and shattered. What looked like rain fell onto the oak floorboards next to Black's feet, and it took Hannah's brain a moment to process that it wasn't rain, but shards of glass. Falling, sprinkling to the floor, dancing around his feet.

She looked up to his face. Black's mouth was stuck open, the last word frozen on his lips. His gaze seemed to be beyond her, beyond the walls of the cabin, his eyes looking at something far distant. Something only he could see.

Then his hand went to his chest and with it, her gaze. That's when Hannah saw the blood expanding along his white t-shirt, blossoming like a red rose filmed in high speed. Opening wide, bright red against faded white, drips of blood creeping over his fingers, hanging for a moment, then falling to the floor, painting the broken glass.

And then he collapsed to his knees.

Hannah didn't scream. She couldn't, because she couldn't even move. She just stared at him, looking in a face that became whiter by the second, processing the flow of blood that wouldn't stop, and knew the father of her child was going to die as she watched.

CHAPTER FORTY-TWO

"Run," was the only word Black said before his body slumped facedown to the floor, his right arm outstretched as if trying to reach something that could have saved him. Hannah was still frozen, first by the look on Black's face, now by the sight of the small pool of blood that widened beneath him, the edge of it creeping toward the side of his head until his thick hair began to soak it in.

Her stomach lurched just as it had at the motel yesterday. She leaned over to vomit but nothing happened except a dry heave so intense she struggled for air. When she finally recovered, she sat up and filled her lungs, then exhaled slowly and steadied her breathing.

Go, Hannah.

When she finally unfroze, she did so with such a rush of thoughts that she ended up just kicking her legs out uselessly. Everything was suddenly clear to her, but the jolt of panic wouldn't let her body cooperate. Black was dead, which meant the plan had failed. They had probably killed Peter as well, which is why he didn't show up. Which probably meant she was next to die. She had to get out of the cabin *this minute* if she had any hope of surviving.

The key. The key. The key.

She said it out loud. "The key." She shoved her hand in her jeans pocket as she kept talking, as her heart kept pounding faster and harder in her chest. "Get the key. Open the cuffs. Grab the gun. Not the front door. Bedroom window."

Yes, bedroom window. Same place you escaped from last

time. Run to that dry creek bed, then follow that down. Don't rivers always lead to somewhere?

Where is that fucking key?

She felt metal for a brief moment with the tip of her forefinger, but her jeans were tight enough she only managed to get two fingers to slide inside. That only resulted in her pushing the key deeper into the pocket.

"*Come on.*" Hannah pushed harder against the opening with the rest of her hand and managed to get all but her thumb in the pocket.

Deeper. There it is. *God, why is it so small?*

It seemed impossible to grasp, and her leg kept twitching involuntarily, kicking out as if her brain were hooked up to electrical impulses, making the key push just out of reach every time she was seemingly close to it.

Finally, *there.* She bent three fingers around it, clawing against her thigh as she did. She pulled to bring the key out, but now her knuckles held fast against the seam of her pocket.

Relax, a distant voice told her.

Hannah didn't know if the voice was her own or of something otherworldly watching over her. But it was so calm, so assuring, that Hannah immediately obeyed. She loosened the ball of her fingers.

Slide it up with your fingers. Don't grab it. *Slide it.*

"Okay," she said, straightening her fingers. Then she used her forefinger and middle finger to coax it up along the inside of her pocket.

"Okay," she breathed. She almost had it. A strand of sweat-stained hair fell in front of her face, and she twisted it away with a shake of her head.

And she almost had it. She was close. Very close.

But close wouldn't save her. The door burst open, and Hannah suddenly saw her father for the first time since she was fifteen.

Billy held a rifle in his hands, and he was smiling.

CHAPTER FORTY-THREE

Billy didn't stand in the doorway for more than a second. If he had, Hannah might have had time to put the key in the cuffs and release herself from the radiator. Instead, he rushed at her. As he did, Hannah's fingers pulled the key from her pocket and the small piece of metal tumbled to the floor next to her thigh. She grasped for it just as Billy reached her. Her hand seized the key at the same moment his large work boot crashed down on her fingers, scattering tiny clumps of dried dirt on the floor around her hand.

The pain seared white-hot through her fingers, shooting up her arm, filling her chest with heat.

"Almost didn't recognize you with the black hair, Hannie. Can't say it suits you, if you don't mind me sayin'." He looked down at the hand under his boot. "Whatcha got there?"

Billy kicked her arm away, the hard rubber toe of his boot driving into her forearm. In a flash, he bent down and picked up the key, put it in his pocket, then stepped back from her.

In that moment Hannah remembered the gun. Since the moment the bullet had struck Black, Hannah's own gun—the one still concealed beneath the radiator—had disappeared from her mind. The only thing she had thought about was getting away, but the gun was still there. She was sure Billy hadn't seen it, but Hannah didn't know if she could even fire it. Her one free hand burned in pain. She slowly tried to bend her fingers but the agony was so intense her fingers might as well have been bending backwards. Broken, for sure. One, maybe two of them. As she watched her free hand swell, she knew she couldn't grab and hold the gun, much less pull the trigger. She could try, but she would fail. And Billy would then kill her.

"Well," he said, looking at her on the floor. "I figured about as much." He turned, aimed the rifle at Black, but didn't pull the trigger. There was no need to, Hannah could tell. If Black wasn't dead, he was unconscious. She wondered if she would live long enough to mourn him.

For everything Black had been, for all the comfort and assurances he'd given, for all his knowledge and his strength, he was human, and his life had just been nullified by a small piece of lead traveling at a high velocity. Black had lived his life minimizing mistakes, calculating and recalculating, planning every move. But he had underestimated Billy, and he paid with his life. Now Black no longer protected Hannah, but perhaps he never really did anyway. Hannah could only truly protect herself, and in this moment, her ability to do even that was gone.

"I figured you and him was workin' together." Billy walked up to her and leveled the barrel of the rifle at her head. "You did have the key to the cuffs, so I ain't buying that he was going to turn you over. What else you got?" Her father set the rifle on the floor and put both hands on her ankles. The touch of his hands flooded her with memories of Thanksgiving night. Of his open palm against her face. Then, his closed fist.

His hands squeezed her ankles and slowly made their way up to her knees, and then snaked up her thighs.

She spit at him with what she could gather in her paper-dry mouth. Most of it landed on his forehead. Billy didn't say a word. His expression didn't change. He didn't even wipe it off.

His hands reached her hips, and his right hand pushed between her legs, which she tried to keep squeezed together. She felt the warmth of his fingers through her jeans.

"Fuck you," she whispered. Then she lifted her free arm and swung it at him, but the attempt was impotent and painful. Her useless fingers slapped his shoulder, and a fresh burst of blinding pain rocked her.

Billy said, "Now you just calm down. If I wanted to fuck ya,

I'd have done it a million times when you were a kid. But you're not my type, Hannie."

His hands reached up her waist, under her sweatshirt, but rather than groping he patted her, checking for weapons. Seconds later he was done, and Billy pulled his hands back and rested them on his knees as he crouched in front of her.

Hannah glanced at the bottom of the radiator, something she must have done unconsciously because it was the exact thing Billy needed from her.

"That's where it is, huh?" He leaned over and reached his arm across and felt under the radiator. Hannah badly wanted to do something. To hit him. Bite him. Anything. But her hand felt as useless as a piece of steak at the end of a fork, just dead meat. Bringing her hand against him would only hurt her and anger him more.

Billy pointed the gun at her face. "Planning on an ambush, were you?"

Hannah noticed the smell of him for the first time, and that same shit cologne—she couldn't remember the name but it came in a red-and-white-striped box, making her always think of a barber shop—mixed with sweat and cigarette breath. The smell suddenly flooded her nostrils, bringing her twenty years and a thousand miles away.

Your momma's just learning a little lesson, that's all, Hannie. Nothin' to be afraid of. See, if she'd done what she was supposed to, everything would be fine. Fact is, she don't listen so well sometimes, so she's gotta be reminded. Like a dog, see? Some hounds learn easy, some learn hard. Your momma, she's a hard-learnin' hound. Can't say whether it's stubborn or stupid, but in the end I don't suppose it matters.

"You killed her," Hannah said. "She should have left a long time before you did."

He smiled and waved the gun under her nose, as if it was a bouquet of freshly cut flowers. "Oh no no no, darlin'. You are so wrong about that. See, she needed me. Once I was gone, she was gone. You see? I was her *direction*. Once I went to prison, she lost her way. So actually, *you* killed her. You fucked it all up, Hannie.

Thought you were being a hero, but you destroyed our way of life. Broke up the *family unit.*"

On the last words Billy reached out with his free hand and squeezed her cheek, pinching it hard between thumb and index finger, like an overly zealous aunt coming to visit. It stung, but there was something amounting to affection in the gesture. Hannah would rather he had outright struck her.

"Now," he said, suddenly bounding to his feet. "You're going to tell me where that husband of yours is, aren't you? Because he has *my* money."

Hannah then remembered the camera. All this was being recorded. Hell, she didn't even need Billy to say anything incriminating. Black's murder was there in vivid detail.

She turned her head toward Black one more time, promising herself she wouldn't look at him again, because the scene was too awful. Except the one outstretched arm, his body was crumpled, not peacefully as if in sleep, but constricted into a tight ball, as if every muscle shrunk in the moment of death, pulling him into himself. Blood painted the floor, but it had finally stopped growing into a wider circle. There simply hadn't been any more left to come out of him.

Don't cry. Don't you fucking cry. Not even for Black. He'll think you're scared, and even if you are, you don't cry. Not for fear, nor for sadness. Not for anything.

"We killed Dallin," Hannah said. "We took him to a motel room, taped him to a chair, and he told us everything. Including the account number to your eight million dollars." Hannah was going to die. She knew that now as clear as she had ever known anything. The past thirty days were full of nothing but lies, but this was one truth that slapped her full force across the jaw. She had maybe thirty minutes. An hour at best. Hell, maybe less than a minute. But she would die this morning, in this cabin. But that didn't mean she had to be silent.

"He pleaded for his life," she said. "He told us everything. About *Justine.*" Her sister's name rolled off her tongue like she was naming a newly discovered virus. *Justine.* "And Connor. All about your plan to make me so scared I had to run. But I'm *not* scared."

"Oh, you're scared all right." Billy no longer smiled.

Hannah ignored him. "Black took the account number and transferred the money to his own account, and you just killed the only person in the world who had that information. So I guess you're kinda fucked now, aren't you, Billy?"

Billy kept his gaze fixed on her but his eyes—wolf's eyes, they'd once been called—narrowed just enough for her to know he believed her.

"Bullshit," he said. "Either you know that account number or your husband's alive. Maybe both. Either way, you know something I need to know, and you're in a tight spot right now. I figure I can find a way to make you talk."

Hannah felt something bordering on calm. She became detached, as if seeing this moment for what it was. Her last one.

She took a deep breath and let the air slip slowly from her lungs before speaking again. "Once he told us everything, I made Black leave the room. Told him I needed a few more minutes with my husband, just to tell him a few things. Private, husband-and-wife-only kind of things. Then the plan was to let him go. Just take the money and disappear for good. Eight million, that was enough, we figured. I convinced Black I could do that. Just disappear, let you all get everything you wanted except that money. There was more money, I knew. But I convinced Black I was okay with letting you all win. I was okay starting over. I could let it all go." She looked to the side, feeling the need to break eye contact with her father, even if for a moment. "And when Black left the room, I told Dallin I was pregnant."

"Well, isn't that good news?" Billy said.

"It's true." Hannah shifted her gaze back to her father. "You would have been a grandfather." She deliberately said *would have*, wondering what kind of reaction that would create. What was she hoping for? For him to say, *oh, darlin', I'm not going to kill you*?

"Well, hell, there are too many fucking brats in this world anyhow."

It had been many years since Hannah had hoped she wasn't

pregnant, but this was one of them. She wanted to be wrong. Wanted to think it was the stress on her body making her late. And this was a perfectly reasonable explanation, probably the most logical, except for the fact she simply knew and it crushed her, because her baby would die with her.

Hannah resisted being baited by him. She wanted Billy to react to her words, not the other way around.

"Dallin didn't have the same opinion," she said. "He was happy, actually, until I told him the baby wasn't his."

Billy barked a short laugh. "Well, there's a whorey twist for you. Such a slut that you're running for your life but you still can't keep those skinny legs closed." He shook his head and smiled, but it wasn't a malevolent or even dismissive smile. There was a look of discomfort, like an athlete grinning through pain. "You fucked the man who arranged every part of your demise." Billy nodded to Black's body.

Again, Hannah ignored the hate in his words. It wasn't very hard to do—she had built up armor for such things many years ago.

"Dallin was very upset when I told him," Hannah said. "He actually cried, and for a moment, the briefest of moments, I felt sorry for him. Sorry that he was too weak to have faced responsibility. Sorry that you were able to force him into doing what he did."

"He coulda done many things to change the course of all this," her father said. "But he didn't. He *wanted* you gone."

"And that's why my moment of pity for him didn't last. I knew he was little more than a pawn in your and Justine's plan, but you can't win a chess game without any pawns, can you?"

"He served a purpose."

She kept her gaze locked on him. "You should have seen the look on his face when I put the duct tape over his mouth. All... confused. Like a dog being beaten for no reason at all."

"Oh, yeah? Why, you torture him and didn't want him screaming?" Another smile, this one barely masking insecurity. Uncertainty. Billy shifted his footing, and his forearm veins pulsed as he gripped the gun more tightly.

"No, I didn't torture him," she said. "No point in that. There was nothing I needed from him. I knew the story behind what happened to me—he told me everything. Black had the account information from him. There was nothing we needed from Dallin. I put the tape on his mouth so he couldn't breathe through it. Then I took a much longer piece and wrapped it twice around his head and face. Covering his nose."

"Bullshit," Billy said.

Hannah didn't want to stop her momentum. "Then you *really* should have seen his face. Eyes bulging at me. Head thrashing back and forth. Skin turning red, then purple. It was awful, to be honest. I almost couldn't take it. I came real close to removing the tape." Hannah studied her father's face, his washed-blue eyes that now seemed clouded. Old. "But then I remembered everything he had done to me," Hannah continued. "And I forced myself to watch. I watched him plead with his eyes, because that was all he could do. Wide-open eyes, to the point I thought they'd burst. I watched those eyes roll up and then finally look at nothing."

For the first time, Billy seemed to have nothing to say. Then he crouched down in front of her, and the smell of sweat and grime filled her nostrils. With his right hand he ran his fingers slowly through her long black hair, causing Hannah to shudder.

"Hannie, darling," he said, his voice little more than a coarse whisper. "You just don't have it in you. You think you do, but when it comes time to pull the trigger, you just can't. Trust me, honey. That's a *good* thing. You don't want to be like me. Always fightin' the rage. Suffering the ball of pain in the stomach that just makes me so fuckin' angry at the world. You think you're like me, but you ain't. I know you didn't kill Dallin, so tell me where he is."

"I'm more like you than you know," she said. "And I've hated you every day of my life for it."

"You didn't kill me when you had the chance," he said.

"I tried. God, I wanted to see you burn."

"Killing is just not in your nature."

"Then give me the gun and let me make up for past mistakes," she said.

That elicited a brief smile. "Aw, that's just self-defense for you and your little one. Anyone could do that." He leaned closer. "Now tell me where Dallin is or *you're* gonna burn."

The word *burn* jolted Hannah, and Billy noticed.

"Yeah, little girl. I'm going to do to you what you wanted but couldn't do to me. See, I got a spare can of gas in the trunk of my car, and I got a lighter in my front pocket. It's going to make things easy, because I'm gonna torch this whole place. They might be able to figure out who you and your boyfriend are, but it's not going to be easy. Have to do some of that DNA testing on your charred bones."

When she was in her twenties, Hannah had gotten into meditation. This was soon after she had met Dallin and years before the use of meditation to help her with her stress was replaced by a wine bottle. She remembered one particular teaching that was focused on pain relief, and the teacher had said how by controlling one's thoughts and by focusing deep within the self, a person could block out any amount of pain. It was a practice dating back to India some 2,500 years ago, and it had been used throughout the centuries to withstand the most brutal of torture. But very few could maintain the focus needed in those most dire of circumstances in the face of such pain.

Hannah always remembered that. Always shuddered at the thought of needing a skill like that. But now she could be minutes away from an unbearable pain and she was certain she would be unable to block any of the agony as she burned alive.

"Why did you always hate me so much?" she asked. "If you're going to kill me, at least tell me that much. You beat Mom, but that just seemed like an outlet for you. Your real hate was always directed at me. What did I ever do to deserve that?"

Billy seemed to think about this for a moment. He looked on the verge of telling her something other than what he ultimately said.

"Because you were always different," he said. "You just didn't fit in, and you knew it. You thought you were too good for us."

"That's not true," she whispered. "I just wanted out. How could I possibly want to stay any longer in a house like that?"

"Like I said, too good for us."

"I didn't deserve your hate," Hannah said. "None of us did."

"Well, Hannie, that's the thing about life, they say. Not a lot of fairness spread around." Billy walked back over and grabbed her cuffed hand, yanking it against the radiator until Hannah thought her wrist would snap inside the cuff.

"Yeah," he said. "You ain't going anywhere. Be right back, darlin'."

Still holding Hannah's gun, Billy then collected the rifle from the floor and went outside, leaving the door open. Hannah was at an angle where the partially open door blocked her view, but she felt cool air around her waist, just as she had from the open window. That air represented the outside, the vast woods, freedom. And it was just beyond her reach.

She yanked against the cuff until the skin chafed into a bloody ring around her wrist, but it didn't do anything but transfer pain from her broken hand to the other side of her body. The radiator didn't budge a millimeter.

Her mind fired thoughts at her almost faster than she could process them.

He's not bluffing. But will he torture me first, hoping for the account number, or will he just set me on fire and watch me burn? I can't scream. He doesn't deserve that satisfaction. I'll suck in the smoke. That's how people die in fires, right? Smoke inhalation. Suck in as much as I can as fast as possible. Maybe I'll die from that before the fire eats my skin. But he wants the account number. I don't have it. Don't even know how to get it. Black transferred the money to the new account and now that died with him. Will Billy believe me, or will he keep hurting me until I say something?

Then she heard a sound, soft but distinct. It was the sound of an approaching car, and she probably wouldn't have heard it except for the fact the front door was open. The road leading to Black's cabin ended there, she knew, so any car coming here was either lost or coming here specifically.

Peter, she thought. Peter was supposed to be here already. It must be him.

She heard a car door open and then close.

Then Billy. "The hell you doin' here? I told you to stay put."

And then silence for what seemed like a lifetime. In that silence her imagination spun at a frenzied pace, and perhaps it was all in her mind, but her hearing seemed to suddenly become superhuman, picking up on the slightest of sounds outside the cabin. A distant bird calling to another. The spiny needles of the pine trees brushing each other in the late-fall breeze. A deer stepping delicately around rocks as it foraged for food.

Then laughing. A low chuckling. Mocking.

"That's about right," she heard Billy say.

More silence, though the air seemed filled with the electric current preceding a lightning strike.

Then a sharp crack. Hannah jumped at the sound, yanking her hand against the cuffs, further tearing the skin around her wrist.

Gunshot.

The echo lasted longer in Hannah's ears than it did in the air, rippling through her brain, fading only to a dull, distant drumbeat. Adrenaline surged through her, heightening every sense, studding her flesh with goose bumps and raising the hairs on her arms.

Footsteps, slow and cautious. Two steps. Stop. Two more. Stop.

A low moan. The scraping of dirt.

Finally, a shadow stretched along the inside of the cabin, a few feet past the front door. A long alien head and body created by the low sun in the sky. Something in one of the alien hands. Hannah knew in that instant that the person casting the thin, stretched shadow wasn't Peter.

The door was silent as it fully opened.

Hannah looked up to the figure of her sister standing with the morning light streaming in behind her. Then her gaze flicked to the gun in Justine's hand.

"I killed Dad."

CHAPTER FORTY-FOUR

Justine's face was cloaked in shadow and the sunlight lit the long strands of blond hair that draped her shoulders. She just stood there, swaying slightly, like a steel suspension bridge in high winds. Hannah didn't know if her sister was drugged, drunk, or in shock, but there was a weakness in her stance, as if the slightest touch would topple her.

Hannah tried to focus her hearing, listening for any sign of Billy in front of the cabin. Justine remained silent, looking down at her older sister, saying nothing else after her murder confession.

Hannah finally spoke.

"He's really dead?"

Justine's answer was simply to walk a few more steps into the cabin and gaze around blankly.

"Justine, did you shoot him?"

Justine finally focused her attention on her sister.

"You dyed your hair," she said.

"Justine, listen, whatever you think of me. No matter the reason why you hate me, we need to work together right now."

"Is Dallin here?" Justine asked, dazed. Again she craned her neck, scanning the room, but now Hannah could finally see her sister's eyes, and it was clear she was firmly detached from reality.

"Justine, I'm going to ask you again. Did you *kill* him? Because if not, he's coming back in here to kill me."

"That was what I wanted all along," Justine said. Hannah had never seen her sister in such a fugue-like state. She wondered how she had been able to drive over here and find the cabin, much less shoot someone. "I wanted you dead," Justine continued. "Out of the way. It's what Daddy wanted, too, but I was the reasonable one. I knew if you were dead it would be a problem. The next best thing was to have you run away."

"Justine, listen very closely to me. There's a key to these handcuffs in Billy's front pocket. I need that key. Can you get it for me?" Hannah was edging closer to hopefulness, which she warned herself away from. She had no idea if her sister would simply raise the gun and put a bullet in her skull at any moment. "Justine, get the key, and then we'll talk this out. I'll tell you where Dallin is."

Justine's eyes widened for a moment at the sound of Dallin's name.

"I need him," Justine said.

Hannah's sense of massive betrayal at the hands of her sister was supplanted by her need for survival, so she didn't respond to Justine the way she wanted to. She just said, "I know you do. So go out and get me the key, and then I can tell you where he is."

Justine's face held a near-catatonic lack of expression. She didn't nod, smile or frown, didn't look at her sister with disdain or distrust. She asked nothing, not even if Dallin was still alive. After a few seconds of silence, Justine turned and went back out the door.

In the moments that followed, Hannah pictured Billy finding that last bit of strength to overpower Justine, just like Grizzly had done with her. He would grab her ankles and pull her down, and Justine, in her zombie-like trance, would topple easily. Billy would take her gun and put a bullet in her head, and then he'd drag himself back inside the cabin to finish off his other daughter. Billy would not allow himself to die until he took everyone else out first.

But it was Justine who finally came back through the open doorway. She held the little silver key in her left hand, and her knuckles were painted in Billy's blood. She tossed the key to Hannah, which clinked a few times on the ground before coming to rest against her leg. Hannah immediately reached for it, pain searing through her broken hand as she tried to squeeze the key between her fingers. She didn't want to ask Justine for help—hell, she wasn't sure Justine even *could* help in her state—so she gritted through the pain until she was able to use enough force to grasp the key and turn it inside the locking mechanism.

The cuff broke open, releasing her left hand, and that moment of release gave Hannah her first sense of hope. She stood and moved for the door, knowing that by doing so her sister would be standing behind her. But Hannah needed a weapon.

She looked outside. Billy was about fifteen feet away, lying facedown in a pool of blood that spread around his torso. His rifle was on the ground next to him, and Hannah ran over and snatched it off the ground, pausing only a moment to check for movement from the body on the ground. There was none.

She looked over at Black's car, remembering the keys were in his pocket.

Hannah held the rifle with both hands and walked back toward the front door. A few steps away she stopped and examined the weapon. She wasn't very familiar with rifles, though Black had one he'd shown her while teaching her about handguns. She put the safety on, pulled back the bolt, and saw the gleam of the round lodged inside. She slid the bolt back in place and removed the safety.

Hannah raised the weapon to eye level as she slowly made her way inside the cabin.

Justine was still standing where Hannah had left her, staring in the direction of Black's body, but seeing through him. Seeing somewhere either far away or deep within.

"If Dallin is dead," Justine said distantly, "go ahead and shoot me."

Hannah didn't need to use the sight on the rifle. At this distance, Justine's head was an easy target. Hannah's finger kissed the trigger of the rifle, teasing it with the lightest of touches.

"He's not dead," Hannah said.

Justine turned, and the smile on her face was the first emotion she had shown.

"Promise?" she asked.

"My God," Hannah said. "You really love him, don't you?"

Justine nodded.

"So what came first?" Hannah asked. "Your love for him or your hate for me?"

"I don't hate you, Hannah. I just need you out of my way."

The woman in front of Hannah was unrecognizable, or perhaps Hannah was seeing her truly for the first time. All they had been through together, every verbal assault, every bruise their mother wore, every night spent huddled on the floor against a bed, wondering what sound would come next from the other room. All those years, and Hannah never knew her sister.

"You think I won't pull the trigger," Hannah said. "You destroyed my life, and now you're just standing there, like I wouldn't do something about it."

"I saved your life," Justine said. "Daddy would have killed you."

"Peter. Where is he?"

"Dead," she said. "Daddy's plan was to come out here well before the meeting. He waited about a mile down the road to make sure no one else was coming to the cabin. I saw Peter's car when I was driving here. It had smashed into a tree on the side of the road. Bullet hole in the windshield. His body was in the front seat. Daddy killed him."

Hannah squeezed her eyes shut for a second and tried to shake off the horror of how easily Justine told her this.

"Stop calling him *Daddy*," Hannah said. "He's not a daddy. He's a fucking monster."

Justine didn't even seem to hear her.

"When Black called and said he had Dallin, Daddy lost his mind. Said he knew you two were working together and that the money might not be coming. He told me to stay put, but I knew he was coming to kill you. I..." She looked down again at Black's body. "I almost listened to him. Thought how easy it would be. He'd come here. Kill the both of you. Find Dallin. And then I'd have everything I wanted." Hannah noticed a tiny bubble of spit on her sister's lower lip, which bobbed as Justine spoke. "I waited too long, but I came. Saw the directions he'd written. I came, but I was too late to save Black. Too late to save Peter." Her gaze shifted back to Hannah. "I'm sorry."

"Put the gun down, Justine."

There was no hesitation. Justine's hand opened and the gun that had been hanging by her side clattered to the floor.

"Kick it to me."

Justine did. Hannah picked up the gun and left the rifle on the floor. The gun felt more familiar, *assuring*.

"Why, Justine?" Hannah held the gun at her side, knowing Justine was no longer a threat. "Why did you do this to me?"

Justine shook her head softly and looked at the floor. "Because you took away everything I had."

"I took you away from a horrible life."

A tear appeared beneath Justine's right eye as she looked back up at Hannah. It would make it halfway down her cheek before running dry. "Our life there worked for everyone except you," Justine said. "Maybe it didn't make sense to you, but it worked for Momma, worked for Daddy. Worked for me."

"He *beat* her," Justine said. "It wasn't *working* for her. Justine, what are you talking about?"

Head still softly shaking. "You made him go away."

"He was going to kill her, Justine. Eventually."

The silence that followed was electric, and though it lasted only a few seconds, Hannah could feel the tension buried within it.

Then Justine whispered, "You never understood, Hannah. You and me, we're not..."

"Not the same?" Hannah interjected.

"No." Seconds passed. Then, "We're not sisters."

What the hell is she talking about?

"You're right," Hannah said. "I don't understand."

"You never knew. But I did. Mom told me before she died, but she didn't want you to know."

Hannah took a step toward her sister, resisting an urge to slap Justine across the face in an attempt to bring her back from the void into which her mind had apparently fallen.

"Why are you doing this?" she asked. "Why are you telling me lies?"

"It's the truth," Justine said. Her voice was flat, emotionless. "Mom had an affair when they had only been married a few years. You were the result of that affair. Dad suspected it but never knew for sure. She told me that's when he started drinking. Hitting her. And it all continued from there. You were the reason for all of it, Hannah."

Hannah started to retort but closed her mouth. Could it be true? Or was this just another manipulation by Justine?

Justine shared physical traits of both her parents, but Hannah had inherited only her mother's features. Hannah had always been verbally abused by Billy, while Justine was always spared. Could it be that Billy always hated Hannah because he suspected she wasn't actually his daughter?

You never fit in, Hannie.

"I don't believe you," Hannah said.

"You don't need to," replied Justine. "Maybe it's not even true, but it's what Mom told me. I believe it. You were never one of us, Hannah."

In that moment, Hannah felt a wave of sudden relief, like someone pumped her body full of morphine. Her instinct was to deny Justine's words, but the thought of actually not being Billy's daughter was an incredible gift. All the rage she felt growing up would have come from her environment and not her blood. Her anger was learned and not genetic. There would be no more excuses—Hannah could finally be her own person.

"Who is my father?" she asked.

"I don't know," Justine said. Something flashed over her face.

Sadness, perhaps. "But someone better than Daddy, I imagine. But he's still my daddy, and I did all of this for him. For us. Daddy needed money, and it was my idea to take it from you. From Dallin. I wanted Daddy to be happy, and I wanted you to be unhappy. But..."

"But you fell in love with my husband," Hannah said. It was obvious. Justine's failed relationships over the years always seemed to have a commonality—her absolute need of the other person. The suffocating, all-encompassing need, one that eventually drove the other person permanently away.

"Yes," Justine said. "I had to kill Daddy because of that. I knew if he killed you, Dallin would be next. And then I would have no one."

There were so many things Hannah wanted to scream at her sister, things about Justine's delusions, her lies about wanting to save Hannah, her complete disregard of her children in the shadow of what she thought was love. A part of her wanted to inflict pain on her sister, to make Justine feel even a portion of the agony Hannah herself had been put through. An even smaller part of Hannah—though larger than she would care to admit—wanted to walk up to her sister and shoot her point blank in her face.

But Hannah knew none of that would accomplish anything but create a black wound in her own soul, something that would fester for the rest of Hannah's life.

Hannah put down the gun and walked up to Justine. She brought her hands up to Justine's face, cradling her head just as she had done as a child, on those nights when the yelling had been so bad nothing could drown out the sound of a family being torn to pieces. On those nights Hannah would hold her, trying to protect her, bring her comfort, and now, as Hannah stood before her, it occurred to her that Justine had never really cried in those moments. Never had been as scared as Hannah assumed she must have been. It was herself she was truly trying to comfort. Justine was not only used to the screams, but she must have been so immersed in Billy's world that the anger and the rage were probably as common to her as banal, dinner-table conversation for other families. Justine had been destroyed before she was even a teenager, and Hannah never realized that until now.

"We are sisters," Hannah said. "No matter what, we are sisters."

Justine looked at her and began to sob, finally grabbing Hannah and squeezing her tightly, holding onto her as if she would otherwise collapse.

Hannah squeezed Justine's back as she spoke. "Dallin is in the Jackson Motel in Issaquah," she said. "Room 24. You better get there fast because he's taped to a chair and probably needs water by now." She stroked Justine's hair. "Maybe you'll have a good life together, but I doubt it. Whatever happens, you have to take care of your boys, Justine. They are all that matter here. Nothing else, understand?"

Hannah pulled back and looked at her sister. Justine squeezed her eyes shut as she nodded. The tears kept coming. Her face flushed a scarlet red, bright and splotchy against the blond hair falling alongside it.

"I'd like to tell you that I forgive you," Hannah said. "But I can't. Maybe someday I will. But the only thing I know for sure is I'm never going to see you again."

Hannah knew these would be the last words she would ever say to Justine. She leaned forward and kissed Justine on her forehead, and when she released Justine's head and stepped back, Justine sank to her knees, buried her face in her hands, and continued to cry.

CHAPTER FORTY-FIVE

Hannah walked over to Black's body and knelt next to him. She knew he was dead. There was an absence of energy that she couldn't define, but knew it was because there was no longer any life in the man on the floor. Nothing could be done, though she felt some guilt for not trying. For not rolling him over, frantically checking for a pulse, staining herself with his blood as she performed chest compressions on him, then shoving ripped pieces of her blouse into the bullet wound to stop the bleeding. For not weeping over his corpse.

But she did none of those things, because she *knew*. There was a stillness in him, like a fallen tree in the woods. Perhaps the tears would come later, but right now she didn't want to feel anything. She just wanted to leave.

There were two things in Black's coat pocket she needed. One was the key to Black's car, which she would drive to the airport. The bags in the trunk of the car were packed, though Black's bag would remain behind. Her luggage contained new clothes, enough for a couple of weeks until she was able to find an apartment and go out shopping on her own. In her purse was her new passport, so perfectly constructed—so Black had told her—that she would have no trouble for at least five years until she needed to have it renewed. Even her resident visa papers were perfectly forged. A Canadian abroad, a single woman by the name of Sylvia Genout—the "t" silent like *merlot*, she would tell people.

The other item in his pocket was one Black had told her about. It was a phone, a smartphone, not the archaic flip phone variety he had used in a disposable manner. This phone was not connected to any provider, but on it was stored all the information she needed to access the bank in the Cayman Islands that contained the money they had transferred from Dallin's account. The phone was locked using retinal-recognition software, but Black had set it up to recognize each of them. *Just in case*, he had said last night. Hannah was thankful for this, because she didn't want to roll Black over and start waving the phone in front of his lifeless eyes, hoping the software would work on a dead person.

Her fingers throbbed as she patted the outside of his right jacket pocket. Broken, she thought. At least the index finger. Maybe the middle.

Hannah felt what she was looking for, and purposefully looked away from Black as her hand burrowed into the pocket, retrieving the key and the phone.

Hannah powered on the phone and looked into the screen. Seconds later it unlocked. Instead of defaulting to a home screen scattered with icons, a yellow digital notepad filled the screen. There was a note typed on it. A note from Black. Her eyes wanted to quickly scan for critical words, important things only, things that might help her in the immediate moment, but Hannah read every word, slowly, as if reading a love letter.

> *If all went well, I was planning to delete this note after we left the meeting with Billy. But if you're reading this, well, I suppose that's not good news for me.*
>
> *Everything you need is on this phone, encrypted in the app I told you about. Not just the account information, but all my notes from years of making people disappear. Use them, Hannah. Follow every instruction to the word. Don't be lazy, don't let down your guard, even for a second. Billy will keep looking for you, as will people much smarter and more capable than him. It's an exhausting way to live, but maybe you can find peace.*
>
> *Remember, Hannah. You can't ever go home. Ever.*

Now, you are Sylvia Genout. Erase the name Hannah Parks from your mind, from your heart, and forever from your lips. Funny, I spent so many years under the name Black that's now who I am. If you're curious, the address book on this phone has one entry, and that's my real name. Only if you're curious. I haven't used that name since the day I escaped from prison, but I suppose there's no harm in anyone knowing it now.

Time for you to leave, Hannah. Delete this note, secure this phone, and sail away. I hear the sunsets are pretty damn good where you're going.

Black

CHAPTER FORTY-SIX

Hannah avoided looking at Justine as she picked up the gun and headed to the front door. She was almost outside before she remembered the video being recorded. She turned and headed to the kitchen where she found the camera, unplugged the cables, and took the device with her. She was tempted to say something to Justine, something like *If you decide to come after me, I'll release this to the media.* But she said nothing. Justine wouldn't have heard her anyway. Her sister was in a distant world.

Hannah walked out the front door.

The body of her father lay in the amber dirt only a few feet from the front door; Hannah realized he was in almost the same position Black's body was, and she felt disgust at Billy having anything in common with Black, even in death.

She briefly wondered about the crime scene she was leaving behind. Two bodies. Fingerprints everywhere. Who knew how long it would even be before Black and Billy were discovered? Would Justine say anything to the police? Would she at least shut the front door so the animals of the woods didn't feast on Black's remains?

Hannah shuddered as her stomach turned at the thought. Maybe she should burn the place down. Destroy the evidence best she could, just as Billy had intended to do while Hannah was handcuffed to the radiator.

Doesn't matter, she told herself. *Just go.*

A small movement ahead of her, on the ground. Hannah thought maybe she didn't see it at all, then there it was again. Billy's left arm, pushing up about an inch along the dirt. He didn't make a sound, but sure enough, he was moving, like some toy animatronic nearly run out of battery life.

Hannah stopped and watched him. Over the course of about a minute each of his arms moved a couple inches forward, his fingers twitching like a spider cautiously feeling for a change in surface. The rest of his body remained still.

Hannah could still hear her sister—and she still considered Justine her sister—softly weeping inside the house. Did Justine shoot Billy just to try to save Dallin? Or did Justine have a fleeting moment of clarity, a flash of all the abuse hitting her at once, opening her soul, making her understand that their father was a monster and nothing else?

How *did* it feel to shoot Billy?

Hannah walked forward, slowly, until both of her feet were next to Billy's head. It didn't escape her that this was the same position in which she stood when she was about to kill Grizzly, about to put the final bullet into the man she had already shot once. In that instance, Grizzly was very much alive, so much so he summoned his energy to overpower Hannah, almost killing her before Black was able to put him down.

Hannah stood, almost wanting her father to come alive, to attack her, in the same inexplicable way a person stands on the edge of a tall building and feels tempted to jump.

But Billy moved no more. Even if he was still barely alive, Hannah knew he was not a threat.

Then he said something. Maybe he opened his eyes and saw Hannah's feet. Maybe he sensed her nearby. Or maybe he was talking to God, telling Him it was a shame they would never meet.

Whatever he said, Hannah didn't understand him. And she didn't care.

"You aren't my father," she told him. Hannah then raised the gun and pointed it at the back of Billy's head. When she fired, the sound made her jump, but only a little. The gun kicked in her hand, but not enough to make her miss. The back of Billy's head came apart, but from Hannah's viewpoint, he still looked like the man he'd always been.

EPILOGUE

The brim on Hannah's sun hat orbited her head, shielding sunlight that was bright but not particularly intense. A summer thunderstorm had rolled through last night, leaving the lake sprawled in front of her a little more full and the trees surrounding it more lush in their greens. The hills around the lake always made her think of Washington this time of year, the shades of green ranging from the lightest of teas to the dark skin of a ripe avocado. But not as lush as Washington. Nor did these hills have the density of the Washington woods, where one hundred yards deep was enough to make you forget from which direction you'd come. It had been a long time since Hannah had been in the Washington woods.

She pushed her sunglasses up along the ridge of her nose. She wore sunglasses the same way the Lone Ranger wore a mask: all the time, and for the sake of anonymity.

"*Volete altro?*" The man's voice was on her right, and Hannah looked up at the waiter. His olive skin was pitted from acne scars, and his deep black hair swept back tight against his head. He carried a small silver tray that he balanced expertly on his hand as if it were simply an extension of his body.

"*No. Solo il conto, per favore,*" she said.

"*Bene.*" He nodded and offered the slightest of bows, then handed her a small piece of paper that listed the cost for an espresso and a small piece of *torta caprese*. He then left her alone, and Hannah knew she could stay here for hours more if she wanted.

Here, there was never a hurry, not even during the summer when tourists swelled the cafés. Here, there was only time.

They knew her at this café, one of the few places Hannah allowed herself to become known, even if the person she was known as was a Canadian woman by the name of Sylvia Genout.

She had coffee here almost every day. Black always had a pastry. The torta was half-eaten on the plate, chocolate crumbs dotting the white porcelain plate, the silver fork upside down on the tablecloth. Black had been distracted by something interesting enough to lure him from cake.

"Mama, look," the boy called out. He was twenty feet away, on his hands and knees atop the sand-red flagstone that swept in a large arc along the top of the cliff. The café looked down onto Lago di Varese, which always looked to Hannah like the kind of water that would never be captured as beautifully in a photo as it looked through one's eyes. Her small villa was nearby.

"What is it?" she asked her son.

Her boy was peering down at something. He turned his head back to her. "A bug! A big one."

Hannah stood and walked over. She could tell it was indeed a large insect, about as long as one of her boy's fingers.

"Not too close, Black," she said.

But Black only leaned in closer, peering at the bug through squinted eyes. He reached out with his right hand, his index finger pointed out.

"Don't *touch*," Hannah said, her tone leaving no room for Black to ignore. He pulled his hand back.

"What is it?" he asked.

Hannah looked down and felt a mild revulsion at the creature. She had never cared for bugs. It looked almost like a large cockroach, but its back legs were longer than the front ones, so the insect sloped forward. Long, spiny antennae probed in front of its head, feeling, sensing. The creature was otherwise still.

"I don't know," she said to her son.

"Can it hurt me?"

"No," she reflexively answered. Then, not wanting to give Black a false sense of security, added, "I don't think so."

She reached down and touched the top of the boy's hair, his thick black hair warm from the sun. His arms and neck were tanned from hours in the Mediterranean sun, and his skin had the smoothness of a child still too young for permanently scraped knees and elbows, though that would surely come.

He craned his head and looked up at her, and she felt herself nearly gasping as he looked at her. It happened from time to time, seemingly more so the older he got. Black had the exact pale green eyes as his namesake, a color that would have blended into the summer foliage surrounding the lake. There were moments where the look just hit Hannah, took her breath away for a moment, as if she was looking at the child-ghost of the man she had only known for a few weeks, five years ago.

"Can I bring it home?"

"No, sweetie. The bug doesn't want to come home with us. I'm sure it wants to go back to its own home tonight."

"Where does it live?"

"I'm sure the bug has a nice apartment nearby. Maybe down by the shore. Probably has TV and everything."

"Really?"

"Maybe," she said.

Hannah leaned down and kissed the back of her son's head, which smelled like lavender from the shampoo she bought at the small grocery store in Biandronno. She ran her fingers one more time through his hair and then went back to her table, leaving Black in his rapt and seemingly mutual fascination with his new friend.

She took one last sip of her espresso, which had cooled but still tasted perfect, a rich, smooth cream on her tongue. She drank too much of it since moving here, but she hadn't had a sip of alcohol since she'd disappeared five years ago, so she allowed herself a few minor vices. The first three months without booze had been the worst, and she realized why rehab programs were often ninety days.

Life wasn't perfect, nor had she expected it to be. Certainly she had enough money not to have to find other resources, though that didn't mean she could live anything but a conservative existence. She'd had to move four times in five years. Being alone with two broken fingers, assuming a new identity, and giving birth to a child was a confluence of events she could never imagine wishing on anyone. And still she ran, because that was what Black had told her to do. Never let down your guard. Never assume you're safe.

A bird effortlessly rode a breeze over the edge of the cliff, making it look much more regal than what it was: a dirty pigeon.

Hannah hadn't checked the news, turned on a TV, or been online during the first month of her disappearance. That was the first thing Black had written in the volume of advice on his phone. *Establish connections to no one or nothing for at least the first month. Don't go online. Don't use a phone. No bank. No ATM. No credit cards. Take out enough cash to last. Don't go out at night where you could meet someone. Be no one. Be invisible. Untraceable.*

She hadn't planned on having broken fingers during the time of her disappearance, and the pain had been constant. She'd bought some splints at a drugstore and had dieted on Motrin for a month as she tried to heal them herself. The bones fused slightly off-center, so now Hannah dealt with swollen joints and limited motion from those digits. Someday—maybe soon—she'd have a doctor break and reset them.

On the thirty-second day of her disappearance, Hannah chanced an Internet cafe in Bruges and opened the world before her for the first time as a new woman. She Googled "Hannah Parks" and was stunned to see the first article that appeared.

It had been dated two weeks earlier. She had frantically clicked the link and read the story as fast as she could, then a second time, and then slowly for a third.

There was not much to it. Justine had walked into Dallin's office one day after lunch, alone and unannounced. Dallin had apparently told his assistant it was fine, since clearly they knew each other. He shut his office door, and less than a minute later there was a shout and then a bang. Seconds later another one. Security broke open the locked door and found Dallin dead on the floor, a single shot to the chest. Justine lay to his side, her head bleeding from the second shot, the gun inches away from her fingertips on the floor. She had left a note behind at home declaring that Connor was Dallin's son and Justine was truly very sorry, and nothing more.

The blood from Billy ran through Justine, and on that day it had boiled enough within her that she could take it no more. Without thinking of her children, Justine took her own life after killing Dallin.

Hannah had consumed as much information as she could that day at the computer, staying no more than two hours to avoid calling attention to herself. She read article after article. There was no mention of Justine rescuing Dallin from the motel, though clearly she must have. Hannah saw the story clearly in her own mind. Dallin loved his boy, but he didn't love Justine. He probably wanted joint custody of the child, or, perhaps, full custody, but did not want to marry her. She had no one left, and in her anger and desperation, she took his life and then her own.

That's how Hannah saw it, and though it was senseless, it was the only explanation that made sense. The media came to a similar conclusion, and this blossomed into suspicion that perhaps the missing Hannah Parks had in fact been murdered as a result of a jealous sister, a straying husband, and a father with a violent past.

Good, Hannah had thought. Let them all think I'm dead.

She had visited several different Internet cafes for the following week, each no more than an hour a day, wiping the cache and history from the computer each time she left.

She cried quietly when she read a brief interview with Hannah's neighbor Cynthia, the one Hannah had asked Justine to let take care of Zoo. Zoo was doing quite well, even though he didn't have the same apartment space he'd been accustomed to. There was even a picture, which shattered her. She missed that dog so goddamn much.

In everything she read, Hannah found no mention of Jill, the web slut/waitress. To the woman's credit, she apparently never said a word to anyone. Jill was probably still up in Silverson, unaware of any news, slinging drinks to anonymous passersthrough, wondering if Black was ever going to walk through the bar doors again.

The moment Hannah realized she could not go back home, she had stopped reading or watching the news. Because in her mind, if she saw enough of a crack of hope she would go claim custody of her nephews. Of leaving everything, nothing was more painful than knowing she couldn't go back to those parentless boys. It was an easy fantasy to assume she would be cleared of all suspicion, a fantasy that played around in her mind when she was too tired being on the defensive every second of the day. But she had done too many things to make a return possible. Yes, she had the video of her time in the cabin, a video that would explain what had happened, to explain why her prints and strands of her hair were found near the bodies of an escaped felon and of her father. But there were other things, things like a burned body in the woods that might eventually be traced to her. Things like false passports. Things like access to eight million dollars in that account.

Hannah knew she might never go to jail, but she would never be given custody of her nephews. In that case, there was no point in returning. Dallin had a sister in New Hampshire who had reportedly requested custody of both boys. Her name was Chelsea, and Hannah had always liked her. Chelsea had always given tight, embracing hugs. Hannah didn't know her well, but she imagined the boys would be safe—and thrive—with Chelsea. Dallin's will left everything to Chelsea in the event both he and Hannah were dead, so Chelsea would be able to raise the boys comfortably. Very comfortably.

A seagull landed on the patio and inched closer to the bug

her boy was still guarding over. The bird bobbed its head and stutter-stepped closer, its eyes black, unblinking beads.

"Go away," Black said. He shielded the bug with hands that wavered a few inches above it. Black shouted again, louder. "He's mine! You can't eat him."

"Aidan, it's okay," Hannah said. She rarely called her son Black in public. That was a special name, a name she always wanted to know, a name forever connecting father and son. In public, though, he was Aidan, which was the *real* name of the boy's father. She never looked at the file on the phone with Black's real name, not wanting to know the man by any name except the one he'd introduced himself with. But finding out was unavoidable in all the articles she had read. Once Black's body was identified, his name was tied to several of the stories about Hannah. Black's real name was Aidan Hainsworth. Former cop, then convicted murderer. So her son had a namesake in both Aidan and Black, but Hannah would always know—and remember—the man as Black.

The third body discovered that day was about a mile from the cabin. It was the body of Samuel Light—a.k.a. Peter—an ex-con with an I.Q. of one-sixty and a penchant for securities fraud. Hannah thought about Peter every now and then, the hulking man who had stayed around to make sure Black and Hannah escaped safely, only to end up getting shot by the man he originally worked for. Another life lost to Billy. Hannah thought about Peter's dream to move to Mendoza, Argentina and run a vineyard. If she still drank, Hannah would happily raise a glass of Malbec in Peter's honor.

For the first three years, Hannah didn't know if she could keep running. More than once she came close to turning herself in, to getting on a plane, going home, and just seeing what would happen. Other times she had come within a cap-twist of drinking again. On a very rare occasion she thought about walking straight into a lake and never coming out. The first years were the worst, but she had always stopped just short of each of those decisions because of her son. Her life wasn't ever going to be normal, but Black deserved the best she could offer. So she had to keep trying.

Hannah kept looking at her boy. He was all she had, and she would never give him up. She wouldn't give up anything, anymore, ever. She had given up too much, and all that remained was hers to keep.

She wondered if she would tell her son about her past. Tell him about who she used to be, who his father was. Who Billy was, and what happened to him.

No was usually the answer she heard in her head.

Billy didn't need to be spoken about. His name didn't deserve the effort of muttering it. She hadn't even had the Billy Dream in over a year, so, like her past, everything was becoming a distant memory, the kind of memory that bled into the realm of *maybe-it-never-happened*. Occasionally, Black would throw a horrible tantrum, the kind involving the lashing out with fists and feet. All kids had such moments, she knew, but when it happened to Black, Hannah saw flashes of her father in her son, and she feared Black had inherited Billy's dark rage, despite Justine's declaration that Hannah was not Billy's daughter. Other times Black would do something so kind or even simply innocent that Hannah knew in her heart her boy had none of Billy's blood in him.

Such were the scales of Black's childhood, tipping ever so slightly one way and then to the other, and only time would truly tell what kind of man Black would grow up to be. All Hannah could do was raise her son with limitless love, compassion, and patience. And hope for the best.

Hannah sighed and looked at her watch. It was just past seven in the evening, late for espresso and cake, but too early for dinner. Tonight, as most nights, they would have a simple dinner at home. There would be two books at bedtime, one in English and one in Italian, and Black would sleep deeply next to her as she lost herself a bit deeper in her own book. Tonight she would finish *The Great Gatsby*, one she had read twice before. This time, she felt Daisy Buchanan's loneliness so achingly that every word spoken by her in the book could have come from Hannah's own mouth.

Tomorrow she would begin again. One sunrise at a time, hoping the brightness of the day would set them free and not expose them like roaches caught in the open by a kitchen light.

A bruise-gray cloud passed in front of the sun. Hannah was jolted by the sensation of looking out her window onto Puget Sound, waiting for the dark to come. Hating the in-between when the sun was rolling through the last moments of its day. Of longing for the certainty of night.

It would be dark here soon enough.

"Aidan, time to go," she said.

Black looked over and asked one more time if he could keep the bug.

Hannah said no.

Black frowned, looking for a moment as if he was going to argue, but said nothing. Then he looked back down at the bug, which hadn't moved the entire time, and tilted his head as he considered it. As the cloud passed and the sunlight once again warmed her face, Hannah watched her boy. She felt her body tense as she suddenly envisioned Black deciding to stomp on the bug, smearing it against the ground. That's what Billy would have done. A young Billy would have played with the creature until he got bored, then he would have killed it.

Instead, Black stood, said something to the bug, then ran over to his mother, laughing.

"I told him I could come back tomorrow and play with him some more," he said.

Hannah exhaled and brought her boy close into her, holding him, running her fingers through his thick hair, and then bending down and kissing the top of his head.

CPSIA information can be obtained
at www.ICGtesting.com
Printed in the USA
FSHW021440021121
85784FS